I0637209

KIMBERLY BROWN

WHERE SECRETS FIND SOLACE

BLACK
ODYSSEY
MEDIA

WWW.BLACKODYSSEY.NET

Published by
BLACK ODYSSEY MEDIA

www.blackodyssey.net
Email: info@blackodyssey.net

This book is a work of fiction. Any references to events, real people, or real places are used fictitiously. Other names, characters, places, and events are products of the author's imagination, and any resemblance to actual events or places or persons, living or dead, is entirely coincidental.

WHERE SECRETS FIND SOLACE. Copyright © 2025 by KIMBERLY BROWN

Library of Congress Control Number: 2025916799

First Trade Paperback Printing: January 2026
ISBN: 978-1-957950-79-2
ISBN: 978-1-957950-80-8 (e-book)

Cover Design by Qamber Designs

To the extent that the image or images on the cover of this book depict a person or persons, such person or persons are merely models and are not intended to portray any character in the book.

All rights reserved. Black Odyssey Media, LLC | Dallas, TX.

This book or parts thereof may not be reproduced in any form, stored in a retrieval system, or transmitted in any form by any means—electronic, mechanical, photocopy, recording, or otherwise—without prior written permission of the publisher, excepting brief quotes or tags used in reviews, interviews, or complimentary promotion, and as permissible by United States of America copyright law.

10 9 8 7 6 5 4 3 2 1

Manufactured in the United States of America

Distributed by Kensington Publishing Corp.

The authorized representative in the EU for product safety and compliance is
eucomply OU, Parnu mnt 139b-14, Apt 123
Tallinn, Berline 11317, hello@eucomplianceprtner.com

Dear Reader,

I want to thank you immensely for supporting Black Odyssey Media and our ongoing efforts to spotlight the diverse narratives of blossoming and seasoned storytellers. With every manuscript we acquire, we believe that it took talent, discipline, and remarkable courage to construct that story, flesh out those characters, and prepare it for the world. Debut or seasoned, our authors are the real heroes and heroines in *OUR* story. For them, we are eternally grateful.

    Whether you are new to Kimberly Brown or Black Odyssey Media, we hope that you are here to stay. Our goal is to make a lasting impact in the publishing landscape, one step at a time and one book at a time. As always, we welcome your feedback and kindly ask that you leave a review. For upcoming releases, announcements, submission guidelines, etc., please be sure to visit our website at www.blackodyssey.net or scan the QR code below. And remember, no matter where you are in your journey, the best of both worlds begins now!

Joyfully,

Shawanda Williams

Shawanda "N'Tyse" Williams
Founder & CEO, Black Odyssey Media

AUTHOR'S NOTE

This is women's fiction with romantic elements. This story contains themes and events that may be distressing to some readers, including sexual assault/sexual abuse, childhood trauma, prison, and murder. Some of this is depicted on page. While written with care, some scenes may be triggering for those with personal experiences related to these topics.

Please prioritize your well-being while reading.

This is a story rooted in healing, protection, and love—but it doesn't shy away from the shadows these characters must face to reach peace. If you choose to continue, thank you for trusting me with this journey.

DEDICATION

To anyone who's ever heard the phrase, *"What happens in this house stays in this house."* You are not alone, and help is available.

National Sexual Assault Hotline: a service of RAINN
Telephone hotline: 800-656-HOPE (4673)

National Domestic Violence Hotline
Telephone hotline: 800-799-SAFE

National Center for Missing and Exploited Children
Telephone hotline: 800-THE-LOST (843-5678)

National Center for Victims of Crime, for all crime victims
Telephone hotline: 855-4-VICTIM (84-2846)

PROLOGUE

TEN YEARS AGO

Alayah Chambers (Age Seventeen)

"**A**LAYAH! **GET YOUR** ass down here right now!"

I sighed heavily at the sound of my mother shouting my name. She was always yelling at me about something. No matter what went wrong, I somehow ended up wearing the blame for it. Closing my calculus book, I stood from my desk and left my bedroom. Before going downstairs, I stopped to check on my little sisters, Adrienne who was seven and Amiyah who was five. They were fast asleep in their bunk beds.

My little sisters were my heart. If nobody else in this house loved me, they did. I'd practically been their second mom since the day they both came home from the hospital. For those girls, I'd give my life. They had no idea the shit I endured to protect them.

"Alayah!" my mother screamed.

I quickly closed their door and headed downstairs. I found her walking around in her work uniform and smoking a cigarette.

"Yes, ma'am?"

"You didn't hear me calling you?"

"I was coming. I was just doing my homework."

"Whatever. Why does this house look like this?" She waved her hands around for emphasis. "You forgot you have chores?"

"I didn't forget. I had to help Adrienne and Miyah with their homework, then I had to cook dinner. After we ate, I got them ready for bed so I could do my homework. I—"

"All I'm hearing are excuses. I don't work like a dog so you can lay around doing nothing."

I relaxed my face so the frown I felt forming didn't show. I'd hardly call my household contributions nothing. My mother worked as a CNA during the day and when she wasn't working a double shift, she was a bartender at night. At home, I was the cook, the maid, the babysitter, and more often than not, a punching bag. But I didn't say that. Instead, I nodded.

"I'm sorry. I'll clean after I finish studying for my exam."

"No, you'll clean now. I have to go to work. Rodney will be here in a little bit, and I don't want him coming home to a dirty house."

I swallowed hard. I hated Rodney. He was the scum of the earth, yet she worshiped the grass that grew from the ground he walked on. I never understood why, though. He came from money, yet she was still working two jobs to support us. He threw her a few dollars here and there or paid a bill or two every so often. Maybe it was the material things he showered her with. Whatever it was, in her eyes, he could do no wrong.

I decided to appease her. The quicker I cleaned the house, the quicker I could get back to my room and avoid that bastard.

She snapped her fingers in my face. "Don't just stand there. Get to cleaning."

She grabbed her bag and headed out the front door. I sighed as I grabbed the basket designated for the girls' toys and began picking everything up. An hour later, the living room was spotless, and so was the rest of the downstairs area. I looked at the clock to see that it was almost nine. I trekked back upstairs and decided to shower so it would be one less thing I had to do when I was done studying.

Grabbing my pajamas and underclothes, I headed into the hall bathroom. Thirty minutes later, I was out of the shower. After moisturizing my skin, I slipped into my clothes and left the bathroom. I placed my school clothes in the hamper in the laundry room, then headed back to my room. As I neared it, I noticed that the door was slightly ajar. I swallowed hard as I approached it. Gently pushing it open, I found Rodney sitting on my bed. He gave that same terrifying smile that always caused me to tremble in fear every time I was alone with him.

"Close the door, and bring your pretty self here," he said.

I didn't move.

I couldn't do this again. I'd been dealing with him coming into my room for three years now. My mother had been with him for five years, and from the moment I met him, he gave me creep vibes. It started with the way he showed me affection. He always wanted to give me a kiss on the cheek or a hug. His hugs were accompanied with compliments of how pretty I was or how I looked just like my mama.

He graduated to making me sit on his lap when she wasn't around. I tried to protest, but he'd always grab me and force me. I'd sit there with tears streaming down my face as he stroked my hair and smelled me.

"You're filling out real nice."

"You're gonna be as thick as your mama."

"You better not be out here giving these young boys a taste of you."

At one point, he started whispering dirty things in my ear as he touched me and himself. I tried to tell my mother he made me uncomfortable. I tried to tell her what he was doing, but she always cut me off. I remembered the first time he came into my room.

My mother was working the night shift at a bar, and he was here with his friends watching a football game. My aunt always fussed at my mother about leaving us in the house with a man that wasn't our father, but she never listened. Adrienne and Miyah were asleep when I went downstairs for a drink. I tried to sneak past them, but he caught me.

"Alayah!" he called, stopping me in my tracks.

"Yes?"

"Come here."

I hesitated before walking over to him. His friends gave me the same creep vibes. They all watched as I entered the living room. Rodney grabbed my arm and pulled me down onto his lap.

"Whatchu doing up, pretty girl?"

I hated when he called me that.

"I was just getting a drink and going back to bed."

He chuckled as he looked around at his friends. "Ain't she beautiful?" he asked, stroking my hair.

"Yeah... She's real pretty," his friend said, eyeing me.

I tried to get up, but his grip around my waist tightened.

"Where you going? I thought you were thirsty." He grabbed a red cup from the table and handed it to me. "Drink."

I shook my head. "I can't."

"Come on. I won't tell your mama. You ever had moonshine?"

"I'm fourteen."

He laughed. "I had my first sip at twelve. It ain't gon' hurt you. Take a sip."

"I just wanna go to bed, Rodney."

"Then take a sip."

I looked at his friends for help, thinking one of them would have the decency to speak up. Alas, they all seemed to be waiting. I grabbed the cup and took a small sip. *The liquor was strong and burned my chest. I tried to hand the cup back, but he shook his head.*

"All of it."

"I don't want to."

He roughly grabbed my face. "Drink it."

Terrified, I quickly drank the disgusting liquid in the cup. My chest was burning so bad that I had a coughing fit. Whatever was in the cup tasted like rubbing alcohol. He and his friends laughed as I ran upstairs when he finally released me. I wanted to make myself throw up, but I knew it would burn twice as bad coming back up. When my coughing finally got under control, I sat on the edge of my bed. All I wanted to do was lay down.

The effects of the liquor hit me quick. I fell back across my bed and stared up at the ceiling feeling like my head was spinning. I wasn't sure how long I'd been laying there when my door opened. My vision was slightly blurry, and I couldn't make out the figure, but I knew it was Rodney.

"Damn, baby girl," he mumbled.

I felt his hands on my body, but I didn't have the strength or mental capacity to stop him. The next thing I felt was his lips on my neck and face, then finally my lips.

"St-Stop..." I groaned, trying to turn my head.

"Shhh!"

I felt my clothes being removed and then the heaviest weight on me and a sharp pain between my legs. I couldn't move. I couldn't speak. I could barely breathe. Before I knew it, I had passed out.

That night, my innocence was stolen, and it was the beginning of the hell I experienced at the hands of my mother's boyfriend. Almost every time my mother went to work and my sisters were in bed, he came to me. When I threatened to tell, he threatened to go after my little sisters or have one of his boys have their way with them.

That shut me up.

I'd been silent. I'd suffered for so long, and I was tired.

"Come here, Alayah," he said firmly.

"No."

He stood from the bed and moved toward me. "What?"

"I said no. You can't touch me anymore."

"Who's gonna stop me? Your mama? She'll never believe you. She already thinks you be out here fucking these boys from the neighborhood. You really think she'd believe I did anything to you?"

"I don't care! You will never touch me again!"

He grabbed me and pushed me up against the desk, bringing his face close to mine. I could smell the liquor on his breath. It was nothing new. He was always drinking.

"Don't make me hurt you, pretty girl," he said, stroking my cheek. "I just wanna make you feel good."

He dropped his hand to the string on my pajama bottoms. No was never an answer. It wasn't a luxury I had with him.

"Stop playing with me, and take these off."

"No!"

I mustered up every bit of strength I had and pushed him off me. He stumbled backward, but quickly regained his footing. His eyes were dark as he glared at me, and I knew if I didn't protect myself, he would seriously hurt me. I fumbled around on my desk for something to defend myself with. My fingers landed on a pair of scissors, and I quickly grabbed them as he charged at me.

As soon as he got close, I raised my hand and stabbed him in the neck. His eyes widened in surprise as he stumbled and stared at the bloody shears in my hand. Something came over me. All the anger and rage I felt for this disgusting man filled me, and all I saw was red. Fueled by anger, I charged at him, stabbing him repeatedly as I screamed like a madwoman.

"You bastard! You'll never touch me again! Just…fucking…die!"

Over and over, I brought the scissors down on him. I wasn't even sure where I was stabbing him at this point, I just knew I wanted him dead. His body had long since gone limp, but I kept going. It wasn't until I heard the screams of my little sisters outside the door.

"Sissy!" Adrienne yelled. "Are you okay?"

"I'm scared!" Amiyah cried.

The knob turned, and I scrambled over to the door to keep them from seeing the horrid sight inside. My pajamas were soaked. When my eyes landed on Rodney's bloody corpse, I dropped the scissors.

"I'm…I'm okay," I choked out. "I just had a bad dream. Go back to bed."

"But—"

"Please go back to bed, girls," I pleaded. "Please…"

I could hear their little feet retreating down the hall. For the longest time, I sat on the floor, staring at the body with blood pooling around it. What had I done?

I was finally free of the ongoing abuse Rodney had subjected me to, but what was the price I was about to pay?

CHAPTER 1

Alayah

Present Day

"**I**NMATES! FALL IN line!"

I drug myself out of my bunk and slipped on my prison-regulated shoes as the door to my bunk opened. It was 6:00 a.m. and time for showers. Grabbing my toiletries, I stepped out the room and waited for the morning headcount before we headed to the community bathrooms. After showers would be breakfast, then work duty, lunch, yard time, then dinner. We'd have a few hours of downtime before it was lights out, only to wake up and do it all over again tomorrow.

This had been my routine for the last ten years.

Ten years.

That's how much of my life had been taken for taking the life of my abuser. It didn't hardly seem fair. I'd been molested and raped for years, and when I snapped, I was punished. Overkill, they said. I'd stabbed Rodney a total of twenty-six times. The prosecutor tried to paint it as a crime of passion. It was so far from that. If anything, what I did was a hate crime because I hated that bastard.

I didn't regret taking his life. Doing so saved me and my little sisters from any further or potential abuse. It saved many other little girls like me. My only regret was not doing it sooner.

My thoughts were interrupted by the guard clicking her counter in my face. She walked past me and finished her count before telling us to follow her. In a single-file line, we headed for the showers. Because of the nature of my crime, I'd been placed in a block with violent offenders. When I first got here, I was terrified. While I wasn't innocent of a crime, I wasn't violent.

I didn't deserve to be held with murderers and child abusers. For the first couple of weeks, I barely slept. I was terrified of someone doing something to me in my sleep, even though I was in a single cell and the door was locked. When I did sleep, I had nightmares about what I had done. All I could see was the blood. All I could hear were the screams of my sisters.

I hadn't seen either of them since I'd been locked up. My mother forbid me to contact them. She refused to accept my calls so I could speak to them. She had every letter I wrote them returned to me. The only reason I knew what they looked like was because Aunt Penny and Uncle Clive brought pictures when they came to visit me. They were the only family I had who truly loved me outside of my sisters. Aunt Penny was my mother's older sister. She and Uncle Clive never had any children, and they loved us like their own.

Kennedy Chambers, my mother, had painted me out to be a monster just like Rodney's family. She told everyone I killed Rodney in cold blood. I was the reason for their trauma. I was the reason she'd lost the love of her life. The story she went around telling was that I'd been trying to seduce him for the longest, and he refused my advances. When I couldn't get what I wanted, I killed him.

My aunt and uncle didn't believe that for a second.

They had been actively fighting my conviction since I was sentenced. While I appreciated their efforts, I told them to just give it up. They'd spent too much time and money trying to bring me home already. I just had to accept that I was going to spend most of my life behind bars. There was too much evidence against me and none against Rodney.

At least none that could be found. Prior to his death, it had been at least two weeks since Rodney had penetrated me. The experts concluded that I wasn't a virgin, and the vaginal trauma could be from regular intercourse. I had no defensive wounds. No cuts or bruises to suggest that I'd been attacked. The only evidence I had were the videos he'd taken of us on occasion over the years. The thing was, he'd hidden them, and to this day, they had yet to be found. Aunt Penny said they tore my mother's house apart looking for the tapes and hadn't found anything.

Without that key evidence, I was royally fucked.

Ten years I'd been down on voluntary manslaughter charge, and I had twenty to go.

"Chambers, stop lollygagging and bring your ass!" CO Judy yelled.

I hadn't realized I was walking so slowly behind everyone else. Whenever I thought about my circumstances, I tended to dissociate, no matter where I was.

"I'm sorry," I said, picking up my pace.

By the time I made it to the showers, the stalls were full. I waited patiently for my turn. Once inside, I quickly disrobed and slipped on my shower shoes before stepping inside. Most of the hot water was gone, so it was lukewarm at best. Still, at least it wasn't cold. Quickly and diligently, I bathed myself, forgoing washing my hair.

Exactly fifteen minutes later, I was being escorted back to my bunk to put my things away and to wait to be taken to breakfast.

I used that time to talk to Carissa, the inmate next door. I sat next to the vent that connected our rooms and spoke softly.

"Good morning, Riss."

I could hear her shuffling about before I heard her voice. "Hey, Lay. How you doing this morning, baby?"

"Same shit, different day."

Carissa had been next door since I got here. She'd looked out for me and made sure none of the other women tried anything with me. She was an older woman in her fifties and had a lot of influence around here. She was well respected by the other women, and what she said was law. I thought of her as the mother figure I needed, and having her on my side had made a world of difference in my time.

"I know that's right. How did you sleep? I didn't hear you screaming last night."

"I slept okay. No recurring nightmares last night."

"That's good to hear. Guess what?"

"What?"

"My man is coming to visit me today."

I smiled. She'd met her boyfriend Eric through the prison pen pal system. For months, they had been writing each other back and forth. It took a while for her to get him on her approved visitation list, but judging by their pending visit, it must have worked out.

"That's wonderful. I'm sure you're excited."

"I am. It's been a while. I need you to do my hair. I have to make sure I look decent for this visit. I can't let the first time he sees me, I look dusty."

I giggled. "You could never be dusty."

She giggled as well. "Thank you, baby. I keep telling you to get you a pen pal. We have nothing but time on our hands. At least have a little fun. Once I get approved for these conjugal visits, I'm gonna have a whole lot of fun."

I shook my head as though she could see me. "Dating is the last thing on my mind, Riss. I don't trust these men as it is. What can we do for each other while I'm in here?"

She huffed. "Use your imagination. Make plans for the future. You won't be in here forever, you know."

"I still have twenty years, Riss. Ain't no future for me when I get out of here. I'll be lucky to find a job making minimum wage."

I often thought about what I would do upon release. I'd gotten my GED a year into my sentence. I'd also gotten my cosmetology license through the vocational program. I did a lot of the girls' hair around here. It kept them off my back and me on their good side. Maybe I could get a job at a hair salon. It had never been my aspiration in life, but it was a useful skill.

I had been on the fast track to a full scholarship to the Black Ivies where I'd planned to major in chemistry and minor in biology. With my conviction, I'd lost all of that. Even when I got out, I couldn't afford to pursue that degree. What kind of job would I be able to get? If I took out a student loan, how would I pay it back? Was forty-seven too late to begin thinking about starting over anyway?

I just didn't know what I would do. Whatever I did, I knew for certain I didn't want to be behind these barbwire fences and concrete walls ever again.

"You gotta speak shit into existence, Alayah. Stop being so damn negative. I've told you about that."

I sighed. "I know, I know."

"You're a beautiful young woman, baby. Any man would be lucky to have you."

"I don't trust men, Carissa. I want nothing to do with them."

"Then get you a lady."

That made me laugh. "In all the time you've known me, have you ever once heard me say I like women?"

"Chile, if you're in here long enough, you'll start to wonder. Being behind these walls cut off from the outside world, you miss intimacy. You miss being held and loved. I don't judge anybody. We're all just trying to live and survive in here."

She was right about that. My fight-or-flight responses had kicked it up a notch in here. I lived in survival mode. I tried to tell myself that if I just made it to see tomorrow, I'd be okay. I'd been telling myself that since I got here. Unlike many of the women who came through those doors, I was still here.

I'd seen girls get jumped and beaten to death. I'd seen a few women get shanked and sent to the infirmary. I'd even known a few who couldn't take it, so they took their lives. While I didn't have much to live for, I still wanted to *live*.

"You wanna know what I heard?" Carissa asked, amusement lacing her voice.

"Humor me."

"My girl Candy…you know how her work duty is assisting the warden, right?"

"Yeah."

"Guess who got approved for a parole hearing?"

"Who?"

"You, baby."

My eyes widened. "What?" I whispered.

Me? Parole?

"The paperwork came through yesterday evening. Don't tell nobody though. You know these bitches act funny when they think you're getting out."

I hadn't heard much else of what she said. The fact that she just told me I was approved for a parole hearing was a wild statement. My aunt and uncle had gotten me a new lawyer about a year ago. When I met with her, she had me go through the process of filling out the paperwork for a hearing. I did it with no hope that it would get approved. I'd all but given up on getting out early, but my aunt and uncle had so much faith in me that I just did it to appease them.

My lawyer, Erica Sawyer, came to see me once a week. I didn't ask about the progress and told her not to tell me anything unless she had a definite answer. She respected my wishes, and we talked about everything but parole. I'd honestly forgotten about it until Carissa said something.

Leaning against the wall, I took a few deep breaths.

This could change everything. It would be the difference in getting out and starting over or serving another twenty years in this hellhole.

CHAPTER 2

KILLIAN LAKE

IT WAS BRIGHT and early on a Monday morning.

I'd woken up at five, gotten in my workout, ate breakfast, and got ready for work. I made it to the law offices of Brennan and Jones around eight, same as I did every morning. I stopped in the employee lounge to make myself a cup of coffee before making my way to my office, only to be stopped by my coworker, Casey.

"Lake! How was your weekend?"

"Same shit, different day. How was yours?"

"It was great. The wife and I took the kids down to the river for a little camping and fishing trip. There's nothing like sunshine and fresh air to make you feel alive again."

"True. I gotta get going, Casey. Have a good one."

Before he could rope me into a long, drawn-out conversation about his family life, I hightailed it down the hall. It wasn't that I didn't like Casey. He just talked too damn much. Messing around with him, we'd be having a thirty-minute conversation with him doing all the talking. I didn't have time for that.

I rounded the corner and passed a few offices only to have my name once again be called.

"Killian!"

I groaned inwardly as I backtracked to the source. Erica Sawyer. She was one of the top attorneys at the firm. Her record of wins was impeccable. I wasn't sure what kind of pull she had, but she always managed to get the job done.

"Good morning, Erica."

"Good morning. Quick question: Do you have court this week?"

"Friday. Why?"

"I have a very sensitive case, and I could use an extra set of eyes. I know how diligent you are."

"Sure thing. What's the case?"

"It's a parole hearing. My client has been in G.S. Glen Penitentiary since she was seventeen years old for a murder that in my eyes was justified as self-defense. I'm trying my hardest to bring her home. Her aunt and uncle have spent a lot of money over the years fighting for justice for her, and I don't want that to be in vain."

I nodded. "I'll take a look at it."

She smiled. "Awesome. A copy of the files is on your desk."

I chuckled. "So you just knew I'd be down to help you?"

"I know you, Killian. You take on a lot of sensitive cases, and I knew once you read this one, you would help if you could."

She was right about that. My workload was always filled with sensitive cases. It had sort of become my thing.

"I'll see what I can do," I said.

"Thank you again."

"No problem."

I left her office and finally was able to make it to mine. Stepping inside, I closed the door and placed my briefcase on top of my desk as I took a seat behind it. As I sipped my coffee, I logged into my computer and pulled up everything I'd need for the day. I then checked and responded to a few urgent emails before finally getting started on my workload.

Grabbing my briefcase, I placed it on the floor next to the desk. My eyes landed on the file folder. Picking it up, I opened it, and my brows immediately furrowed at the sight of the name.

Alayah Chambers.

It couldn't be her. I hadn't heard her name in years, but I never forgot what landed her behind bars. Her story was one of the main reasons I'd decided to pursue a career in the criminal justice system. Alayah had not only been my classmate from elementary school all the way through high school, but she was my friend. I remembered her being shy and timid, yet sweet and so damn beautiful.

She had the most beautiful natural curls that were always wild and free. Her skin was caramel colored, smooth, and peppered with freckles. She was the first black woman I'd ever seen with freckles. Her beauty was unmatched.

She didn't talk to too many people, but I'd been lucky enough to get partnered with her for a science project. Being that we spent a lot of time together working on it, I got to see a side of her that most people weren't privy to. Not only was she beautiful, but she was smart as hell, and she was goofy—both qualities I found attractive.

"Damn," I mumbled as I read through the file.

I knew why she want to jail, but I'd never seen all the details laid out in black, white, and color pictures. The gruesome images of Rodney West almost made my stomach turn. There was so much anger and rage packed into the twenty-six stab wounds he'd received to his neck, face, and chest. He was unrecognizable. There were pictures of Alayah covered in his blood after the incident. There were pictures of her bloody bedroom. It was a horrible sight.

The file mentioned she'd accused him of molesting and raping her for years. She gave detailed accounts of several instances and even alleged that there were tapes—tapes that had never been found. The details alone should have been an indicator that she was telling the truth.

I thought back to all the times I got the feeling that something was going on with her back then. I'd met Rodney a few times when I went to her house to work on our project or study, and he was always affectionate with her. He was affectionate with her sisters, but especially with her. I remembered how blank her face would go when he hugged her or kissed her cheek. I remembered the sigh of relief she'd breathe when he left the room or the house.

I thought back to one of those moments. We were in the kitchen studying for an exam when he came in. I saw the way her shoulders tensed when he walked into the room and came to stand behind her. Stooping, he kissed her cheek.

"Hey pretty girl," he said, squeezing her shoulders.

"Hey, Rodney," she mumbled.

He looked at me. "Killian, right?"

"Uh, yes, sir."

"You two studying hard or hardly studying?" He chuckled at his own joke as he stroked Alayah's hair.

"Studying hard," I answered. "Well, I'm studying. Alayah already seems to know the answers."

"My girl is a smart one."

She slightly shrugged his hands away. "We have to finish studying."

"Okay, baby." Again, he kissed her cheek. "Nice seeing you again, Killian."

He patted my shoulder as he walked away. She sighed heavily, seemingly shaking away the feelings his hands left behind.

"I don't like him. Don't let the niceness fool you. He's an asshole."

She said that with so much venom in her voice. I didn't say anything. When it was time to go, she walked me to the door to say goodbye.

"If I don't pass this test, I'm blaming you," I jested.

"You'll do fine, Killian. You're smart."

"Not as smart as you."

She blushed. "I'll see you at school."

I hesitated for a moment before pulling her in for a hug. Her body tensed momentarily, then relaxed as she hugged me back. From his spot on the couch, I could see Rodney watching us.

"See you," I said, finally pulling away.

I remembered her coming to school the next day looking completely out of it. She was present, but mentally she wasn't there at all. I asked her what was wrong, and she brushed it off as she was just tired from taking care of her sisters and doing chores.

I let it go because I'd met her mother. I heard the way she spoke to her and saw the way she treated her. There were times I'd helped her clean or volunteered to cook dinner while she helped her sisters with homework just so she wouldn't get in trouble. I thought about all of that as I sat looking at her file.

Regret filled me.

Why hadn't I said anything? Why hadn't I made her tell me what was going on?

Only God knew what she had gone through the last ten years behind bars. I prayed that she was surviving. I knew this time had changed her, but I hoped she'd at least begun to heal.

Closing the file, I sat back and ran my hands down my face. I stood from the desk and left the office with the file in hand as I made my way to Erica's office. She was clicking away on her keyboard when I walked in.

"Hey," she said, looking up. "Did you read it?"

"I did."

"What do you think?"

"She deserves to be free."

"I agree. Reading over it had me looking at her mama sideways. How didn't she know? I'd notice if my man were looking at my daughter. I'd notice the changes in her."

"You've never met Kennedy Chambers."

Her brows furrowed. "You have?"

I sighed as I took a seat and began explaining the nature of my relationship with Alayah and the things I'd seen and heard.

"You think Kennedy will come to the parole hearing?" I asked.

Erica shrugged. "I don't know. She and his family have been notified. I know his people are coming. They are adamant about protesting Alayah's release." She shook her head. "I have to get her out, Killian. The justice system failed her. Her mother failed her. She was a victim, and they treated her like shit at that trial. I'm praying that this new judge will review everything and have mercy on her. She shouldn't have had to do ten years, let alone thirty."

I sighed. "I agree. I hate I can't work with you to represent her. I'd have to recuse myself."

"It's fine. I'm just glad we're on the same page."

"I do want to go to the hearing though. I need to lay eyes on her."

Erica smiled. "Maybe you can be a friend to her when she gets out. I say *when* because it's going to happen, I don't care what the victim's family has to say. She's been punished enough."

I nodded in agreement. "When is court?"

"Next Tuesday. I'm going to give her the news today. Hopefully she'll accept the date. She's basically accepted her fate. With her aunt and uncle fighting for justice so long, she feels bad about all the time they have dedicated to her case. They are the only family she really has."

"What about her sisters?"

"According to them, her mother hasn't let them see or speak to her."

I shook my head. I knew how much she loved her little sisters. They were her babies, and she cared for them as though they came from her.

"Damn. I knew that woman was a piece of work." I stood from the chair. "Let me get out of here and refocus my energy. If I think about the shit too long, I'm gonna get mad all over again."

"Sounds like you cared for her at one point."

"I did. I've always regretted not asking her to be my girl when I had the chance."

Erica smirked. "Well…there's always second chances."

I didn't say anything as I stood and left the office. I didn't know about a second chance here. A lot of time had passed. I wasn't sure what kind of person Alayah had become. Prison had a way of changing people—hardening them. I hadn't seen this woman in ten years. I hadn't visited. I hadn't written. As far as I knew, she wouldn't want anything to do with me, and I couldn't blame her.

CHAPTER 3

Alayah

AGE FIFTEEN

"**R**ODNEY, PLEASE..." I *begged in a whisper. "I don't wanna do this."*

"*Ain't I good to you, Alayah?" he asked, stepping closer to me. "Don't I spoil you for being my good girl?"*

He slipped an arm around my waist and pulled me to him. I could smell the familiar stench of liquor on his breath. I wanted to throw up. He was delusional if he thought buying me things would make up for what he was doing.

"*Answer me," he demanded, his grip tightening. "Am I not good to you?"*

I fought back tears as I answered. "Yes."

"*Don't I tell you you're my pretty girl?" His lips fell to my neck.*

"*Yes."*

"*I would never hurt you. I just wanna make you feel good the same way you make me feel good."*

He grabbed my hand and placed it on his crotch, rubbing it up and down.

"*I need you to take care of that for me, pretty girl. Take care of me, and I'll take care of you. Take off your clothes."*

I couldn't hold back the tears as I slowly backed away from him and began to undress. This wasn't right. I was fifteen now, and his visits to my room had become more and more frequent. I'd long since stopped fighting him off after he almost choked me to the point of passing out. There was nothing I could do but take it. I had to lay there with his weight on top of me…his sweaty skin against mine…his heavy breathing in my ear as he violated me.

I wondered if he said the same nasty things to my mother that he said to me. I wondered how he could lay up with her after violating me time and time again. I'd watch him hug, kiss, and grope her like he loved her so much, all the while knowing what he was doing to me. I watched her serve him like he was some sort of fucking king when he was nothing but a pervert who liked little girls.

"Rodney, please… You're hurting me," I begged.

I felt like I was suffocating beneath him. He was being so rough, and it was hard not to scream into the darkness surrounding us.

"It hurts!"

He covered my mouth. Evil eyes bore into mine as I struggled to breathe. My hands clawed at his as my headboard lightly tapped against the wall. Forever seemed to pass, and when he grunted, I'd never been so relieved for him to be finished. He rolled off me, panting heavily. I covered my face and cried silently as the bed shifted and he stood to his feet.

"Stop all the damn crying," he said harshly. "You might as well get used to this, Alayah. I'm never letting you go."

"No…no stop," I screamed.

I popped up in bed, and I could hear the yelling of the inmates around me, telling me to shut up. By now, everyone knew when I was having a nightmare. My screams were so loud that they woke up the whole cell block. I heard my cell door unlock, and in walked CO Judy with her flashlight.

"You good, Chambers?"

I nodded. "I'm sorry. I had a nightmare."

She shook her head. "I thought those were getting better."

I wiped my hands to down my face and took a deep breath. "My parole hearing is in a few hours," I revealed.

"*Ahhh.* That makes sense. Honestly, I hope you get out of here, Chambers. You never deserved to be here anyway."

She offered me a warm smile as she backed out of the room and closed the door. I pushed myself up until my back touched the wall of the cell. Pulling my knees to my chest, I wrapped my arms around them and rested my head on my knees. I looked at the pictures of my sisters. I missed them so much. They were seventeen and fifteen now and had grown into beautiful young women.

I wondered what they were like—if they were happy and healthy. Had what I'd done caused them any severe trauma? My aunt and uncle refused to tell me anything about them that might make me feel bad or trigger me. I appreciated that, but still…I just needed to know.

Maybe if I got released, I could try to repair my relationship with them. They were old enough to make decisions for themselves. Then again, Kennedy had forbidden any interaction thus far. What would stop her from continuing to do so? She had custody of them, so as far as the law was concerned, what she said goes.

I sat in that same spot until it was time to get up for morning showers. I could never go back to sleep after one of those dreams. It had been a little while since I had one. Maybe it was the fact that I would be seeing Rodney's family today. Erica told me they were protesting my release, so they would be there.

When I first got here, I got letters from them telling me that they hated me and would never forgive me for what I did. His mother came to visit me once, and I left the visit in tears. She called me everything but a child of God and told me I was going to burn in hell.

She didn't believe that her son was capable of such vile acts. I wouldn't wish what he did on my worst enemy, but I prayed that another young girl would come forward and prove that I wasn't lying. I couldn't have been the first and only one. I just couldn't have.

"Chambers!"

The sound of my name being called broke me from my thoughts. I was sitting at the table picking over my breakfast because I couldn't eat a thing. When I looked up, CO Sellers was standing over me with handcuffs.

"Time to go. Your lawyer is waiting."

I stood and dumped my tray before holding out my hands to be cuffed. Sellers led me from the cell block, and we made our way to the room where Erica was waiting. When the door opened, she smiled at me.

"Good morning, Alayah," she spoke.

"Good morning."

"How are you feeling?"

I shrugged. "I'm here. I don't have any hope of being released, but I'm willing to try."

"That's all I need. We've prepared for this. Everything is in place for when you go home because you *are* going home. I have full faith in that."

"Is my mother going to be there?"

"I'm not sure. She was given notice, but I can't be certain that she will show up. Your aunt and uncle are already on their way to the courthouse, though. She sent you some clothes and shoes, too. I'm gonna step out and let you get dressed."

She pulled out a bag and placed the clothes and shoes on the table. After patting me on the back, she left me with the guard to change. I took a deep breath. Today, my life would change—or it would remain exactly the same for twenty more years.

I stood in the back waiting with the guard for my turn. My heart raced, and my hands were clammy. I kept taking deep breaths because I feared I would pass out from nervousness. Erica was so confident that I was going to be granted parole. I wasn't sure what she had up her sleeve, but I had no choice but to trust her.

What seemed like forever went by before it was my turn. When I walked into the courtroom, the first people I laid eyes on were my aunt and uncle. They sat huddled together with hopeful smiles on their faces. Even though they weren't supposed to touch me, my aunt stood and kissed my cheek.

"We love you," she whispered.

"I love you, too."

As I went to sit, my eyes landed on Mr. and Mrs. West, who both wore frowns on their faces. Behind them were a few other family members I'd met while my mother was dating Rodney and a lot I didn't know. My heart fluttered thinking I would see her when I looked around the room, but she was nowhere to be found. Who I did see, however, caused my eyes to widen.

Killian Lake.

I hadn't seen him since before my arrest, but I would never forget his face. Time had been good to him. He still looked like the seventeen-year-old boy I used to have study sessions with, just more mature and devilishly handsome in his suit. He offered me a warm smile. I didn't return it—just focused my attention on the parole board. In the middle was the woman I assumed to be in charge. She was a beautiful black woman who looked like she played no games. She introduced herself as Andrea Lemon and then introduced her colleagues.

"You may be seated," she said.

As soon as my handcuffs were removed, I took my seat.

"Good morning. This is a parole consideration hearing for inmate Alayah Chambers, CDC number 290451. Ms. Chambers, are you ready to proceed?"

"Yes, ma'am."

"Very well. Ms. Chambers, you are currently serving a thirty-year sentence for the murder of one Rodney West. By our calculations, you have served ten of those years. Can you tell us about the crime you committed?"

"Yes, ma'am."

I slowly stood. Behind me I heard my uncle whisper, "You got this, baby girl." I took a deep breath before training my eyes on the parole board.

"My mother began dating Rodney when I was twelve years old. From the moment I met him, he made me uncomfortable. It was the way he looked at me or the way his touch lingered too long. He told us—me and my sisters—that he was going to be our new daddy. He did everything to make us like him or to try to gain our trust, but something about him never sat right with me.

"The older I got, the more I noticed the change in the way he acted toward me. He became very affectionate, always wanting to hug or kiss me or touch me in some way. He made me sit on his lap when I didn't want to, and when I tried to get up, he would tighten his grip on me. He would…he would smell me and make inappropriate comments about my body and my looks.

"When I was fourteen, he forced me to drink a cup of moonshine in front of him and his friends. When I passed out, he came into my room, and that was the first time…the first time he raped me—"

"She's a liar!" Mrs. West screamed, jumping to her feet.

"Ma'am, one more outburst, and you will be removed from this room, do you understand me?" Ms. Lemon asked.

Mr. West guided his wife back into her seat and held her close.

Ms. Lemon turned back to me. "You may continue."

"*Um*...that was the first time. After that, he started coming into my room when my sisters were asleep and my mother was working. Sometimes he would just touch me while he touched himself. Other times, he would make me touch him. Most times, he forced himself on me. I threatened to tell, but he said he would go after my sisters next. They were just little girls...I had to protect them. So I took it. For years, I took the abuse so they wouldn't have to.

"The night...the night I killed him, he came into my room drunk. I was tired...so tired of him doing whatever he wanted to me. I said no, and when he came at me, I grabbed a pair of scissors and stabbed him in the neck. I was terrified that he'd keep hurting me, so I kept stabbing him over and over. I just wanted him to stop. I didn't plan to kill him; I just wanted him to stop."

I sniffled as I finished telling my story. Repeating those details was triggering me in the worst way. My chest felt tight, and it was getting harder to breathe. I rested my hands on the table to steady myself and my breathing.

"Ms. Chambers, are you okay?" Ms. Lemon asked, her voice full of concern.

"Yes, ma'am. I just...I need a moment."

"Get her some water."

A few seconds later, an officer appeared with a cup of water. I thanked him before chugging the entire cup.

"You can do this," Erica said, gently rubbing my back. "Take some deep breaths."

I did as she stated, and after a minute or so, my breathing returned to normal. I stood upright and faced the parole board again.

"I apologize."

Ms. Lemon nodded. "How do you feel about your actions now, Ms. Chambers?"

I paused. "Would you like me to be honest?"

"Please."

"I am sorry that I had to take a life in order to protect myself and my sisters, but I do not regret it. I wasn't safe in my own home. My mother didn't protect me. My life was in danger, and if I hadn't protected myself, I was going to continue to be abused or die fighting him off. I will never apologize for protecting two innocent little girls and choosing to live, even if it meant having my freedom taken."

Ms. Lemon looked at the others, then back at me. "So, you accept full responsibility for your actions?"

"Yes, ma'am."

"How have you spent your time while incarcerated?"

"I read as often as I can, and I journal. I was able to earn my GED and my cosmetology license. It's not something I ever dreamed of doing, but many of the women in my cellblock came to me to do their hair for visits or birthday and holidays. They just wanted to feel beautiful in spite of their circumstances. I'm glad I was able to help them with that."

Ms. Lemon smiled softly. "According to your records, you have been a model inmate—not a single infraction in ten years. How did you manage that?"

I smiled softly. "My cellmate became a motherly figure. She looked out for me and told me how to survive my time. She protected me." I looked behind me at my aunt and uncle. "Then there is my Aunt Penny and Uncle Clive. They constantly prayed for me and showed me love from the outside. They are all I have in this world since my mother has cut me off from my sisters."

Ms. Lemon nodded. She and the other board members took turns asking me various questions such as how my thinking had changed since committing the crime, what was planned if released, where I would live and work, and how I would manage potential triggers or high-risk situations. Erica had briefed me on the types of questions they would ask, and I tried not to make it sound like my answers were rehearsed.

"Two final questions, Ms. Chambers," Ms. Lemon said. "First, how do you think your crime impacted the victim's family?"

I looked over at Rodney's family. "I know they hate me—I've been told such to my face. I can imagine they miss him and still grieve for him, but I grieve for what I lost because of him, too."

"Why do you think you should be granted parole at this time?"

"Honestly, Ms. Lemon, I don't have much hope in being granted parole, but I would like to go home before I'm forty-seven years old. I did a horrible thing in the heat of the moment, but a horrible thing was done to me for much longer. I fully realize that I committed a crime, but I was a victim. No one could save me, so I had to save myself. Ten years in prison is nothing compared to the hell I lived in that house. I just want a chance to live and be completely free."

Ms. Lemon nodded. She spoke briefly with the board members before turning back to me.

"Thank you, Ms. Chambers. You may be seated."

"Thank you."

I took a seat, unsure of how to feel. The board's faces were hard to read, but that was to be expected. Of course, they had to have poker faces in this line of work. I wasn't sure if I had helped or hurt my case with my candid honesty, but I couldn't lie. Only time would tell.

CHAPTER 4

Killian

I SAT IN the back of the room, with my heart racing as Alayah recounted what lead to her committing murder. I felt sick to my stomach knowing that she was going through all that. I hated myself even more for not saying anything when I suspected something was wrong. When her eyes met mine earlier, all I saw was the seventeen-year-old girl I'd been crushing on for the longest time.

One thing I could say was prison hadn't hardened her looks. She was still as beautiful as the last time I'd seen her. Today, she was dressed in a white button-down shirt, navy blue slacks that hugged newfound curves, and matching heels. Her curls were just as wild and free as I remembered, only her hair was longer. A fresh face highlighted the freckles I'd loved so much long ago. And those eyes—those same beautiful brown eyes made my heart stop.

She was more than beautiful outside. She was beautiful inside, in spite of the ugly thing she'd done. I prayed the parole board would show her grace.

Turning my attention back to the front of the room, it was time for the victim's family to speak. Mrs. West stood and headed to the podium with her husband at her side. She glared at Alayah for a moment before speaking.

"There is no greater loss than a parent burying their child. Rodney was my son. I carried him for nine months. I nurtured him and took care of him. I raised a good, respectable, hardworking man, and I refuse to believe he did any of the things he was accused of. For five years, he helped the woman he loved raise her children. He loved and cared for them like they were his own, and that very child he took care of took his life from him.

"Alayah Chambers is a murderer. She stabbed my son twenty-six times in his face, neck, and chest. She deserves to rot in jail for what she's done. My family will never see my son again. We will never have peace in his death. Seeing her walking around free while he rots in the ground will never sit right with me. I beg of you, please keep this animal where she belongs."

One by one, several of the West family members spoke on behalf of Rodney. When it was time to have someone speak on behalf of Alayah, more people than expected spoke for her defense. There was her aunt and uncle; Ms. Snider, our favorite teacher in high school; a few correctional officers from the prison; as well as the warden.

Everyone said so many good things about her, but the one thing they all agreed on was she was not a troublemaker, and she wasn't vengeful. They all described her as someone who was quiet and kept mostly to herself. That was the truth.

I was a little confused when the board excused themselves from the room. Alayah was taken to the back. I stood from my seat and went to speak with Erica.

"What's going on?" I asked.

"They are deliberating."

"Now?"

"Yes. Killian, I've been working on this case for a year. Andrea owed me a favor. I had them look over every file, every transcript, every testimony with a fine-tooth comb when I presented this. I watched the tapes myself. Something was very wrong in that trial. There was no way they should have thrown the book at her the way they did. If she gets parole, this isn't over. I'm looking into everybody involved."

"You think something dirty went down?"

"I'd bet my life on it. I haven't told Alayah this because she has enough on her plate, but I plan to have the entire case reviewed."

"Can I help you?"

She looked surprised. "I don't know, Killian. I don't want you getting too close to this considering your past with her."

"I won't. Whatever I can help with, I'll do it. I owe her that much."

She sighed. "We'll talk."

I nodded and headed back to my seat. It wasn't long before Alayah was being brought back in at the same time the parole board took their seats. Ms. Lemon motioned for her to stand.

"Ms. Chambers, I first want to extend my deepest apologies for all you have had to endure. We did not make this decision lightly. When this case was presented to us, an extensive number of reviews took place before we granted this hearing. That being said, we have taken into account the facts of this case and the testimonials given here today."

She gave a sympathetic look, and I wasn't sure what was coming after that.

"Let me say this: While it is not my place to convict, I believe that you were not handled as a victim. Your previous council failed you. The people who were supposed to protect you failed you, and so did the justice system. I will not allow you to be failed today."

She looked over at the Wests. "Before I read this verdict, let me remind everyone to conduct themselves in a professional manner. Any outbursts or unacceptable behavior will result in arrests. Do I make myself clear?"

The room fell silent, but several heads nodded. Ms. Lemon turned back to Alayah.

"Parole is granted on the grounds that you will live with your aunt and uncle as well as gain and maintain legal employment. You will be required to meet regularly with a parole officer, avoid contact with known criminals, and adhere to every condition that will be provided to you in writing. Any violation of these terms could result in your return to custody. Do you understand and agree to these conditions?"

Alayah stood frozen for a moment. It was as though she didn't hear what was said.

"Ms. Chambers, do you understand?"

"Y–Yes…" she whispered.

"I hate to send you back, but we have to get the paperwork processed. You should be released within the next twenty-four to forty-eight hours. And Ms. Chambers?"

"Yes, ma'am?"

"Make the most of this second chance. So many don't get one."

"Yes, ma'am. Thank you…thank you…"

It was at that moment, she eased into her seat, and her shoulders slumped. She released an audible cry that shook me to my core. Erica gently rubbed her back as she whispered to her. Her aunt and uncle stood and reached for her. As they shared a tearful embrace, the West family stormed out of the room.

I stood from my seat to exit as well. Looking to the front, I noticed Alayah's eyes on me. I offered her a warm smile and mouthed, *"Congratulations."* I was proud of her. She deserved to have this freedom. I just prayed that when the case was revisited, she would finally have justice.

"Hello. Hello! Where y'all at?"

It was Sunday, which meant I was having a family dinner with my parents; my sister, Bridget; her husband, Collin; and my five-year-old niece, Ellie. This was a staple in our family once my sister and I moved out. Every Sunday, unless we had a prior engagement, we gathered at our childhood home for a meal that was sure to induce a food coma.

"Uncle Killian!"

I heard the head full of beads and the sound of my niece's bare feet on the hardwood floor before I saw her. She came running full speed at me with her arms outstretched. I tucked my keys away and prepared to catch her as she jumped into my arms.

"Hey, princess," I said, scooping her up. "How's my favorite niece?"

She giggled. "I'm your only niece, Uncle Killian."

"You are. I missed you, Ellie."

"I missed you, too. Guess what."

"What's that?"

"I got all gold stars at school, and I was student of the week."

"That's my girl. I'm proud of you, baby."

"Thank you!" She held out her little hand and smiled at me.

"What?" I asked, feigning ignorance.

"My monies. You promised to give me monies if I did good in school, and I did. You gotta pay me."

I laughed as I reached into my back pocket for my wallet. Ellie absorbed everything and forgot nothing. Opening my wallet, I held it out for her to pick what she wanted.

"You can pick one bill."

She tapped her finger against her chin as though she was thinking hard before reaching in and plucking a fifty-dollar bill. I just knew she was going to grab the hundred.

"Thank you, Uncle Killian."

"You're welcome."

I placed her on her feet, and she grabbed my hand, then led me into the kitchen where my mom and sister were. From the window, I could see my father and brother-in-law standing by the smoking grill chatting it up.

"Mommy, look! Uncle Killian gave me some monies for doing good in school this week!"

She waved the fifty-dollar bill around excitedly. My mother laughed.

My sister just shook her head. "I've told you not to spoil her so much, Killian."

"I don't remember that conversation."

I walked over to hug and kiss both of them before stealing a piece of bacon my mother had cooked to put in her cabbage. She popped my hand and shooed me away.

"I'm gonna put you out of my kitchen. You do this every Sunday."

"You should be used to it, then."

She rolled her eyes. "How's your week been?"

I blew a breath. "It's been…something. Hey, Ellie, why don't you go outside with Daddy and Grandpa for a second. We need to have grown-up talk."

"Okay."

I waited until she was on the other side of the door.

"Ma, do you remember Alayah Chambers? She was my partner on a science project, and we used to study together."

"The little freckled-face girl you were crushing on?"

"That's her."

Bridget snapped her fingers. "The one that…you know, killed her mama's boyfriend?"

"That would be her, too."

"What about her?" they both asked.

"She was granted parole."

"Good for her," my mother said. "That poor girl never deserved prison time. Now that mama... She should have been under the jail. You can't tell me she didn't know what was going on."

"Mama, these women don't care," Bridget said, waving her hands. "Some of them just want a man to say they have one, and some of them are jealous of their daughters, like there is some kind of competition."

My mother sighed. "You're right about that. But to allow your boyfriend to continuously rape your daughter and say you didn't know? Come on, now. That poor girl would have been showing signs or something. She should have gotten therapy, not a thirty-year sentence."

I nodded. "I agree. I wish I knew then what I know now. Maybe I could have helped her. It's crazy how her lawyer didn't fight for her and the law refused to acknowledge the abuse she suffered. I read the court transcripts and watched the tapes. They focused more on her mental state at the time of the murder than what lead her to it."

Bridget touched my shoulder. "This is really weighing on you, huh?"

"It's always weighed on me, sis. I've been to that house. I watched that man interact with her and how uncomfortable she was just breathing his damn air."

My sister shook her. "You were a kid, Killian."

"I was old enough to know something wasn't right."

My mother placed a hand on my other shoulder. "Baby, there was nothing you could have done if she denied it. A friend of mine went to that trial. That man threatened to do the same to her sisters if she told anybody. She probably would have taken that secret to her grave if she could have. I don't want you blaming yourself for things beyond your control, you hear me?"

I sighed. "Yes, ma'am. Erica is looking to have the case reviewed. I'm planning to help her. Maybe we can get the conviction overturned and her record expunged."

She offered me a smile. "I hope you two are successful."

Truthfully, I hoped we were, too. An overturned conviction wouldn't change the time she'd already served, but at least it wouldn't count against her anymore. My thoughts drifted back to seeing Alayah at the parole hearing. She had always been beautiful, but her as a grown woman... She was gorgeous.

I remembered the day I was going to ask her to be my girlfriend, but I chickened out. We'd been studying together for a few months, and our friendship had grown into something different.

She wasn't as shy around me. She cracked jokes or played around with me. Sometimes she even talked shit. My friends teased us about us being a couple, but she always insisted that we were just friends.

"You never wanted a boyfriend?" I asked one day during lunch.

She looked up at me curiously as she took a sip of her juice. "I don't know."

"What do you mean you don't know? You like being single?"

She shrugged. "Boys don't really pay attention to me, Killian."

"Trust me, they look. You're just so busy looking elsewhere."

"What would they be looking at? I don't look like the other girls at this school."

"So. You don't need to look like anybody but you. These other girls do too much. You...you are naturally beautiful, Alayah."

She blushed. "Killian, stop."

"I'm serious. You're always so put together. You don't show a whole lot of skin like some of these girls."

"I thought y'all liked that."

I waved her off. *"My daddy says you have to leave something to the imagination."*

"And just what are you imagining?"

My face began heating up. I couldn't tell her I'd imagined kissing her every day for the last couple of months. I couldn't tell her that her scent was like a warm hug every time she came near me. I damn sure couldn't tell her I had to count to twenty to calm my raging hormones every time she stared at me with those beautiful brown orbs.

"Hello? Earth to Killian?" She waved her hands in my face, breaking me from my trance. *"Where did you go?"*

"My bad. I was just thinking."

"About?"

"I'd rather not say."

She giggled. *"You must have been imagining something. I'd hate to know what runs through the minds of teenaged boys."* She took another sip of juice. *"What about you?"*

"What about me?"

"You questioned me. Don't you want a girlfriend? I haven't seen you with anybody the whole school year."

I twiddled my thumbs. *"Well, there's this one girl. I'm not sure if she'd be into me though."*

"Why not? You're handsome, smart, and very likeable."

"Thanks. Would you...you know date me?"

She swallowed hard. *"Um...if you were into me, maybe, but you aren't. We're just friends who study together."*

That stung. *"Right...just friends."*

I was too afraid to ask after that. I never imagined that just two weeks later, she'd be arrested for murder. There were so many stories going around the school about what happened. People were asking me questions like I would have the answers. A few people made jokes, saying that it could have been me that was next on the chopping block. I didn't find that shit funny at all.

I got into a couple fights after it all went down, mostly from defending her and myself. I begged my parents to let me go to her trial, but they said I didn't need to hear the gory details. At the time, it pissed me off. I felt like she'd think I'd abandoned her, too. Sadly, I did. Time passed. I graduated and went off to college. My thoughts of her slowly went from every day, to occasionally, to not at all.

Erica putting that file on my desk pulled everything from the back burner to the front. I knew it wouldn't be long before it began to simmer, and I had to see her.

CHAPTER 5

Alayah

"**I** CAN'T BELIEVE my baby is leaving me," Carissa said, cupping my face.

I gave her a teary smile. We were in my cell while I packed up my things. My release was only an hour away, and I still couldn't believe that I was leaving these walls behind. While I wouldn't miss this place, I was truly going to miss Carissa. For ten years, she was the only mother figure I had in here. She treated me just like a daughter, and for that, I would always have love for her.

"I'm gonna miss you so much."

"I'm gonna miss you, too, Riss. Thank you for all you've done for me the last ten years. I'll never forget you."

"I know you won't. Promise me, you won't come back here, baby. You survived, but you don't belong here. Promise me you're gonna do something with your life. I want you to be happy. Go find you a man and let him love you and give you a shitload of babies."

I giggled as she swiped my tears. "I promise."

She kissed my forehead and pulled me in for a warm, motherly hug. "I love you, Alayah. I mean that."

"I love you, too."

Our embrace lasted for a while before we parted ways, and she grabbed my hand.

"Come on. The ladies are waiting to celebrate with you."

She pulled me out of my cell, and I immediately teared up at the sight. The ladies had decorated a table just for me. There was food, drinks, and gifts. Music was being played. Somebody had even made a little cake. They clapped and smiled as we approached them.

"You guys didn't have to do this," I said as I made my rounds hugging each of them.

One woman, affectionately known as Juicy, waved me off.

"Of course we did. It's not every day our lil' baby gets parole. We're gonna miss you around here, boo. Not the screaming in the middle of the night, but we'll miss you."

"Definitely not the screaming," Luna agreed. "Who's gonna do my hair now? I'm gonna be back to looking like a damn bird."

I giggled. "Luna, I showed you how to take care of your hair."

"Yeah, but it's better when you do it."

I shook my head as the rest of the ladies nodded in agreement.

"Open your gifts," Juicy urged.

Carissa ushered me into a seat. I looked around at the gifts all wrapped in newspaper. I didn't know what to open first. Closing my eyes, I randomly picked one. When I opened it, I found handmade little paper roses and a vase made out of a toilet paper roll and pebbles. The second gift was a handmade purse fashioned out of chip bags. I already knew that came from Luna. She'd made them for several of the ladies on the block. There were a few hand-drawn cards and pictures and a journal.

My heart was overjoyed at the love they showed me.

"Thank you all so much," I whispered, fighting back tears.

"You get out of here and make us proud," Juicy said.

All I could do was nod as Carissa massaged my shoulders. They allowed me to have a moment before Luna turned up the radio.

"Alright. Enough of this sad shit. Today is a happy day. We're gonna eat good and party a little before you say goodbye. Get your pretty ass up, mama."

I giggled as she pulled me from my seat and started dancing with me. Time seemed to fly by after that. We ate and had a good time, and before I knew it, CO Judy was calling my name.

"Chambers! Let's go! You're outta here!"

I hugged the girls again before gathering my gifts and taking them to my cell to place them with my other things. With my box in my hand, I made my way to the door where CO Judy was waiting. With one last look back, I offered the girls a tearful smile before I left them forever. The entire way to the front and through the check-out process, my heart raced. This was it. It was really happening.

I was going home.

The walk to the gate seemed to be the longest of my life. The rays from the sun warmed my face. The air was cool and fresh. The sounds of nature seemed to amplify outside of the barbed-wire fences. Everything was so beautiful now that I could take it in from the other side.

I could see my aunt and uncle waiting beside their car. She clung to him with tears streaming down her face as I got to the entrance of the gate. The minute it began to open, they started toward me. When there was just enough space for me to slip out, I broke into a run to them. Placing my box on the ground, I fell into their arms, crying profusely.

"You're free," Aunt Penny whispered, kissing my cheeks.

"We're so happy to have you home, baby girl," Uncle Clive added.

"Thank you." I pulled back to look at them. "Thank you for never giving up on me. I don't know how I'll ever repay you—"

Aunt Penny placed a finger to my lips. "None of that. You are our niece—practically our daughter. We love you. There's nothing in this world we wouldn't do for you."

She kissed my cheek and pulled me back in. It felt so good to hug them. I could feel the love flowing through them and into me. I needed that like I needed air to breathe and food to sustain me. They loved me. They'd spent thousands of dollars fighting for me for ten years. Every week, they were there for visitation. And now, they were the first people I saw when I stepped out of prison and back into normal life.

I wasn't sure what lie ahead for me, but as long as I had them in my corner, somehow, I knew I'd be okay.

We pulled up at the home I'd spent much of my childhood in. Everything was just as I remembered it. Uncle Clive still kept a neatly trimmed yard. Aunt Penny still had the beautiful rosebushes lining the front porch. The tire swing I used to push my sisters on still hung from the big oak tree, and the familiar birdhouse my uncle and I had built was still there, too.

As happy as I was to be here, I was too nervous to get out of the car. Every negative thought flooded my brain. What if I couldn't survive out here? What if my aunt and uncle decided they didn't want to help me anymore and put me out before I could take care of myself? What if I was doomed to go back behind those barbed-wire fences and concrete walls? I was so lost in thought that I didn't hear my uncle open the back door.

He stooped down and took my hand. "What's wrong?" he asked.

"I'm scared."

"What are you afraid of, baby girl?"

"That I'm not gonna make it out here."

"Listen to me: Penny and I didn't fight this long and hard to get you out to let you fall by the wayside. You're home. This is your home for as long as you want it. We will always be by your side, Alayah. If you don't believe anything else, believe that."

I looked from him to my aunt who simply smiled and nodded.

"We can take all the time you need," Uncle Clive said. "When you're ready, we'll go inside."

I sat there for a moment with my eyes closed. Fear was once my worst enemy. It was the one thing that held me captive for so many years. Fear of speaking up caused me to be subjected to unspeakable acts. It led me to taking a life that ultimately cost me my freedom. I was free now. Rodney was dead, and he could never hurt me or anyone else again. I had a second chance at a new life, and I had to make the best of it.

Opening my eyes, I turned to my uncle. "I'm ready."

He nodded and stood to help me out of the car then grabbed my belongings. I followed my aunt up to the front door. When she opened it, the familiar scent of lavender and honey floated into my nostrils. I hesitantly stepped in behind her. Aside from new furniture and new paint on the walls, it looked almost as I remembered. I slowly walked around the living room, looking at the pictures on the walls. There were several of me and my sisters.

I stopped in front of one of the three of us from the last Christmas we spent together. I was sitting on the floor, and the two of them were sitting on my lap, all three of us wearing big smiles. There was so much pain behind my smile, but I always managed to put on a brave face for Adrienne and Amiyah.

Reaching out, I touched their faces. I missed them so much. If nothing else caused me pain, it was not being able to see or talk to them in ten years. Tears pooled in my eyes as I looked at the picture.

"Do they still come over?" I asked.

"Adrienne comes whenever she wants," Aunt Penny said. "She's the rebel of the two of them. Her and your mama don't get along, but Kennedy refuses to let her come live with us. Amiyah is a little more timid. She doesn't like confrontation and tries her hardest to appease your mother. Sometimes she comes with her sister, but she mostly calls or FaceTimes us."

"Are they safe with her?"

She sighed. "I'd like to think so. I always ask Adrienne if there is anything going on that we need to know about. She always says no. I do know that Kennedy has a new man. She's been with him for a while, but he isn't allowed to stay over or be around the girls without her being there."

I gave a sigh of relief. At least she learned from me. It would kill me to learn that she'd allowed yet another man to do to my sisters what Rodney had done to me.

"I miss them so much, Auntie."

She came up behind me, resting a hand on my shoulder. "I know, baby."

"I need to see them."

"Kennedy knows you're living here. The day of your parole hearing, she called and cursed me out for allowing it. Apparently, Rodney's mother called and told her everything. She forbid us to see the girls as long as you are here."

The tears in my eyes stung so bad as I tried to hold them back. It was no use. Before I could stop it, I was in full-blown tears. My knees weakened, failing to hold me up as I fell to the floor and cried. All I wanted was to see two of the four people who'd ever really loved me. I wanted to hold them and hug them and tell them how much I thought of them every single day for the last ten years.

I wanted to tell them how sorry I was that I'd committed such a vile act while they were present—that I'd done it to protect them from suffering the same fate I did. I accepted what I'd done, but I was a victim. If I hadn't done something, Rodney would have preyed on me until I was no longer desirable to him. If it wasn't me, there would have been some other helpless little girl, and I'd be damned if it had been my sisters.

"Come on, baby," Uncle Clive said, helping me to my feet. "Let's get you to your room. Maybe you should lie down for a bit. Today has been a lot. You get some rest and then come eat dinner with us."

I allowed him to lead me down the hall. We came upon the bedroom I'd slept in as a child. When he opened the door, I was pleasantly surprised to find that they had completely transformed it with new furniture fit for a woman of twenty-eight. There was a black queen-sized bed with matching nightstands and a dresser. The bedding held a pretty black, white, and gold pattern.

The white walls had a few pictures with positive affirmations on them. In one corner of the room was an oversized white papasan chair. In the other was a black desk and bookshelf combo. The bookshelf was filled with all kinds of books I couldn't wait to read. I smiled, remembering telling my aunt about all the time I spent in the prison library. I'd always loved reading, but prison only deepened that love.

"Do you like it?" Aunt Penny asked.

"I love it." I turned to face them. "Thank you. I love you both so much."

I went into their arms, the one place I'd always felt safe. If I had to start over with anybody at my side, I was forever grateful that it was them.

CHAPTER 6

Killian

"REMIND ME AGAIN why Pops couldn't come to the grocery store with you," I said to my mother.

It was Sunday, which meant we were having Sunday dinner. It wasn't unlike my mother to wait until the last minute to come to the butcher's section to grab whatever meat she planned to cook for the day. She claimed she liked to get it fresh so it would be at its best.

"You want to eat, don't you?" she sassed me.

"I'm just asking, woman."

"*Mmm-hmm.* Well don't ask. If you must know, your father went by the nursing home to see your grandparents."

"And Bridget?"

My mother stopped walking and placed her hand on her hip. "You got something better to do, son?"

"Nah, I don't."

"Good." She dug into her purse and shoved a piece of paper into my hand. "Go get the things on this list and meet me at the butcher's."

I sighed. "Yes, ma'am."

She patted my face before walking off. Looking down, I saw that the list was a mile long. Shaking my head, I grabbed a cart and started walking up and down the aisles, collecting the items on the list. I turned down the baking aisle and stopped in my tracks. There stood Alayah with her aunt. They spoke softly for a moment, before her aunt walked off and went down another aisle. Alayah busied herself with examining something on the shelf.

She looked so beautiful with a fresh face. She wore a simple pink maxi dress that hugged her curves and a pair of sandals. Her mass of curls was wild and free. I stood still, contemplating if I should say anything. She hadn't seen me, so it would be easy to back off the aisle and come back later. Apparently, that thought didn't register to my feet as they started moving in her direction. They had a mind of their own as I moved around the cart to stand next to her.

"Alayah…" I said softly.

She turned to face me, a stoic expression on her face. "Killian."

"It's good to see you. I'm glad you're home."

"Yeah… Me, too."

She turned back to the items she was previously looking at. That should have been my cue to walk away, but I stood there awkwardly, still talking.

"*Um*…how has it been?" I asked.

"It's not prison."

"Right. Well, are you adjusting? Do you need anything?"

She sighed as she turned to me. "What are you doing?"

"I just—"

"I don't like small talk. I also don't like when people feel like they are obligated to speak to me just because they see me. It's awkward enough having people stare because they know my face."

I shook my head. "I'm sorry. I wasn't trying to make it awkward. I just wanted to check up on you." I paused for a moment, carefully choosing my next words. "I've thought about you over the years. I wish I could have come to see you."

"Be glad you didn't. Prison is depressing, and visitation only reminds you that you're not going anywhere."

"I can only imagine. You look good."

"Yeah, well, thank God I don't look like what I've been through. Listen, Killian, I have to go."

She started to walk away, but I stepped in front of her.

"Maybe we could catch up sometime."

"Why? You wanna hear about my last ten years behind bars? You didn't hear enough in the courtroom? That's why you came, right? To spectate?"

"What? No. Erica and I work at the same firm. I didn't even know she was your lawyer until she asked me to look over the case to help her. I had to recuse myself because I know you—"

"Correction: You *knew* me. You don't anymore. I'm not the same girl you knew in high school. I never want to be that version of myself again. Have a good day."

She turned to walk away, and this time, I let her. I wasn't trying to piss her off, but maybe approaching her wasn't the best idea. We were friends once upon a time, so I thought maybe she could use a friend on the outside. Ten years was a long time to be locked down and not forge a friendship of some sort with the women she was housed with. But she wasn't there anymore. She didn't have to be a loner out here, but I could understand that her trust was all fucked up.

I sighed heavily as I grabbed my cart and continued my shopping. Fifteen minutes later, I met my mother at the butcher's. She glanced over at me, and her brows furrowed.

"What's wrong?" she asked.

"Nothing."

"Don't lie."

"Ma—"

"Killian Lake."

I sighed. "I saw Alayah just now."

She looked around me. "Where is she?"

"Somewhere around here."

"I'd love to see her."

"She doesn't want to be bothered, Ma. She was cold as ice just now."

She gave me a sympathetic look. "*Awww*, baby. Don't take it personal. She was locked away for a long time, and she has a lot of trauma. She's adjusting. You never know what she's dealing with in being home again. I can't imagine it's been easy for her."

I nodded. "You're right. We were friends. I just—"

"You missed your friend. I get it, baby. I know how guilty you felt when she was arrested. You internalized all of that. I know you feel like you could have done something to help her, but the reality is, you couldn't have done a thing. You had no proof, and she didn't accuse him until after he was dead. I know that's hard to accept, but you couldn't save her. Again, I don't want that on your conscious, you understand me?"

"Yes, ma'am."

She offered me a light smile as she cupped my face and kissed my forehead.

"You're a good person, Killian. Don't let anybody or any circumstance make you feel less than that."

She turned away from me and refocused her attention on the butcher preparing her meat package. I knew she was right, but that didn't stop my mind from wandering. I thought back to the day I found out Alayah had been arrested.

It was a normal Friday morning. I walked into school like I did five days a week. The moment I stepped in the building, I got weird looks from way too many people. There were several groups huddled together talking quietly among themselves. As I passed each of them, their eyes darted to me, causing my brows to furrow.

"What the hell is going on around here?" I mumbled to myself.

I kept making strides to my locker, my eyes scanning the hallways for Alayah. Her locker was right across the hall from mine. She was never late to school, so I expected to see her there, but she wasn't. Maybe she was eating breakfast. I didn't think much of it as I opened my locker to grab my first-period books.

My friend Kadeem came up to me with the same weird look on his face.

"Yo, why is everybody looking like that?" I asked, closing my locker.

"You ain't heard about your girl?"

"My girl? My girl who?"

"Alayah."

"What about her?"

"She got arrested, man. She killed her mama's boyfriend."

"Get the fuck outta here, Kadeem. Alayah? She wouldn't hurt anybody."

"Swear to God. She stabbed that nigga up last night."

He pulled out his phone and pulled up a social media post. Staring back at me was a picture of Alayah being led out of her house covered in bloody clothes. Police cars and ambulances were on the scene, and neighbors were gathered around. My eyes widened as I read that she'd stabbed Rodney West a total of twenty-six times, and his face was beyond recognition.

"This can't be right," I said, shaking my head as I handed the phone back to him. "Alayah wouldn't do that unprovoked."

"Shit, I don't know the story, but she definitely did that shit. You see all that blood? It looks like a massacre."

I opened my locker again and grabbed my backpack before starting back toward the main entrance.

"Where you going!" Kadeem called after me.

I ignored him. I had to see Alayah. Something had to have happened. She wouldn't just snap like that.

I drove all the way to the police station that day. I wasn't sure why I thought they would let me see her. I saw her mother, sisters, and who I now knew were her aunt and uncle waiting and crying. My first mind told me to go over there, but I stopped my feet from moving. What the hell was I supposed to say? Defeated, I left the police station and went back home. My parents hadn't left for work yet, and when I walked in, they both looked at me with knowing gazes.

The television was turned to the news station, and the story was playing. I didn't go to school that day. Instead, I sat in my room watching the story on every local outlet that played it. I scrolled my social media, reading every theory my classmates had about what really happened. Some of them thought Alayah was sleeping with Rodney. Some said he must have done something to her because she was too quiet to ever do something like that.

There were so many speculations with no real truth behind them. Kadeem texted me later to tell me there was an entire assembly, and the principal urged anyone who was having problems to speak with the guidance counselor if they needed help. They never said Alayah's name, but they didn't have to. Everybody knew who and what he was referring to.

For weeks on end after the details came out, several people asked me if I knew anything or if she was telling the truth. I said nothing, but every question brought back a memory. It was her behavior or little things she said and did. All the signs of abuse were there, yet somehow they were missed. I felt like I failed her as a friend. As much as I spoke with her, as much as I'd been to that house, I should have known...I should have known.

CHAPTER 7

Alayah

ONE OF THE conditions of my parole was that I found a job. I think my biggest fear was going for an interview and having someone recognize my face. I'd been home for two weeks now, and other than going with my aunt to the grocery store, I hadn't left the house. I spent most of my time in my room reading or in the backyard in the garden.

In prison, my first work duty consisted of maintaining the garden. It was supposed to help build vocational skills, boost mental health and self-esteem. I can admit that it gave me a sense of pride in growing something with my own two hands. My aunt grew most of her fruits and vegetables and had been doing so since I was a kid. Growing up, my sisters and I used to help her when we came over. In a way, it made me feel closer to them since I couldn't see them.

Today, I was going with my uncle to his mechanic shop to start my training. His receptionist was going on maternity leave soon, so he'd graciously offered me her job temporarily. Once she came back, he said he would find something for me to do if I wanted to stay there. I appreciated him being so accommodating. I was a little nervous with meeting everyone. There was no telling how they would react to me.

I got up bright and early to get myself together. Technically, it wasn't an office job, but I would have my own office. He told me to dress comfortably, so I threw on a white V-neck that I tucked into a pair of green cargo pants, along with my white slip-on canvas shoes. I slicked my curls into a low ponytail and borrowed a few pieces of jewelry from my aunt to accessorize.

"You look so good," she said, beaming with pride. "Turn around. Let me see you."

I giggled. "Aunt Penny, this isn't the first day of school, and I'm not a kid."

She waved me off. "I don't care about any of that. This is your first job."

"Given to me by my uncle. I didn't earn it."

She cupped my face and peered into my eyes. "It's still something to be proud of, baby. Most people who come home from prison come home to nothing. Celebrate your wins, even if you had a little help getting there, understand?"

I nodded. "Yes, ma'am."

"Good. Now, spin for me!"

I playfully rolled my eyes, and I spun so she could get a three-sixty look at me. My uncle came to the room door with a smile on his face.

"You look great, baby girl."

"Thank you."

"Alright, Clive," Aunt Penny said. "Don't let those men in there get in my baby's face."

"Oh, they have already had that pep talk. They know not to look in her direction."

I shook my head. I didn't even want to think about a man. They were the last thing on my mind. As far as I was concerned, they could stay as far away from me as possible. I didn't need one, and I didn't want one—not as my man, not as a sneaky link, not as a friend.

My thoughts drifted back to Killian.

Once upon a time, he'd been my friend—my best friend at that. I knew he cared about me, and I shouldn't have expected him to try to contact me after I was arrested, but it hurt me that I never heard from him. Seeing him in the courtroom, then in the grocery story fueled that hurt because why would he want to talk to me now? Maybe it was childish. Maybe I expected too much. It wasn't like I reached out to him either, so it was what it was.

"You ready to go?" Uncle Clive asked.

"Yes, sir."

"All right, baby. We're gonna head out."

He pulled my aunt into his arms and kissed her sweetly. That made me smile. He'd always been the most loving and caring man and the only father figure I'd ever had. If I were to end up with a man one day, he had to be like my uncle.

"I'm gonna bring you two some lunch later," Aunt Penny said. She cupped my face again. "Have a great day, Alayah. I love you."

"I love you, too, Auntie."

She kissed my cheek then ushered us out of the room. I followed my uncle out to his car and climbed in. The drive didn't take more than fifteen minutes. I'd been to his shop often as a kid. Usually, he let me help him change a tire or pass him a few tools. Today would be interesting to say the least.

When we got there, he introduced me to the crew. There was a mixture of younger and older men and one woman. I didn't miss the lustful stares or the overly friendly smiles. The woman, who he introduced as Londyn, offered me a warm smile.

"You are gorgeous," she said, snapping her fingers.

Her nails were long, and I wondered how she did any work with them. She was a beautiful girl with flawless butter-pecan skin, full lashes, bone-straight weave down her back, and a body I was sure most women went under the knife for.

"Thank you," I said, returning the smile.

"Londyn is gonna try to make you her best friend," Uncle Clive warned.

She giggled. "I absolutely am. It's tough being the only female mechanic on the team, girl. They treat me like I'm delicate and don't know anything when I could run circles around them."

The men all spoke up in protest.

My uncle quieted them down. "All right, all right. Introductions are over. Get back to work."

"We'll talk," Londyn said, winking at me.

She left me with a smile as they dispersed back to their assignments. Uncle Clive led me down the hall to the office where I'd be working. He knocked softly before opening the door. Inside stood a very pregnant woman at a copy machine.

"Morning, Charlene."

"Good morning, Mr. Clive." She turned to face us and smiled. "You must be Alayah. Nice to meet you."

"Nice to meet you, too."

"I'm gonna leave you two to get better acquainted. I'll be right out front if you need me, baby girl."

"Okay."

He kissed my temple and left the room. Charlene gathered her papers and waddled back behind the desk.

"Your uncle is a very sweet man."

"He is."

"You ready to take my place?"

"I might as well be. I don't know anything about being a receptionist."

"Lucky for you, I'm a great teacher. I have a pretty simple organization system. The hardest part will probably be entering data. Everything else is pretty much basic customer service. You greet customers, take calls, schedule appointments, handle complaints, and take payments. Don't pay these men in here any mind. They will fuck anything with legs, and a pretty little thing like you is right up their alley."

I swallowed hard. "I peeped that. I'm not interested. I just want to do my job and go home."

"That's the spirit. Well, we're about to open. You'll simply shadow me for the day. Tomorrow, I'll see what you've learned."

I took a deep breath and nodded. I was a little nervous. This was my first day at my first job as a twenty-eight-year-old woman. This wasn't what I had in mind, but it was better than nothing, and I was grateful for it.

Today will be a good day, I told myself.

Lunchtime rolled around before I knew it. I was feeling confidant in my new job duties already. Granted, we hadn't done anything too complicated. Tomorrow would tell if I had really learned anything.

Aunt Penny brought Uncle Clive and me lunch. While he ate in his office, I decided to go to the break room to enjoy my meal. When I walked in, a few of the guys were also on lunch. I gave a light smile and took a seat in the back. I ate quietly for a minute or two before the one Uncle Clive introduced as Theo came and took a spot in front of me.

"How you doing, beautiful?" he asked, flashing his gold grill at me.

My brows furrowed as I swallowed my food. "Fine."

"Why you looking at me like that?"

"Because you just invited yourself into my space."

He chuckled. "My bad, shawty. I was just being hospitable. I didn't mean to ruffle your feathers. Mr. Clive never said he had such a beautiful niece. Where you been hiding?"

I stared at him with a blank expression, hoping he would get the hint. He continued to sit there, waiting for me to answer.

"Oh, you one of those playing-hard-to-get women. I know that type all too well."

Something about that statement sent a chill up my spine. He was giving off predator vibes, and I didn't like it.

"Look, I'm just trying to eat so I can get back to work."

"And I'm just trying to get to know you a little. You don't have to be so cold, pretty girl."

Pretty girl.

The sound of that caused my heart to race. I squeezed my fork and tried to control my breathing. Those two words would forever haunt me. It didn't matter that Rodney was dead and gone. The significance of those words lived rent free in my head.

The sound of approaching footsteps caused my gaze to shift. Londyn walked in, and her eyes immediately fell on me. She stood there for a moment, looking between me and Theo before walking over.

"Theo, didn't Mr. Clive say to leave this girl alone?" she asked.

"I was just being friendly—"

"Well, take your friendly ass on somewhere. Go on. Git."

He kissed his teeth as he pushed off from the table and stood. He looked back at me like he wanted to say something, but Londyn smacked the side of this head.

"Bye!"

He waved her off before going back to the table he'd come from. Londyn turned to me and motioned to the chair.

"You mind if I sit?"

I shook my head no. "Thank you."

"No thanks needed, girl. These men can be creepy, and I don't just mean the ones that work here." She shook her head as she opened her lunch bag. "So, how's your first day been so far?"

"It's been okay. Charlene is very thorough."

"She's good at her job."

"How long have you been here?" I asked.

"Five years. Mr. Clive was one of the few people willing to give me a chance. You know men think they own and run the world. God forbid a woman do the same job as a man and do it better than him. Anyway! I take it you're new to town?"

"No. I grew up here."

"Really? Now that you mention it, your face looks very familiar."

I swallowed hard. "Well, you know what they say: Everybody looks like somebody."

"True, but I swear I've seen you before. Did you go to Eastpoint?"

Slowly, I nodded. I knew where this was about to go. I was hoping to avoid this shit.

"What year did you graduate?"

"I, *uh*...I didn't graduate."

"Oh. Did you drop out or something?"

"Or something."

She eyed me curiously before a grin broke out on her face. "I can tell when I'm being nosy. I'm sorry. I won't pry. Anyway, we should hang out sometime."

"I don't know—"

"I promise I'm not that pushy. I just don't really have many people I consider a friend. Mr. Clive and Mrs. Penny are angels, so I figured you were good people. You seem quiet and out of the mix. I just got a vibe we might make good friends. Plus, you're gorgeous. Pretty girls like pretty girls."

"Are...Are you hitting on me?"

I'd been in prison a long time, so it wasn't uncommon that women in there found me attractive.

Londyn laughed out loud. "What? Girl, no! Well, if I had a little liquor in my system, I might want to rub on your booty a little bit, but I'm strictly dick, love. I just give credit where credit is due. I mean, your auntie is a baddie, too, for her age."

I blew a breath of relief. "Just making sure."

"Why? Are you—"

"No. I'm not interested in women, men…nobody. I'm just focusing on me at the moment."

"I get that. My money is the only thing that makes me cum right now." She offered me a warm smile. "So, what do you say? You wanna hang out sometime? We can take it slow—maybe go out for lunch at work. I get the feeling you aren't too trusting of people."

I hesitated for a moment. She read me right. The only people I'd trusted in ten years outside of my aunt and uncle were locked behind bars. I knew I had to learn to trust other people on the outside at some point. Londyn seemed nice. I'd make sure to ask my uncle about her, but what could it hurt being friendly?

"Okay," I said softly.

She clapped gleefully. "Awesome! Don't worry. I'm gonna make sure you're comfortable here. Let me give you the rundown on everybody."

My lunch hour seemed to fly by listening to Londyn talk. I mean, she never stopped talking, but she seemed like a genuine person. I'd just have to get used to her. When lunch came to an end, I headed back to the office with Charlene. My uncle stopped me to check in, and I told him about lunch with Londyn. When I mentioned Theo, the frown on his face told me that maybe I shouldn't have said anything.

He walked me to the office and told me he would take care of it. What did that mean?

"You had a good lunch?" Charlene asked.

"It was okay."

"Well, I hope you're energized and ready to jump back in."

"I'm ready."

We were about to get started on the next task when a slight commotion out front caught our attention. Charlene peeped through the blinds, and we saw that my uncle had Theo out front giving him what looked to be a stern talking to. I couldn't hear what he was saying, but he had his finger in that man's face and a frown on his own.

Theo raised his hands in surrender and shook his head frantically. The only thing I could make out was Uncle Clive saying, *"Don't fuck with her."* He left Theo standing there rubbing the back of his head. Charlene closed the blinds and sat back down.

"I wonder what that was about." She shrugged as she signed into the computer.

I didn't say anything. I just hoped I hadn't opened a can of worms.

CHAPTER 8

Killian

"MS. THOMPSON, MY name is Killian Lake, your defense attorney. How are you today?"

"I gotta get outta here. I didn't do anything."

"I understand your concern—believe me, I do. Right now, I just need to get your side of the story. In order for us to have the best defense, you have to tell me everything. Can you do that?"

"I'll tell you whatever you want to know."

"Good. Now, before we begin, I must emphasize that everything you say to me is protected by attorney-client privilege. It's crucial that you don't discuss this case with anyone else. Anything you say outside these walls can and will be used against you. Do you understand that?"

She nodded. "Yes, I understand. Thank you for taking my case. My mother had to put her house up to get me a good lawyer. You have to help me."

"I'm gonna try my best. You just work with me. Now, can you walk me through what happened on the night of July 7 when Mr. Owen Davis was found dead?"

Ms. Thompson sighed heavily. "I was at home most of the night. I did go out around eight-thirty to pick up some groceries.

It took me a little longer because there was an accident, and I had to drive around it both ways, but I was back by ten."

"Do you always pick up groceries so late at night?"

"I'm a nurse. I go to work eleven at night and get off at seven in the morning. Sometimes I work a double shift, so I don't get off until three. I'm tired. I go home, shower, and try to get some sleep. I get whatever errands I can get done when I wake up."

"Did you see Mr. Davis at all that day?"

She nodded slowly. "He asked me to come see him. We had lunch and ended up having a very heated argument. There were witnesses, and I might have said some incriminating things to him, but that doesn't mean I killed him. I didn't even know Owen was dead until the police showed up at my door the next morning."

"What were you arguing about?"

She avoided my gazed and the question. "Nothing."

"Again, Ms. Thompson, if you won't tell me the truth, I can't help you."

She sighed. "He wanted to call things off."

"Call what off?"

"Our…entanglement."

"So, you two were romantically involved?"

"Yes. I loved Owen. I would never hurt him. I was just upset. He'd been stringing me along for years. Even when I found out he had a wife and tried to end things, he just kept pulling me back. He told me at lunch that she was becoming suspicious and we needed to cool it for a while. I was upset because he'd been promising me for a whole year that he was going to leave her."

"I see," I said, making a note of her confession. "Can anyone confirm your alibi for the night in question?"

"My neighbor. She saw me come home with the groceries. We had a whole conversation in the driveway, and I have a receipt from the store at my house."

"Good, good. That's helpful. Now, the prosecution claims they have DNA evidence linking you to the crime scene. Can you think of any reason your DNA might be present in Mr. Davis' home?"

She hesitated. "Well, I was at Owen's house earlier that week. His wife was out of town visiting her mother."

I shook my head. This was one thing I hated about being a lawyer. People omitted vital information that could help their case for the sake of saving face.

"That's crucial information, Ms. Thompson. Why didn't you mention this to the police?"

"I was scared," she exclaimed. "I thought it would make me look guilty."

"And I understand, but withholding information only makes things worse. Case in point: Look where you're sitting. Is there anything else you haven't told me or the police?"

Again, she avoided my eyes.

"Ms. Thompson…"

"Just one thing."

"Which is?"

"Two days before his murder, his wife confronted me. Apparently, she's been suspecting him of cheating for a while and had cameras installed in the house. She saw me there and came to my job to confront me in the parking lot."

I sighed. "Alright, Ms. Thompson. The good thing is you said she has cameras in the home. We can get a warrant to have her turn over the video evidence. The downside to that is hopefully she hasn't destroyed it. In that case, we would have to go through the security company to get the footage, and that could take a little longer. I really wish you had told the police this. This is time-sensitive information. I'm gonna see what I can do as far as getting you bail, but I won't make any promises."

She nodded repeatedly before bursting into tears. I stuck around long enough to comfort her before leaving the room. I stopped by the chief's office and told him I needed a search warrant for Mr. Davis' widow before heading home for the day. No sooner than I got in my car did my phone ring with a call from my best friend, Kadeem. I answered on Bluetooth.

"What's up, man?"

"What's good, my brotha?"

I sighed. "Long day."

"Sounds like you need a drink."

"I damn sure do."

"Meet me at Kinko's. We need to catch up anyway. It's been a minute since we linked."

"Bet. I'm headed that way."

I hung up and rerouted my destination. Ten minutes later, I was walking into the bar and grill. I spotted Kadeem at a table talking to a server who was clearly flirting with him. The old Kadeem would have taken the bait, but my boy was a changed man. He didn't even crack a smile. I shook my head as I headed in his direction. He gave me a nod before sending her on her way and standing to greet me.

"Killian Lake," he said, slapping my hand. "Good to see you, man."

"Good to see you, too." I took a seat at the table and got comfortable. "How's the family, man?"

"Blessed, highly favored, and forever growing. Kyah is pregnant with our second baby."

"Congratulations. How does Parker feel about being a big sister?"

He grinned. "She's excited. She can't keep her hands off my wife's belly, and she's forever talking to the baby. Baby girl is hoping for a brother. Truthfully, so am I. I need somebody to balance out all that estrogen, man."

"As someone who grew up in a balanced household, it ain't all it's cracked up to be. Sometimes the estrogen is still just as overpowering."

"I guess I better prepare then, huh? What's been up with you? How's life at the firm?"

"It's life, man. Same shit, different day."

"I'd think you'd be rolling in excitement. Criminal law can't be boring."

"It's not boring at all. Overwhelming at times? Yes. Dumbass criminals? Absolutely. Some of the shit I hear and see, it's like you can't make this up."

"It's *First 48*, huh?"

"Just like *First 48*. I couldn't live a life of crime. I'm no punk, but I'm not built for jail."

"Say that again. I don't know how career criminals do it."

I shrugged. "Some people get conditioned to life behind bars. They can't function on the outside. Some of them have no ambition. Others are products of their environment. You have biological and psychological factors, substance abuse, social and family influence, poverty, mental health issues, and employment issues, man. It's a lot that goes into building a criminal. Add to that, the system doesn't protect those it wasn't built for either."

"You said a mouthful there. We look injustice in the face every day, and most times, ain't shit we can do about it."

I nodded and paused for a moment. All this talk about injustice made me think of Alayah. There were too many women like her behind bars—women who were victims and were now doing hard time for finally putting an end to their abuse. I contemplated telling Kadeem about her. He was the one who broke the news to me in the first place back in the day. He was one of the few people who understood the way Alayah's arrest made me feel.

"What's on your mind?" he asked, noting my silence.

"You, *uh*...you remember Alayah Chambers?"

"Our classmate? The one who got arrested for offing her mother's boyfriend?"

"Yeah, her."

"What about her?"

"She's out on parole."

"Oh, shit! How do you feel about that? You've seen her?"

I nodded. "I was there when they granted her parole. I recently saw her in the grocery store. That didn't go how I expected. She really isn't trying to have anything to do with me, man. I just wanted to make sure she was doing well, see if she needed anything. She basically told me to piss off."

Kadeem chuckled. "Were you expecting things to be the way they were in high school, Killian? She's been through a lot. She's probably done some things she's not proud of. Prison has a way of changing people. They don't trust easily after being locked up for so long. You gotta remember she did a ten-year bid. Nobody would be the same after that."

"I know that, man. I get it. I just...I miss my friend. I feel guilty about not being there for her. I could have written or visited or something—anything to let her know she wasn't alone."

"You're putting too much guilt on yourself, just like you did back then. Give her some time to get reacclimated to civilian life. Don't be pushy. I'm sure you care. Just don't do the most."

"I don't do the most."

He laughed. "You can. I'm gonna leave it at that though. I think you need to get laid, my brotha—take some of that stress off you."

I waved him off. "My mind ain't even on a woman right now."

"You mean any other woman."

I took a sip of my drink. "I see what you did there. I won't lie, she's been heavy on my mind. But I'm gonna take your advice… well, I'll try."

Kadeem shook his head. "I know you. I know when you're passionate about something, you can't let it go. Just be careful. Sometimes when we wanna do good, we unintentionally cause more problems."

"I hear you."

I changed the subject so Alayah didn't consume my thoughts. I'd been praying for her. I prayed for peace, healing, and her happiness. After all she'd been through, she deserved that.

CHAPTER 9

Alayah

A **WEEK HAD** gone by, and I was settling in at Uncle Clive's shop pretty well.

Charlene was a great teacher. She'd not only shown me step-by-step instructions for daily duties, but she wrote me a little manual in case I forgot something. I had another week to learn all I needed to know because she would be going on maternity leave very soon. She was already walking around groaning and rubbing her belly like she was having contractions. The last thing I wanted was for her to go into labor in the office.

Currently, I was walking around the shop taking inventory while Charlene was on lunch. It had been a pretty quiet day. After Uncle Clive threatened Theo, he didn't even look in my direction, and the others followed suit. I didn't come here to make trouble. I just wanted my space respected.

"You working hard or hardly working?" Londyn asked, rolling from beneath a car.

"I'm just appearing to look busy," I jested. "I'm doing inventory. Just trying to keep busy. An idle mind is the devil's playground."

"Chile, you said a mouthful. I think about all kinds of shit when I'm bored. Like, dumb shit. For instance, how do our brains remember that we forgot something, but we can't remember what that thing was? Or the fact that nothing is really on fire, more like fire is on things—"

I laughed. She was so random.

"Londyn, do you smoke when you're alone?"

She grinned. "Sometimes. These are not my high thoughts, though. Those are much deeper. You smoke?"

"No."

"Edibles?"

"Nope."

"Damn, girl. What do you do for fun?"

I shrugged. "I like to read."

"Oh! You read smut, don't you? You know those quiet, innocent-looking girls always like stuff like that."

I shook my head. "I like romance books."

"But you aren't trying to have your own romance story." She shook her head. "My friend, my friend."

The sound of the door alarm alerted me to a customer. Since Charlene wasn't back, I had to take care of them.

"I'll talk to you later, Londyn."

"Okay, boo."

She slid back under the car while I headed back through the back door to the office that led to the front entrance.

"Welcome to Clive's. How can I help—"

I stopped as my gaze met Killian's. He offered me a warm smile.

"Alayah."

"What are you doing here?"

He held up his hands in surrender. "I come in peace. I just need a tune-up. My usual mechanic is swamped, and he referred me here."

I sighed as I grabbed a work order form and began filling it out. He watched me intently, but remained quiet, only answering the basic questions until I reached for his keys.

"Can we talk?"

"About?"

"You. I just want to know how you're doing, Layah."

Him calling me that softened my heart a little. It reminded me of the friendship we'd shared once upon a time.

"I'm fine, Killian. My uncle got me this job. I'm keeping out of trouble—just going through this transition with my head down."

"I'll ask again: Do you need anything?"

"No. I have everything I need right now."

"What about a friend? You could always use one of those, right?"

"I'm sure being friends with me would do more damage than good. You have a reputation now, don't you? Big-time lawyer. I'm sure you shouldn't be seen with the likes of me."

"What do you mean the likes of you?"

"You know exactly what I mean, Killian. You shouldn't be seen canoodling with a criminal, especially a known murderer."

He shook his head. "Is that all you see yourself as—a criminal? A murderer? That's not how I see you at all. You survived something some people wouldn't have. You protected your sisters from a monster and sacrificed yourself to do so. How many people do you know would have been able to carry a fraction of what you've carried for so long? You are strong, resilient, and deserving of a second chance because the first one was taken from you. Maybe I don't know this version of you, but I see you, Layah."

I struggled to fight back the tears threatening to spill from my eyes. He stepped close to the counter and gently reached for my hand. I jerked back slightly, but he still held his hand out to me. With trembling fingers, I slowly placed my hand in his palm, watching his fingers close around it. He cupped my chin, then slowly lifted my head so my gaze would meet his. We stared at each other for a moment, until the sound of the back door opening broke our trancelike state.

I looked back to see Londyn standing there with a wide-eyed expression. Slowly, I pulled away from him and grabbed his keys.

"Am I interrupting something?" she asked "I can come back—"

"You're fine, Londyn. Did you need something?"

"Yeah. Can you call Mr. Kelton and let him know his car is ready?" She handed over the work order and his keys.

"Sure thing. *Um*, Mr. Lake is getting a tune-up. Can you take care of that?"

"Yep."

I slipped the work order and his keys into a plastic cover and handed it to her. Her pretty brown eyes bounced between us before she slipped back out the door she'd come in. I took a step back from the counter.

"You can wait here, or I can call you when it's done."

"I have a few errands to run with my Pops, so just call me."

"Will do."

"Layah?"

I sighed heavily. "What?"

"Keep my number."

"Why?"

"In case you ever need me. Maybe I can I take you out for a coffee sometime—just to talk."

"I'll think about it. Bye, Killian."

"Don't say bye. That's too final. I'll see you later."

"See you later."

He gave me that million-dollar smile of his as he backed out the door. I watched as he climbed into the car with his father until well after he was gone. I wasn't sure if I was ready to rekindle my friendship with him. Building a bond with Londyn was enough already. Did I really want to reconnect with someone who knew my dirty secret?

"Did you bring lunch today?" Londyn asked me, popping her head into my office.

True to her word, we'd been eating lunch together every day this week. I had to admit, I liked her a little more every day. I was still getting used to her talking so much, but she was cool people.

"I was just gonna grab some chips or something from the vending machine."

"No, ma'am. You can come with me to get something. I'm just going to grab my purse. Meet me out front."

She closed the door, not giving me a chance to protest. Beside me, Charlene giggled.

"Go ahead, girl. Londyn doesn't take no for an answer."

"I've grown to understand that," I said, standing. "I'll be back in an hour."

"Take your time. We'll be here," she added, rubbing her belly.

I grabbed my crossbody and headed out of the office. As I rounded the corner, I bumped into my uncle.

"You headed to lunch?" he asked.

"Yes. Londyn invited me to go with her."

He chuckled. "I told you she was going to make you her best friend. Enjoy yourself, baby."

He kissed my temple, then walked past me. I continued out front. Londyn came prancing out the side door, waving for me to follow her. She headed for this beautiful black-on-black pickup truck with pink accents. Once she unlocked the door, I climbed inside. The inside was decked out in pink as well.

"This is nice," I complimented. "I didn't take you for a pick-up truck kind of girl."

She giggled. "It belonged to my dad. After he passed away, I restored it and made it my own." She cranked up and pulled out of the parking lot. "I always see you ride with Mr. Clive. You don't drive?"

"I, *uh*...I never learned."

"What? Girl, where the hell have you been? We're gonna fix that. I wouldn't be your bestie if I didn't teach you how to drive."

"You don't have to do that—"

"Alayah, please don't piss me off. Friends help friends. Give me a couple months. You'll be driving like a pro. I'll even take you to take the test, and when you pass, we're going to celebrate."

I had to admit, her gesture made me smile. I hadn't had a real friend on the outside since...well, since Killian. I thought back to his visit earlier. He was still the nice boy he was in high school, except now he was a nice man. A nice, handsome, grown-ass man.

I shook that thought from my head because where did it even come from? I refocused my attention back on the road. Londyn turned into this burger spot and parked her truck. We hopped out, and I threw my shades on before we walked inside. I'd been having home-cooked meals since I'd come home, so this was going to be interesting.

I settled on a double cheeseburger basket with fries and a vanilla milkshake. Londyn ended up getting the same, and we grabbed a table while we waited for our order to come out.

"So," she said with a smile, "that guy from earlier. He was cute, right? He seemed to be into you."

I shook my head. "It wasn't like that. We used to be friends in high school. That's it."

"Really? Well, if you were interested, you two would make a cute couple. Those would be some pretty babies."

"You can have him if you want him."

She laughed. "Girl, don't tell me that. It's been a minute, and once I put this cat in his lap, it's a wrap."

We shared a laugh. Londyn was a mess. The more I got to know her, the more she reminded me of my girls back in the pen. The server brought our orders out shortly after, and that burger looked heavenly. It was so juicy with just the right amount of everything on it. The fries were crispy, and the milkshake was smooth and creamy. Tasting everything was like an explosion of flavors in my mouth.

"Oh my God…" I moaned my satisfaction.

"It's good, right?" Londyn asked.

"It's heavenly."

"That itis is gonna kick in, and I'm not gonna be good for shit."

"Me either."

"So, Alayah, I feel like I've told you all about me, but you're still a mystery, babe. This friendship can't be one-sided."

I swallowed my food and wiped my mouth. "I'm sorry. I like you, Londyn. You seem like good people. I just… Trust is a hard thing for me right now."

"Why?"

I contemplated telling her the truth. I wasn't sure how she was going to react. When you told people you spent ten years in prison for murder, you'd expect them to avoid you like the plague. I didn't want that to be my life from here on out.

Before I could respond, a shadow appeared over me, causing me to look up. Glaring down at me was Mrs. West with a phone in her hand. She snapped my picture with the bright-ass flash on.

"It must be nice to be able to go out and have a regular meal like regular people," she said nastily. "Too bad my son will never be able to enjoy this again."

"Mrs. West, now isn't the place or the time."

"Oh, it's the perfect time, you murderous little bitch." She started getting loud, garnering the attention of the people in the restaurant. "Hey, everybody, isn't it crazy that my son is in the grave while his murderer is sitting here eating a fucking cheeseburger? She gets to walk around free while he rots in the ground."

Londyn sprang from her seat. "Lady, you need to walk the fuck away."

"Bitch, don't speak to me," Mrs. West snapped. "Your friend is a cold-blooded murderer. She killed my son—stabbed him beyond recognition, then sullied his name with lies."

"I didn't lie," I said, springing to my feet. "Your son was a despicable, sorry excuse for a man. I guarantee I wasn't his first victim, but I will be his last."

She slapped me so hard my head snapped back.

"You lying whore," she screamed, trying to come at me. Londyn stepped in between us, clocking Mrs. West in the nose in the process. A few of the servers grabbed Mrs. West and carried her out of the establishment. Londyn turned back to me.

"You're bleeding," she said, grabbing a napkin to dab my lip.

I hadn't even felt the blood trickling from it. Grabbing the napkin from her, I sprinted to the bathroom with tears in my eyes. I knew this day would come; I just didn't think it would be so embarrassing. I stayed in the bathroom until Londyn came knocking on the door.

"Alayah? Honey, open the door."

I took a few deep breaths and wiped my face before finally opening the door. She stood there with a sympathetic look along with my purse and a bag of food in her hand.

"Come on, boo."

She grabbed my hand and pulled me out of the bathroom. Instead of going out the front, we went out the side door and made our way to her truck. We got in in silence and drove back in silence. She didn't say anything until we were settled in the parking lot.

"You wanna talk about it?" she asked softly.

I sniffled. "I might as well. You already heard it."

She turned to me, giving me her full attention. "Did you really murder her son?"

I nodded. "That man raped me from ages fourteen to seventeen. He told me if I ever said anything, he'd make sure the same thing happened to my little sisters. I had to protect them. They were too young to have their innocence stolen by some nasty ass, perverted man. I just...I couldn't take it anymore. I told him no, and he tried to attack me. For the first time, I fought back. I grabbed a pair of scissors, and I stabbed him—only I couldn't stop. Stopping meant I had to keep enduring that pain, and I couldn't do that.

"I spent ten years of my life in prison paying for his death. My named was ruined because of his family and my own mother. They painted me out to be this sexual deviant. They got on that stand and told that jury I was promiscuous, and I'd been trying to get that man to sleep with me. They wanted to call it a crime of passion because I stabbed him twenty-six times. Overkill, they said. I caught a manslaughter charge. Ain't that a bitch? I was his victim for three—nearly four years—and he's the one getting justice."

Just thinking about it again fueled my anger. I wish I had punched that old bitch dead in her mouth. Londyn stared at me for a moment before reaching out and grabbing my hand.

"Good for you for protecting yourself and your sisters when no one else could or would. You have nothing to be ashamed of, Alayah. Your story is one so many women share. Some of them never get out alive. I'm so sorry you had to go through that and even more sorry that you were punished for it."

She pulled me into her arms and hugged me tightly. I sat frozen for a moment before I finally hugged her back. I needed that more than she knew. Her energy felt sincere, and I could see why my uncle encouraged me to be friendly with her. The way she stood up for me with no hesitation spoke volumes to her character.

Maybe I did need a friend after all.

CHAPTER 10

Killian

AGE SEVENTEEN

I SPOTTED ALAYAH at *her locker as I strolled the halls before second period. I'd had a test in my first-period class, and thanks to studying with her, I'd aced it. I slapped hands with a few of my friends as I made my way toward her. She was just standing there, looking in the locker like she'd lost something. Sneaking up behind her, I poked her side, causing her to jump.*

"Hey, pretty girl—"

"Don't do that," she snapped, "and don't call me that."

She looked at me with angry eyes, confusing me. We had a playful relationship. She'd always laugh at my attempts to scare her, but today…today seemed different.

"I'm—I'm sorry. I was just playing around like we always do."

"Well, I don't feel like playing today."

She grabbed her history book and slammed her locker shut before storming off down the hall. I stood there for a moment before going after her. I caught her on the empty stairwell, gently grabbing her arm. She jerked away and pushed me.

"Don't touch me!"

I raised my hands in surrender and took a step back. "What's wrong with you?"

"Nothing is wrong with me. I just don't want you touching me. I'm tired of people touching me without my permission."

My brows furrowed. "Who touched you without your permission?"

"Nobody. I just...It's nothing."

"You know you can trust me, Layah. You know that, right?"

Her pretty brown eyes pooled with tears as they met mine. She slumped against the wall and collapsed to the floor in a fit of tears. For a moment, I stood there, not knowing what to do. Dropping my backpack, I took a seat beside her and pulled her into my arms. We were late to second period that day.

She never elaborated on what she meant. She never spoke on it again. In fact, when I saw her during study hall, she seemed to be in good spirits. She was laughing and talking like she hadn't broken down in my arms earlier. I wanted to ask her if everything was okay, and when I did, she told me she was just emotional because she was on her period. She apologized for spazzing on me and asked me to forget about it.

I hadn't forgotten about it though. I beat myself up about that shit for the longest. If I'd just said something...if I'd just made her tell me what was going on, maybe she could have gotten the help she needed.

I sat back at my desk, thinking about Alayah. She'd been an ever-present thought since seeing her at the mechanic shop. By now, she was settling in at her new job. I prayed that she had a happy, healthy, and smooth transition back into civilian life. Still, I couldn't seem to shake her.

Two weeks had gone by, and she hadn't used my number. I mean, I never expected her to, but I was hopeful. I was trying to give her space like Kadeem and my mama told me to, but it was like an itch I couldn't scratch. I wanted to see her...I *had* to see her.

Standing from my desk, I left my office and headed down the hall to Erica's. I gave a light tap, and she gave permission for me to open the door.

"What's up, Killian?" she asked, looking up at me. "You look a little perplexed."

"I am." I took a seat across from her. Leaning forward, I clasped my hands in front of me. "Are you still looking into the Alayah Chambers case?"

"I am. I'm actually about to go see her in about twenty minutes."

I swallowed hard. I wanted to ask her if I could go with her, but I didn't want to be pushy.

"Would you like to come?" Erica asked, seemingly reading my thoughts.

"Was I that obvious?"

She giggled. "You have a horrible poker face, Killian. I don't mind you tagging along since I assume you plan to help me with the case."

"I'll help any way I can."

She eyed me curiously. "I sense there is more to your history with Alayah."

I sighed. "I told you I had a thing for her back when we were classmates. We were friends, but I never got up the nerve to ask her to be more."

"Why not?"

"I didn't think she would want it. If she wasn't studying, she was taking care of her sisters. Her mother would have never let her have a boyfriend anyway."

Erica scoffed. "I need to meet this mother."

"Trust me, you wouldn't be meeting much. How she still has custody of her other children is beyond me."

"According to the police reports, the other two couldn't corroborate Alayah's story. CPS did a visit and didn't find anything that would deem her unfit. The house was clean, they had food, clean clothes and shoes, proper bedrooms, and neither of them had been touched. If anything, they were just very sad about their sister. They loved her very much."

"They did. She was more of a mother to them than a sister. I hope they get to reestablish a relationship."

"Me, too." There was a bout of silence between us before she spoke again. "Well, give me a few minutes to finish up what I'm doing, and we can head out."

"Okay." I stood and headed for the door, stopping when she called my name.

"Killian?"

"Yeah?"

"Try not to go in there with googly eyes, okay?"

I kissed my teeth. "Bye, Erica."

Her laughter rang in my ears as I closed the door behind me.

Erica and I stood on the front porch of Mr. and Mrs. Easton's home. My heart felt like it was resting in the pit of my stomach. Maybe it wasn't a good idea for me to tag along. I was never one to hide my emotions or feelings. I just knew seeing Alayah would stir up all the feelings I buried so long ago. Before I had a chance to bow out, the front door opened, and there stood Mr. Easton.

"Ms. Sawyer. Good to see you."

"Good to see you, Mr. Easton. This is Killian Lake. He works at the firm with me and will be acting as my co-counsel."

He extended his hand to shake mine. "Nice to meet you, Mr. Lake. Wait…have we met before?"

"Yes, sir. I brought my car into your shop for a tune-up a few weeks ago."

"Oh! Right. Well, won't you both come in."

He opened the door wider to allow us entry. Nervously, I stepped inside.

"Thank you for continuing to help my niece," Mr. Easton said, leading us into the living room.

Erica smiled. "Of course. We didn't fight this hard to give up now. There is much work to be done. While I know we can't take back the guilty verdict, we are going to do everything we can to make sure everyone knows she was telling the truth. My goal is to get her conviction overturned. She deserves that justice."

"I agree." Mr. Easton looked behind him and called out. "Penny! Alayah! The lawyers are here!"

I swallowed hard as I heard footsteps approaching. Erica stood, and so did I. When they rounded the corner, it felt like my feet were stuck in place. I couldn't move. I didn't think I was even breathing at this point. Today she was dressed in a pair of joggers and a tank top. Her curls were pulled into a sleek, high ponytail.

Those beautiful brown eyes bore into me, holding me captive. "Who is this?" Mrs. Easton asked.

I couldn't answer her because I couldn't find my voice.

"This is Killian Lake," Erica said, "my co-counsel."

She slapped my arm, breaking me from my trancelike state. I averted my eyes long enough to speak.

"I apologize," I said, extending my hand. "It's nice to meet you, Mrs. Easton."

My eyes fell back on Alayah, who was still looking at me with her arms now crossed and a frown on her face.

"You two know each other?" Mr. Easton asked, looking between the two of us.

Alayah nodded. "We went to school together." She stared at me for a moment before taking a seat next to her uncle. "Why are y'all here?" she asked quietly.

Erica spoke up. "I just wanted to touch base with you on a few things. I know you disclosed some things to me that you may not have disclosed to your aunt and uncle. I would need your permission to discuss them now."

Alayah gave a hard swallow, letting me know that she knew exactly what Erica was referring to. Slowly, she nodded. Mr. and Mrs. Easton looked back and forth between each other.

"What's she talking about, Alayah?" her aunt asked.

Alayah took a deep breath. "I was pregnant," she said just above a whisper. "I had a miscarriage."

Both the Eastons' eyes widened.

"When did this happen?" Mrs. Easton asked. "Why didn't we know about this?"

"I was a fresh seventeen. I didn't need a parent notified."

"Did Kennedy know?" Mr. Easton asked.

Alayah shook her head. "No. Rodney took me to the hospital. My mama was working that night. The girls were asleep. I'd been having really bad cramps all day long, and it just got worst that night. I couldn't sleep because I was in so much pain. When I got up to use the bathroom, there was just so much blood on my sheets. I didn't want to ask him for help, but I knew something was wrong."

Tears welled in her eyes as she paused in her story. I was shocked to hear it because it wasn't in the court records or any of her files.

"I was in denial about the pregnancy. I knew my period was late, and I just couldn't face the fact that I could be carrying that man's child. The girls were asleep, so he left them in the house and made me get in the car and drove me to the hospital on the other side of town. They told me I was having an active miscarriage at eight weeks. Everything moved so fast. Within thirty minutes of being seen, the baby was gone. They gave me a D and C, kept me for a few hours, and then sent me home with meds. Rodney didn't even go in with me. It would have been so easy to just tell them what he was doing to me, but I was scared. He told me before I went inside that if I said anything, I'd be sorry."

The Eastons sat with shocked expressions. The room was so quiet that you could hear a pin drop. Nobody was expecting that. Erica cleared her throat before speaking again.

"I've contacted the hospital he took you to. They do have it in their records that you were seen. I put in a formal request with a judge to have those records subpoenaed, and it was granted." She reached into her bag and produced the documents. "Hopefully, we can find some DNA record of the baby on file. Do you remember signing a consent form for genetic testing or anything like that?"

Alayah shook her head. "I was pretty much in a daze by the time it was over. The doctors were talking, but it all sounded like gibberish to me. I just wanted to get out of there, so I just signed the papers and agreed to whatever they said."

Erica nodded. "Okay, so if they did genetic testing, your baby's DNA is on file. It's logged into their system. You would have gotten a notice or something explaining your results."

"I never got anything," Alayah said. She paused for a moment, seemingly contemplating her next words. "So...you could do a DNA test?"

"Yes. Since we can't get a sample from Rodney, we can try to get DNA from a family member. I suspect they will say no. Worst-case scenario, we would have to get a court order to have one of them tested. The tough part is getting enough evidence to prove any new findings would have changed the outcome of the first trial. Now, the judge that signed off on the subpoena owed me a favor, but I can only ask for so much without bringing him something substantial."

"So basically, I'm screwed?"

"I wouldn't say that—"

Alayah stood, shaking her head. "I don't wanna do this. I don't want to relive this nightmare over and over again. I already have to deal with dreaming about this shit. I don't want to go through that hell again, Erica. I appreciate what you're trying to do. I know you think I deserve justice—and I do—but I've already lost ten years of my life. If there is a chance I can live peacefully, I want that...I *need* that. Please drop this. I got out, and I'm home. Just let me try to have a little slice of normalcy."

Without another word, she left the room. A few seconds later, I heard a door slam. We all sat looking at one another, still digesting what we'd just learned. Erica packed up the papers and placed them back in her bag.

"I won't push her," she said softly, "but I'm gonna continue to work on this. There are too many Rodneys in the world and not enough Alayahs brave enough to fight back. Her story deserves to be told correctly."

The Eastons nodded.

"Give her some time," Mrs. Easton said. "This...This is a lot. She's only been home a few weeks. She's still hurting, and she misses her sisters terribly. My niece isn't in the best headspace right now. Just please...give her a little time."

Erica sighed and nodded as she stood. "I hear you. We're gonna get going."

I stood and extended my hand. "It was nice to finally meet you both. Alayah used to talk about you all the time. I'm glad she has you to come home to."

Mr. Easton offered a warm smile. "Me, too. I'll walk y'all out."

He stood and led us to the front door. He stood on the front porch as we made our way back to the car. As I was climbing in, I felt eyes watching me. I looked up to see Alayah staring out of what I assumed was her bedroom window with her arms crossed. Our gazes met briefly before she pulled down the shades, disappearing from my view. I found myself sighing heavily.

"Don't worry," Erica said, breaking my gaze. "We're going to win this for her."

I nodded. I sure as hell hoped so.

CHAPTER 11

Alayah

I'D BEEN IN an emotional slump for days now.

First, I was dealing with Mrs. West posting my picture on social media and dragging me for filth. She and her family called me everything but a child of God, and my mama was right in the comments with her. The only reason I knew about it was because Kennedy had the nerve to tag my aunt, shaming her for allowing me to live her.

I overheard my aunt and uncle talking about it before I walked into the room. They tried to keep it on the hush-hush, but it was too late. Seeing my picture and my name being sullied left a sour taste in my mouth. My feelings were hurt, and the whole thing pissed me off. I had my aunt print out the post and the comments in case I needed it at a later date.

Then there was the news from my lawyer.

After Erica and Killian's visit, I went into my room and cried my eyes out for what felt like hours. I'd pushed the memory of that miscarriage to the back of my mind for the longest. I wasn't sure what made me tell her that in the first place. We were just talking about my history one visit, and it just spilled out like word vomit. I didn't think it would do much to help my case anyway, and I'd almost forgotten that I told her about it.

That was until she brought it up. Now it was all I could think about. That night was so traumatizing. After being in the hospital all those hours, Rodney took me back home. The drive was so awkward. He kept looking at me like he knew he'd fucked up. When we pulled into the driveway, he shut off the car and turned to me.

"You know not say anything about this," he said calmly.

I nodded, avoiding his gaze.

"Good. I'll get this prescription filled." He reached out cupped my chin, forcing my eyes to meet his. "We'll be careful next time."

My heart sank.

Next time.

That let me know that his sick, twisted ass had no plans to stop doing what he was doing to me. He didn't feel like he was wrong at all, and he had no remorse about it. I walked into that house in pain and defeat. After stripping my bed and cleaning the mattress, I put on new sheets and climbed in.

I didn't sleep. Instead, I lay in the darkness until sunrise, praying for death to just take me from the nightmare.

My mother came home yelling about the wet sheets in the washer. I had to lie and say I got my period during the night. She didn't care either way. She called me stupid for not knowing when my period was coming on at seventeen. I just had to take it because what else was I supposed to say?

The past few days had been tough on my mental. I could feel myself slipping into a depressive state. Uncle Clive let me take a few days to get my mental together, but being cooped up in the house was only making it worse. He and Aunt Penny had been trying so hard to give me space but also to make sure I was still okay.

They'd done so much for me already, and I hated to burden them with any more than I already had. I was shocked when they handed me a bank card with my name on it.

Apparently, they had been depositing three hundred dollars into the account every month for the last five years. Uncle Clive told me they always had faith that I would come home, and they wanted me to have something to start me off with. When they showed me the statement, I was overcome with emotion. Between their deposits and earned interest, the balance was almost twenty thousand dollars.

I hadn't spent much on anything because I'd barely left the house if it wasn't for work. Today, I decided to finally venture outside. I told Aunt Penny that I was going to take a walk to clear my head. She'd offered to walk with me, but I declined, stating I just needed some time alone. I packed my small crossbody with the phone, bus pass, and bank card she and my uncle had given me and left the house. I didn't have a destination. I just walked until my feet carried me to the last place I should have been.

My childhood home.

As I sat on the bench across from the house, I just stared at it, memories flooding my mind. I could see me chasing my sisters in the front yard as we played tag. I could see us making snowmen that were melting before we finished because snow in South Carolina never stuck on the off chance we got any. I remembered those hot summer days when I would spray them down with the water hose as their laughter filled the air.

I missed them so much.

My aunt and uncle had tried to reason with my mother to let me see them a few days after I got home, and she cursed them from here to hell. She threatened to beat my ass if I ever came anywhere near my sisters, yet here I was. I wasn't afraid of her. There wasn't much that scared me these days about another woman.

I'd been sitting there for a good hour, hoping to get even the smallest glimpse of the girls. There were no cars in the yard, so I wasn't sure if anybody was home. I felt defeated as I watched the bus rolling to a stop at the corner. It was probably best if I hopped on and made my way home.

Just as I stood to walk to the bus stop, a little red two-door coupe pulled into the yard. I stood frozen as I watched the doors opened, and my sisters got out with their backpacks.

My heart swelled in its cavity.

They'd grown into such beautiful young women. Adrienne favored me so much when I was her age, and Amiyah looked more like our mother. They were laughing and talking as they made their way up the front steps. Their smiles made me smile. Even if it was only a first glance, they seemed to be doing well.

I knew I should have left. I knew I had no business being there, but my feet carried me across the street and into the front yard. Adrienne was busy trying to open the door while Amiyah was snapping selfies on her phone. The moment I came into view, her head spun around. Our gazes met for a moment before she frantically slapped our sister's arm.

"What, Miyah? Damn."

Adrienne spun around, and her eyes landed on me. Their stares were piercing as we looked at one another in complete silence. I couldn't find the words to speak. I'd dreamed of this moment, prayed for it, and now I didn't know what to say.

"You should leave," Adrienne said coldly. "Mama is on her way home, and I don't wanna hear her bitching at us for letting you in." She tried to open the door, but I stopped her.

"Wait!"

Her hand lingered on the doorknob. Slowly, I made my way up the steps, stopping a few feet shy of them.

"I've missed y'all," I said quietly. "I thought about you every day while I was away."

Adrienne scoffed. "While you were away? You say that like you just went on vacation. You went to jail. Telling Uncle Clive and Aunt Penny to tell us you love us doesn't make up for the fact that you abandoned us. You didn't call. You didn't write us. You just left us here with Mama."

I shook my head. "That's not true. I wrote you, but the letters always came back. I called, and she refused to accept them—"

She cut me off. "It doesn't matter now. You can't be here."

"Adrienne, please," I begged, tears lacing my voice. "I love you, both of you. Next to Uncle Clive and Aunt Penny, you're all I have. I did what I did to protect us all. You have no idea what—"

I paused. There was no need to disclose what Rodney had said he'd do to them. I wouldn't have them bearing any of that guilt.

"I just want to make up for lost time," I said softly.

Adrienne shook her head. "Mama said we can't see you. She's already a bitch most of the time. I'm just trying to survive these last couple of months, and I'm out of this house for good."

I could see I was fighting a losing battle with her. I turned to my baby sister.

"Miyah?"

She was hesitant, looking between me and Adrienne. I wasn't sure what she was going to say or if she'd say anything at all.

"Miyah, you already know how Kennedy is," Adrienne reminded her. "We don't want no bullshit with her."

"She's our sister, Adrienne," she said softly. She looked back at me. "But she's right. Mama will have a fit if she finds you here. You know how she likes to go off. I don't wanna get in trouble."

Adrienne didn't say another word, just opened the front door and went inside. Amiyah stood there for a moment, then she did something I didn't expect. She rushed into my arms and hugged me tightly.

I stood there frozen for a moment before wrapping my arms around her. Tears spilled from my eyes as I cradled her against my body. She would never know how much I needed this.

"I love you," I whispered. "I love you so much. I'm so sorry."

"Miyah, get your ass in this house," Adrienne yelled.

She pulled away from me. Going into her bag, she pulled out a scrap piece of paper and a pencil before scribbling something down on it.

"That's my number," she said, thrusting it into my hands. "If you have a phone, text me."

I looked down at the paper and wiped the tears from my eyes. "Thank you."

She offered me a light smile. "I'll work on Adrienne. She's not the hardass she thinks she is."

She kissed my cheeks before going into the house and closing the door. I stood on the porch for a moment, clutching the paper in my hands. It wasn't what I hoped for, but it was a start. After stuffing the number in my crossbody, I hurried down the front steps and back across the street. Just as I made it to the end of the street, I looked back to see a car pulling in the yard. I paused in my stride to see my mother getting out.

She still had her youthful look, still as beautiful as ever. It was a shame she had the looks, but her spirit was so damn evil. I never understood why she hated me so much. I tried to be a good daughter. I tried everything I knew to make her proud of me…to make her love me, and nothing was ever good enough. It was like my very existence pissed her off.

How could I compete with hate?

If she didn't want me, I would have preferred she'd gotten an abortion or given me to someone who did want me. She could have given me to my aunt and uncle for that matter. Instead, she chose to keep me so she could mistreat me. I wondered if her hatred of me fueled her denial about Rodney. There was no way she couldn't have known. I wasn't a mother, but when it came to my sisters, my instincts were always on point. She *had* to have known something.

I was so deep in my thoughts that I didn't realize she was staring at me, squinting. Anger found its way to her face when she realized who I was. Throwing her things on the ground, she began storming across the street. I turned and sped toward the corner where people were getting on the next bus. I climbed on and quickly swiped my bus pass before taking a seat. The closer she got, the more anxious I became. I prayed everybody boarded quickly so we could leave.

I didn't fear Kennedy. I simply didn't want an altercation with her right now.

She tried to get on the bus, but the driver stopped her.

"You need a bus pass, ma'am."

"Fuck you and your bus pass. Come here, bitch," she yelled at me.

"Ma'am, you need to vacate this vehicle before I call the cops."

She glared at him before her eyes settled on me. "Stay the fuck away from my house and my kids. If I catch you over here again, your ass is mine."

She turned and stormed off the bus. Everyone was looking around, trying to figure out who she was talking to. I relaxed my face, trying to match their concern and hide my guilt. Settled into my seat, I watched as she made her way back down the street. I knew in my heart that this wasn't over. The shit had only just begun.

CHAPTER 12

Killian

I TOSSED MY wallet and keys into the bowl beside my front door and kicked off my shoes.

Today had been a long day, and all I wanted to do was sip on a beer, kick my feet up, and watch some football. I headed into the kitchen to grab the beverage and something to snack on while I relaxed. I'd just settled on the couch and turned on the television when my phone began to ring.

I groaned. I just knew it was work calling, and I'd just left the place. Begrudgingly, I placed my items down and dug in my pocket to retrieve the phone. My brows furrowed as I read the unfamiliar number on the screen.

"Hello?"

There was silence on the other end of the line. I pulled the phone from my ear to make sure they hadn't hung up, and sure enough they were still there.

"Hello?" I said again.

"Killian."

The sound of her voice made my ears perk and me sit up straight.

"Alayah?"

"It's me. Do you have a second?"

"Yeah, yeah, I do. What's up?"

"Can we meet somewhere so we can talk?"

I looked at the clock. It was almost six.

"Yeah, we can do that. It's almost dinnertime. You wanna grab something to eat?"

She hesitated for a moment. "Sure. I'll meet you at Rusty's."

I smiled softly. Rusty's was a diner I used to grab us lunch from during school hours from time to time. Since I had a free period before lunch, I'd go out for food and bring her something back. On occasion, I took her there with me.

"I could pick you up," I offered.

"No. I'm already on the bus. I'll just meet you there."

"Oh. Well, okay. Just let me change out of my work clothes, and I'll head out."

"Okay."

She didn't say goodbye or anything else before hanging up. I stood from the couch and took my things back into the kitchen before going to my bedroom. I changed into a pair of sweats and a plain white tee then slipped my feet into my slides. After grabbing my wallet, phone, and keys, I left the house. The drive only took about fifteen minutes. When I stepped out of the car, I could see Alayah sitting in a back corner by herself with her head down.

I walked into the building and was greeted by Ms. Toni. She owned the diner and still worked, even at her age of sixty-five. She smiled as I approached the counter.

"Hey, Ms. Toni," I said, returning her smile.

"Hey, baby. You're here later than usual. I always see you at lunchtime when you come in."

"I know. I'm meeting a friend." I nodded in Alayah's direction where she was seated in a half-circle booth in the back corner.

"*Oooo*. She's a pretty thing. You'll have to introduce me."

"You know her, Ms. Toni. That's Alayah."

"Alayah…Alayah…" She paused for a moment, then her eyes widened. "You mean *that* Alayah."

"Yes, ma'am."

"Bless her heart. I didn't even recognize her. When did she come home?"

"It's been a few weeks, really about a month now."

"Good for her. I always hated that they locked that child up." She shook her head. "I see that mama of hers from time to time. She needs her ass beat for letting that happen to her child."

"Well, you know everybody isn't fit to be a parent."

"They sure aren't. Come on. I'll walk you over. I want to speak to her."

She rounded the corner and led me to the back where Alayah sat, plucking at her nails.

"Hey, Layah," I said, sliding in the booth beside her.

Even though I made sure to put some space between us, she inched away just a little and offered me a tight-lipped smile.

"Hey, Killian."

Ms. Toni took a seat beside her and reached for her hand. "Hey, baby. I'm so sorry I didn't recognize you."

"It's okay, Ms. Toni. I don't mind not being seen right now."

Ms. Toni gave a sympathetic smile. "You were a beautiful girl, but you've grown into such a gorgeous young woman. These curls are still wild and free." There was a short bout of silence before she spoke again. "How are you, baby?"

"I'm okay. I'm here."

Ms. Toni nodded. "I hope things haven't been too hard on you. You deserve some peace. I'll be praying for you, sweetheart."

Alayah offered a half smile. "Thank you. I appreciate that."

"Can I hug you?"

She nodded slowly. Ms. Toni wrapped her arms around her and squeezed tightly. When she pulled away, she cupped Alayah's face and kissed her forehead. She lifted her chin and spoke softly to her.

"Don't hold your head down. You have nothing to be ashamed of, you hear me?"

"Yes, ma'am."

"Good. I'm gonna send Wanda over here to get your orders in a second. It's on the house."

She didn't give me time to protest before she slid out of the booth and fled the table. I sat back, adjusting in my seat. My gazed drifted to Alayah, who was nervously plucking at her nails again.

"What can I do for you?" I asked.

"I, *um*...I need some legal advice."

"About your case?"

She shook her head. "No, no not about that. It's my sisters. I want to know if I have visitation rights as their sibling."

I sighed. "Well, siblings don't have automatic legal visitation rights like a parent would. Now, some jurisdictions do recognize the importance of sibling relationships, and they will allow you to petition for visitation rights in certain circumstances."

"Like what?"

"The most common are instances where foster care or adoption separates siblings, divorce or separation of parents with children from different relationships, or the death of a parent. In other cases, they consider what is in the best interest of the child and the nature of the existing relationship between the siblings. If they are old enough, the courts might consider their wishes. It really all depends on the jurisdiction."

"So basically, I'm screwed."

"I wouldn't say that."

"What judge is going to take me seriously, Killian?"

"Did something happen?"

She sighed. "I, *um*...I went to the house. I know I shouldn't have, but I was emotional and missing my sisters. I really needed to see them."

"Did you?"

She nodded. "For a few minutes. Adrienne wants nothing to do with me. She seems so angry. And Amiyah...I feel like I have a chance with her. She gave me her number, and she hugged me. Killian, I needed that so bad."

Tears laced her voice as she spoke, and I could tell this was weighing heavily on her.

"I've had to live without them for ten years. I know they have a lot of questions and even more feelings about everything. I just want to sit down with them, and I can't. Kennedy has already threatened me if I came near them again."

"Wait. You saw your mother?"

"Don't call her my mother," she snapped. "And yes, I saw her. She pulled in the yard right after I walked away. She damn near chased me on the bus. If the driver hadn't stopped her, she would have gotten on and tried to fight me. I'm not afraid of her. I could have held my own, but who wants to fight the person that gave birth to them? Even if she deserves to have hands put on her, I don't want that to come from me. I'm not that person."

"I know you aren't. I can try to help you—"

"Nah. Don't worry about it. It'll just be a waste of time and money."

"I wouldn't want your money."

"Surely you wouldn't do all this work pro bono. I couldn't ask you to do that, and I won't ask you to do that."

"I wouldn't let you pay me, Layah, and you aren't asking. I'm offering."

"No. I'll figure something out." She was quiet for a moment before grabbing her bag. "I should go."

She went to get up, but I gently touched her arm. "Alayah, please. You're already here. At least have something to eat. I'll take you home."

She peered down at me, then slowly sat. Quietly, she picked up the menu and looked it over. I kept quiet as I did the same. It wasn't long before Wanda came over to take our orders. I smiled as Alayah opted for the same meal I used to bring her back in the day: a double bacon cheeseburger with chili cheese fries and a vanilla milkshake.

"You still have a hearty appetite, I see," I said when Wanda walked away.

"After eating prison food for so long, you appreciate a good meal."

"What's the first thing you ate when you came home?"

She smiled softly. "Aunt Penny made all of my favorites— fried chicken, baked mac and cheese, cabbage, rice, cornbread, and a sweet potato pie."

"I know that itis kicked in."

"I definitely overindulged." She peered over at me. "I should apologize for how I've treated you when I've seen you. It doesn't excuse it, but it's been a lot on my mental. Being home hasn't been the easiest."

"I get that. You're adjusting to life on the outside again. Ain't much has changed around here. Same old River Point."

"What's changed with you?"

I chuckled. "Nothing but age."

"No girlfriend? Kids?"

"Nah. I'm single. I have a little one, but she's not mine. My sister has a five-year-old little girl named Ellie."

I pulled out my phone and pulled up a picture of Ellie and me. Her little face was plastered against mine, and she wore the biggest smile while holding up her award trophy.

"She's adorable. She looks like you."

"That's my baby. Running my pockets every chance she gets. I swear she doesn't forget a thing. I told her if she got all gold stars at school, I'd give her some 'monies' as she likes to call it. I walked into my parents' house the other week, and she met me at the door with her hand out."

"Well, you made a promise. You had to see it through."

"I know, I know."

"I would have thought you'd be married with kids by now. I remember how important family was to you."

"It's still important. I have family dinners with them every Sunday. We do birthdays and holidays. We take a family trip during the summer months, and we have an ongoing group chat. It's safe to say those people stay in my business," I added with a chuckle. "As far as marriage and kids…I don't know. I guess I haven't met the right woman yet. I'm sure the big man upstairs will send me my rib one of these days."

"Good luck with that. I'm sure you'll make a great husband."

"What about you?"

"What about me?"

"Do you eventually wanna…you know, date? Get married?"

"No. I don't want to have to explain my history to anyone. My den mother has this man she met through the prison pen pal system. She tried to get me to sign up for it, but I declined. I want no parts of a prison romance. Did you know they have this Prison Bae group on social media? Somehow my picture got on there, and there were several men that looked me up and sent me letters over the years."

I tried not to laugh. "Wow. I mean you've always been a beautiful girl, Layah. Somebody would want you."

"You sound like my friend Londyn. No thank you."

I smiled. "You made a friend?"

She blushed. "I was kind of forced into this friendship. She's a mechanic at my uncle's shop."

"Is she nice?"

She nodded. "She's very nice. A little crazy, but nice."

"Does she know about...you know."

"She does. I really didn't have a choice in telling her. Rodney's mother rolled up on me while I was out to lunch with her one day. Things got heated and embarrassing, and Londyn was there for me. I had to come clean."

"Run that back. She ran up on you?"

"She was yelling about how funny it was that I was out enjoying lunch while her son rots in the grave. She called me a murderer and a lying whore before she slapped me."

"You should press assault charges, Alayah."

She shook her head. "I don't want to go through all of that, Killian. I knew this was coming eventually. I couldn't avoid the family forever."

"Nobody has the right to put their hands on you."

"Don't you think I know that? If anybody knows that, it's me. I just want to move on with my life. I don't want to see another police office, courtroom, or inside of a jail again. They will never forget what I've done, just like I'll never forget what he did. We all have to live with it."

I could see that I was fighting a losing battle. She didn't deserve to be further abused by the West family, but if she didn't want to do anything about it, what could I do to stop her? We sat there quietly until Wanda brought our plates out. Both of us picked over the food, not really eating much. There were barely any words passed between us until I asked her if she was ready to go.

The car ride to her home was silent as well. She sat looking out the window with her chin rested on her hand. She seemed to be in deep thought, so I didn't bother her. When we pulled up to the house, she sat in the car for a moment before finally speaking.

"I apologize for making things awkward," she said softly.

"You didn't. I just...I don't really know what to say to you, Alayah. I don't wanna set you off."

"How about we just don't talk about prison or my life before that?"

"It's bound to come up."

"It doesn't have to. I won't bring it up if you don't. If you wanna be friends, act like you just met me and you're getting to know me. Pretend I didn't live this whole other life for the last ten years."

"That's easier said than done."

"Then be delusional with me."

I chuckled. "Delusional, huh?"

She shrugged. "Most people go through life being delusional about one thing or another."

"Are you really gonna let me be your friend again?"

She was quiet for a moment. "We'll see. Good night, Killian."

"Good night, Alayah."

She climbed out of the car, and I waited until she was safely inside before I pulled off. This wasn't the meetup I expected, but maybe over time, we really could become friends again.

CHAPTER 13

Alayah

"**BABY, YOU HAVE** to press the gas," Londyn said, laughing.

"I *am* pressing the gas."

"You're going five miles an hour, Alayah. Put some power in it."

"I don't wanna crash."

"You're barely moving, and we're in an empty parking lot. You're fine."

I sighed as I pressed the gas a little harder. True to her word, Londyn was teaching me to drive. She wasn't a bad teacher, but I wasn't trying to wreck her car. Uncle Clive taught me a little back in the day since Kennedy refused to. She didn't want me getting any ideas about driving her car. If she ever sent me to run errands, I always had to take the bus. Even then, I had to take my sisters with me. It was her way of ensuring that I wasn't off doing anything I wasn't supposed to do.

"That's it. You're doing great," Londyn encouraged. "In a few months, you'll be driving like me."

"No offense, Londyn, but your driving scares me a little."

She scoffed. "I'm not even that bad."

"It's the road rage."

She laughed. "Listen, these people will have you seeing red. Everybody shouldn't own a car."

I shook my head. We'd been out here for an hour. I appreciated her teaching me, but I was okay with my bus pass for now. Even if I learned to drive, I didn't have a reason to have a car anyway. I rode with my uncle to work, and if I left the house without him or my aunt, it was on the bus. I was cool with that.

My lesson went on for another hour before we decided to go get something to eat. It was Saturday, and unlike many mechanic shops, Uncle Clive didn't work weekends. He said he wasn't going to slave six days a week, and he wouldn't make his staff do it either. This was the first Saturday since I'd been home that I'd actually left the house.

After the fiasco at lunch the other week, I was a little nervous to go out with Londyn again for fear of further embarrassment. However, she'd come over to the house when I tried to get out of it and talked me into coming with her. I found she could be a little pushy, but I got the feeling that was just her personality. It wasn't a bad type of pushy, more like an I'm-not-gonna-let-you-wallow-in-your-feelings kind of pushy.

We walked into Burger Bliss, a new-to-me fast food place in River Point. It was already busy, but Londyn insisted we stay because the food was good. We waited in line for at least ten minutes before we got to the front. When my eyes landed on the cashier, my heart skipped a beat. Adrienne looked at me with a blank expression. There was a momentary stare off before she finally spoke.

"Welcome to Burger Bliss. What can I get started for you today?"

"I'll take a number three with extra pickles, a sweet tea, and a side of ranch," Londyn answered.

"Is that for here or to go?"

"Here. You can put hers on my order, too," she added, motioning to me.

Adrienne looked to me. "What can I get you?"

I was hurt that she was acting like she didn't know who I was. I understood she could hold up the line being friendly, but she was looking right through me.

"I'll have the same," I whispered.

"That will be seventeen forty-three."

Londyn swiped her card. Adrienne handed her the cups and her receipt.

"I'm gonna go to the bathroom," I said to her.

"Okay. I've got your drink."

"Thanks."

I headed around the corner to the bathroom. Once inside, I locked myself in a stall. I practiced deep breathing, attempting to calm my nerves. As together as I tried to keep it, my sisters were the one thing that could always trigger me. A week had passed since I'd shown up at the house. I hadn't had the nerve to text Amiyah because I didn't know if Kennedy was checking their phones after seeing me. The last thing I wanted was to get either of them in trouble with her.

I hadn't even put her number in my phone to avoid temptation. It was safely tucked beneath my mattress. Maybe one of these days I would get up the nerve to use it. I hated to feel like I'd searched them out for nothing. Given the look Adrienne had given me, it was possible she was already feeling that way.

I stayed in the bathroom for a good five minutes, trying to pull it together. I could hear people coming in and out. When it was quiet, I opened the stall door and walked out the same time as the bathroom door opened. Adrienne walked in and stood in front of me with her arms crossed.

"How did you know I worked here?" she spat.

I shook my head. "I didn't—"

"You're lying."

"I'm not, Adrienne. My friend picked this place. I've never even been here. It's just a coincidence."

"You mean like you showing up to the house, right? You know Mama threw a fit when she got home? She saw you leaving. Me and Miyah had to deal with the backlash of that. She cursed us both out and threatened to beat the black off us if we ever spoke to you again. She told us to call the police if you came anywhere near us. If you want to stay out of jail, you need to leave us alone, Alayah."

I shook my head. "I can't. I love you. I need you both, Adrienne."

"Is that worth doing time over?"

"I've done ten years," I yelled. "Ten years to protect you and Amiyah so you wouldn't have to go through the same thing I did. You were too young to understand what was going on back then, but you get it now. That man raped me, Adrienne. He came into my room damn near every week for three years. He raped me, he *kept* raping me, and he threatened to have his friends do the same to you and Amiyah if I didn't comply."

Hey eyes widened as tears slipped from them. "Wh–What?"

Tears pooled in my eyes and spilled down my cheeks. I reached out and cupped her face.

"I couldn't let anything happen to either of you. You were more than my little sisters. You were my babies. I loved you like you were my own. I would have done anything to protect you and Miyah. That's the truth. I'm sorry I left you with Kennedy, but I just couldn't take it anymore. I couldn't. I just...I snapped."

She broke into tears, and all I could do was pull her into my arms and hold her as I cried with her. If I could have picked her up the way I did when she was younger, I would have. Gently, I stroked her back in a soothing manner as I kissed her temple.

"I love you," I whispered. "I'm so sorry."

For the longest time, we held each other. I think she needed that just as much as I did. Once she finally stopped crying, she pulled away. I grabbed a paper towel and dabbed her eyes.

"You've grown into a beautiful young woman," I said, offering a warm smile.

"Thank you." She reached out to touch my face. "At least prison didn't make you ugly."

I giggled. "At least there's that."

"You said that girl was your friend?"

"Yes. Her name is Londyn. She works at Uncle Clive's shop."

"Is she a friend or a *friend?*"

I laughed. "You think I went to prison and got turned out?"

She raised her hands in mock surrender. "I'm just saying. You were with a bunch of women for a long time. Things happen. I wouldn't judge or blame you for that. She's pretty."

"Not in this case. She's just a friend. She was giving me an unsolicited driving lesson today."

"How did it go?"

"I should probably keep my bus pass."

We shared a light laugh. She grabbed my hands and squeezed them.

"I'm sorry for how I acted. I really am glad you're home. I'm gonna get Miyah, and we're gonna come see you."

"I don't want you getting in trouble, Adrienne."

"The worst she'll do is slap us around."

"That's not okay."

She shrugged. "It wouldn't be the first time I fought her off. We're old enough to make the decision to see you. She had no right to keep us away. She was just doing it to be spiteful. I don't care anymore. I'm seventeen. She can't keep telling me what to do."

I sighed. There was the defiant nature my aunt told me about. If she and Amiyah snuck off to see me, there would be hell to pay. As I opened my mouth to say something, the door opened, and a uniformed worker stuck her head in.

"Adrienne, what's taking you so long?"

"I'm sorry, Ms. Carrie. I was just talking to my sister. I haven't seen her in a long time."

"Well, I'm sorry to break up this little family reunion, but we have customers, and you're needed."

"Yes, ma'am." She turned to me and came into my arms for a hug. "Please come back to see me."

"I will." I kissed her forehead. "I love you."

"I love you, too."

We parted ways, and she left the bathroom. I washed and dried my hands before leaving as well. When I joined Londyn at the table, she looked relieved.

"What happened to you? I thought I was gonna have to come get you."

I sighed as I sat down. "The girl that took our order, she's my oldest little sister."

Londyn gasped. She looked around me and back at the counter. "Now that I look at her again, she does look just like you. Damn, the resemblance is uncanny. Y'all got the same daddy?"

"No. I've never met my father. I don't know anything about that man."

"Oh. I'm sorry, boo."

I waved her off. "No need to be sorry."

"So did you two talk? I take it that's why you took so long. Sis acted like she didn't know you at first."

"We talked. It got a little heated there for a moment, but I think we're okay now. She made me promise to come back here and see her."

"Wait. Why here? They can't come to Mr. Clive's?"

"My…mother, she won't let me see them. She's banned them from the house as long as I'm there and threatened me if I come around them."

"Pardon my language, but why is she being such a bitch about it? They *are* your sisters."

I swallowed hard. In telling her that I killed Rodney, I didn't tell her that my sisters saw the aftermath.

"My sisters…they were in the house when it happened."

"Oh my God!"

"Yeah."

"But you would never hurt them. I know I don't know you that well, but I can't see you intentionally hurting anybody. You did what you did to protect the three of you. It's not like she did anything to protect you. *Ugh!* Now I want to fight her for you."

"No need for that. I'm a firm believer in karma coming back for you. She may not feel it now, but she will reap the seed she's sown."

"Amen to that. My daddy always said that unjust doesn't profit. You can fool man, but you can't fool God."

I nodded. One day, Kennedy was going to pay for the part she played in my childhood. I would never believe that she didn't know. I just didn't want to believe that she knew and chose to let it keep happening. The truth would come to light, and I had a feeling that when it did, I'd be heartbroken all over again.

CHAPTER 14

Killian

I PULLED INTO the parking lot of the bar downtown. It was Thursday night, and I was taking a much-needed mental break from work. Most days, I brought it home with me, so there was rarely a time when I wasn't working. After being nose deep in paperwork all day, I needed to get away from work and my house. I'd originally called Kadeem to see if he could meet me, but he and his wife were having a family night with their baby girl.

I couldn't be mad at that. One of these days I hoped to have a family to do nights like that with. A wife and a few babies to come home to was one of my biggest goals. I could already see me spoiling the whole family and then complaining about it later.

After locking my car, I headed inside to the bar area. It wasn't too busy for a Thursday night. I took a seat at the bar and motioned for the bartender. When I got her attention, she smiled and switched over to me. She leaned across the bar, exposing an ample amount of her cleavage.

"What can I get for you, handsome?" she asked, batting those long eyelashes.

"Let me get a Jack and Coke and an order of hot wings and fries with extra ranch."

"Is that all?"

"Yes, ma'am."

"*Oooo*, a man with manners. We don't get too many of you in here. You must be a good boy. Your mama raised you right, didn't she?"

I chuckled. "Yes, ma'am. She did."

"I like that. I'll put your order in and get right on that drink."

"Appreciate it."

I tuned into the game on the flatscreen above the bar. The basketball game was in the second quarter, and one of my favorite teams was playing. The bartender came back with my drink, and I took a sip.

"Good?" she asked.

"Perfect."

"What's a handsome guy like you doing here all by your lonesome?"

"I just needed to get out the house for a minute."

She gave me a flirty smile. "So you came to see little ol' me?"

I smirked and shook my head. She was cute—beautiful even—but I'd never had a thing for thirsty women.

"I get off at ten if you want to meet up later."

"I'm good, love."

She looked taken aback by my decline. With a slight frown, she walked away, leaving me to my drink. I paused watching the game momentarily to look around the space. My eyes landed on the door, and a smile spread across my face. Alayah walked in behind the woman from the mechanic shop. She looked a little nervous and slightly out of place, but man was she beautiful.

Tonight, she was wearing a white fitted tee, a pair of distressed jeans, and a pair of sandals. Silver accessories adorned her neck, ears, and wrists. Her curls were pulled up into a tight topknot, drawing focus to her beautiful face, including those freckles.

She looked around the space until her eyes landed on me. I could see the breath of relief leave her chest. She motioned for me as her friend lead them to a table. Grabbing my drink, I slid off the stool and made my way over.

"Good evening, ladies."

"Hey, Killian. This is my friend Londyn. Londyn, this is my… this is Killian."

I extended my hand. "It's nice to officially meet you."

Londyn shook my hand. "Nice to meet you, too. I'm gonna give you two a few minutes to talk while I go grab a drink. You want something, Alayah?"

"Maybe a soda or some water."

Londyn rolled her eyes. "Okay, girl."

She walked away, leaving us alone.

"I'm so happy to see a familiar face. I don't know why I let her talk me into coming here. I feel so out of place, Killian."

"You'll be fine, Layah. This is a chill spot. Not much happens. Outside of it getting a little loud during games, this is a relaxed crowd." I reached out and covered her hand with mine. "Don't worry. You're safe with me."

She offered me a slight smile and squeezed my hand. "I know."

We shared a momentary gaze before Londyn sat back down at the table. She looked between the two of us as she placed a canned soda in front of Alayah.

"Am I interrupting something?" she asked, dropping her gaze to our hands.

Alayah quickly pulled her hand way. "No. I told you, Killian and I are just friends—newly reconnected friends at that."

Londyn shrugged. "So there's really never been anything there?"

"No."

"Well…"

Alayah and I answered at the same time. Her head jerked in my direction.

"I…*uh*. I might have had a crush on you in high school."

"I knew it," Londyn exclaimed. "My radar is never wrong."

"Wait," Alayah said. "Are you serious?"

I nervously rubbed the back of my neck as I nodded. "Yeah."

"You never said anything."

"I didn't think there was ever a right time to say anything. You always had a lot going on, Alayah. I cared too much about you to complicate things further. Besides, your…Kennedy would have never allowed it. It was a wonder she let me come over to study."

She thought for a moment. "I guess you have a point."

"I did almost ask you out once. Remember when you asked why I didn't have a girlfriend? I told you I had my eye on someone, but I didn't think she would feel the same."

"I remember that."

"I was talking about you."

She thought for a moment. "You asked me if I would date you."

"And you said maybe if I were into you, but I wasn't and that we were just friends who studied together."

Londyn cackled. "Sir. That was your in right there. You should have said something."

I shook my head. "I know. I was scared, okay? I was your Average Joe, and honestly, I thought she was out of my league."

"You two would make a beautiful couple," Londyn professed.

"I'm just happy to have my friend back," I said. "I want her to be happy. This is a new start for her. That's what I want her to focus on."

"*Awww!* He's considerate!"

Alayah rolled her eyes. "Londyn, please don't start."

"I'm sorry, I'm sorry. I'll dial it back." She turned to me. "I can be a little extra from time to time. I'm a girl's girl. I've only known her a few weeks, and I love her already. She deserves a happy ending after all she's been through."

I nodded. "I agree." I lifted my glass, and Londyn followed suit. "To happy endings."

"To happy endings," Londyn repeated.

Alayah hesitated for a moment before she grabbed her soda and clinked our glasses. "To happy endings."

I ended up sitting with them for a little while—that was until the bar started playing music and Londyn wanted to dance. She spotted someone she knew and dragged them out onto the dance floor leaving Alayah and me alone.

"She is quite the character," I said, watching her dance.

"She is," Alayah agreed. "She reminds me a lot of the girls back in prison. They were very lively in spite of their circumstances."

"Did you consider them friends?"

"No. They were family. We looked out for each other. My den mother, Carissa, she protected me from day one. She never let anybody get too close to me or threaten me. Even when I woke up the whole block with my nightmares, she never let them give me too hard a time. She was proof that not everyone conforms to their circumstances. Prison could have made her hard, but she was the most loving person there."

"You sound like you miss her."

"I do miss her. Next to Aunt Penny, she's the closest thing to a mother I've ever had. I loved her."

"I'm sure she loved you, too."

"She did. I can't violate my parole by having contact with her though." She grew quiet for a moment before taking another sip of her soda. "So, is this typically how you spend your Thursday nights?"

"*Nah*. I'm usually face deep in work I've brought home. If I ever go out anywhere, it's with Kadeem."

"Kadeem…Kadeem Lynch? From school? You two are still friends?"

"We are. We spend a little less time together these days, though. I'm busy with work, and he's married—"

"Married! Kadeem, the boy who had a different girlfriend every week, got married?"

I laughed. "Don't do my boy like that. He's a changed man. Yes, he got married. They have a beautiful five-year-old little girl, and they're expecting a baby."

She smiled softly. "Good for him. And he's faithful?"

I chuckled. "He is. Kyah doesn't play that. I guarantee she would have his balls if he ever cheated. He knows he has a good one. I think you two would make good friends."

"Let me settle into this friendship with Londyn before you pass me off to another female. Look at her." She pointed to the dance floor where Londyn was twerking on some man. "How different would I have been if we'd been friends in high school? I can see her being the pretty, outgoing popular girl and me being her quiet, shy, introverted best friend. She would have dragged me to every party and danced on me just like that."

"And I bet you would have had the time of your life."

She circled the rim of her drink with her nail. "If things had been different, I would have. I feel like I missed out on a lot of life, you know? Not just the last ten years, but in general. Maybe something crazy like get a secret tattoo or piercing."

"Oh, so you wanted to live on the wild side?"

She giggled. "Maybe for a moment. Just to feel normal."

I nodded as I motioned for the server to bring us our tab for the night. She returned a few seconds later with the receipt. I reached for my wallet and handed her enough to cover the bill plus a tip.

"Keep the change," I said, standing.

"Where are you going?" Alayah asked, brows furrowed in confusion.

"We're about to get out of here. Come on."

"Where are we going? I can't just leave Londyn."

"I think she will be fine." I motioned to Londyn in a corner of the bar, tonguing down the guy she was dancing with. "Just send her a message and let her know you're with me."

Alayah looked around me before pulling out her phone. She tapped away on it for a second before tucking it away and standing. I extended my hand, and she took it, allowing me to lead her out of the bar. We headed to my car, and I opened the door for her.

"Don't get me into any trouble, Killian."

"I won't. I promise. We're gonna have a little fun."

"What kind of fun?"

"You'll see."

She eyed me skeptically but got in the car. I rounded the driver's side and climbed in. Pulling out of the parking lot, I headed to the other side of town. She said she wanted to feel normal, so why not give her a little slice of that? When I pulled into the parking lot of the tattoo parlor a friend of mine owned, Alayah's eyes widened.

"You're really taking me to get a tattoo?" she asked.

"You said you wanted one."

"I—I was just talking. I didn't think you'd actually bring me here."

"Well, we're here now. What do you say?"

She laughed. "Killian! I don't even know what I would get."

"Something meaningful. What means the most to you right now?"

She thought for a moment. "Freedom."

"I'll get one with you."

"Matching tattoos?"

"What better way to commemorate our friendship?"

"You know Londyn is gonna be jealous, right?"

I grinned. "She'll live. We were friends first."

She smiled. "Okay. Let's do it."

We got out of the car and headed inside. Micah, my friend, was standing at the counter looking at the computer. When he saw us, a smile spread across his face.

"Killian, my guy!" He came around the corner to slap my hand. "How you doing, man?"

"I'm good. Can't complain."

He looked over at Alayah. "And who is this beautiful sistah?"

"This is my friend, Alayah. Alayah, this is Micah."

"Nice to meet you, Alayah."

He went in for a hug, but she took a step back the same time as I extended my arm.

"She doesn't like people in her personal space," I said.

"I apologize. I grew up in a hugging ass family. Please forgive me."

"It's okay," she said softly.

"So, what brings you here tonight?"

"Alayah wants to her first tattoo," I answered.

"*Ahhh!* An ink virgin. What were you thinking? Small, big, medium?"

Alayah thought for a moment. "*Um*...probably something small. I don't know how much pain I can tolerate. Maybe a few words?"

"Did you have an idea?"

"Something that celebrates freedom. I, *um*...I recently came home from prison."

Micah's eyes widened. "Oh! Well, that's certainly something to celebrate. I won't get in your business, but this seems like a personal tattoo, so I want it to really mean something. Most people I know that went to prison did something that was their last resort. What pushed you?"

Alayah swallowed hard. "Fear."

Micah nodded. "I got you, beautiful. Come on over here."

He led us to his workstation and settled at his desk. While he sketched out something, Alayah and I looked around at his work. My boy was talented. He was a few years older than me, and I met him one summer when I came home for break. My sister and I randomly decided to get tattoos and came to his shop. We hit it off, and he's been my go-to guy ever since.

"All right. What do you think?"

Alayah and I turned to look at the sketch he'd drawn. It was a quote that read, *Beyond fear is freedom* with a few butterflies. She smiled and reached out to touch it.

"It's perfect," she said softly.

"Where do you want it?"

She looked down, contemplating a spot for a moment before holding out her arm and pointing to the inside.

"Right here."

"I got you. Just let me trace this onto the transfer paper, and we can get started. You can have a seat. I'll be right back."

"Okay."

She took a seat on the bench and got comfortable.

"You need me to hold your hand?" I jested.

She playfully smacked my arm. "No, I don't, but be on standby."

I grinned. "I got you, love."

"You're gonna get this too, right?"

"I'm gonna pass on the butterflies—"

"*Aht aht!* You said matching. That includes the butterflies."

I chuckled. "Fine, man. I'll go let Micah know."

I was happy to see her smile. I had far too many memories of her doing anything but that. If there was any way I could make that happen for her, I would.

CHAPTER 15
Alayah

I WOKE UP this morning with a little extra pep in my step, and that was new for me. I smiled as I looked down at my tattoo. It wasn't as painful as I thought given that Micah had used numbing cream on my arm. The tattoo was beautiful and reminded me that I was free. I was no longer a prisoner, and there was nothing on the outside left to fear.

Rodney was dead.

I'd paid my debt to society.

I deserved to live.

Thursday night reminded me of that. From sitting in that bar with two people I considered friends to the impromptu visit to the tattoo parlor, I was reminded that I wasn't where I used to be. I thought it would have been harder to open up to anyone again, but Londyn made it easy, and Killian...well, Killian knew me when I was innocent.

I smiled to myself as I thought about him. He, too, had gotten a tattoo last night. Where I'd gotten mine on my arm, he added his to the chest piece he already had. When he took his shirt off, I had to look away. I felt almost ashamed to see him without it. It wasn't just the fact that I'd only ever seen him clothed, but I felt an attraction that I hadn't even fathomed to be possible.

Rodney had successfully turned me off from guys, but Killian wasn't just any guy. He'd always been so nice and sweet to me. I felt safe with him around. Days that he came over to study, I took comfort in knowing that I wouldn't be touched while he was there. By the time he left, Kennedy would be home from work, and those were the nights Rodney left me alone.

Rodney hated when he came over.

He would find every reason to come into the kitchen where we studied. He put on an award-winning act in Killian's presence, but from afar, he glared at me with threatening eyes. He silently dared me to let him touch me, and I never did…he never did. That's why Killian admitting he had a crush on me threw me for a loop. All that time, I just assumed that he was being nice.

I guess I was wrong.

I shook the thoughts from my head as I finished up my morning journaling and prepared to start my day. Today I had a meeting with my parole officer, Ms. Vera. We were set to meet every other week until she felt like she could trust me fully. She said once I showed good behavior and progress, she would recommend it be dropped to once a month. She was a nice older woman who didn't do too much. I'd heard horror stories from my bunkies about their parole officers being the bane of their existence. Thankfully, she wasn't like that.

I got up and showered then dressed in a pair of jeans, a graphic tee, and a pair of sneakers. After packing my crossbody with my essentials, I left my bedroom and went into the kitchen. Aunt Penny and Uncle Clive were sipping their morning coffee. I greeted them both with hugs and kisses to the cheek.

"Good morning," I said.

"Good morning, baby girl." Uncle Clive eyed me. "You look like you're in a good mood."

"Must have been that late night she had," Aunt Penny said, smirking.

I giggled. "I was in before my curfew."

"Yeah, but you never stay out late. You and Londyn must have had a good time."

"It was fun. We ran into Killian, and somehow, he and I ended up at a tattoo parlor—"

"You got a tattoo," my aunt exclaimed.

I held out my arm for them to see. She smiled as she ran her fingers over it.

"It's befitting. I'm glad to see you finding yourself." She gave me a slight side eye. "Killian, huh?"

"We're just friends, Auntie."

She held up her hands in mock surrender. "I didn't say anything. It's good you rekindled a friendship and made a new friend."

Uncle Clive chuckled. "Londyn didn't really give her a choice."

"She didn't, but it's okay. I think she'll be a loyal friend."

"I know she will. Anyway, I meant to ask if you needed a ride to your parole officer."

"No, sir. I'll take the bus and just walk from there. It's not too far."

"You sure?"

"I'm positive. I'm heading out. I don't wanna be late. Love you guys."

"We love you too, baby," they both said.

I kissed them goodbye and left the house to make my way to the bus stop. It was loading as I approached. After swiping my bus pass, I settled into a seat in the back. The bus pulled off shortly after.

The ride to the downtown area didn't take long at all. I walked into the building with ten minutes to spare and took the elevator up to the fifth floor where Ms. Vera's office was located and knocked on the door.

"Come in!" she called.

I turned the knob and walked in to find her behind her desk putting on her makeup. She looked up at me with a smile.

"Don't mind me. I got a late start this morning."

She capped her lipstick and put her things away. Reaching into her drawer, she pulled out the familiar urine sample cup.

"Do we have anything to worry about?" she asked, standing.

"No, ma'am. I'm clean."

"Alright then. You know the routine."

I nodded as I took the cup from her and went to the bathroom in her office. I wasn't a fan of having her watch me pee in the cup, but at this point I was used to it. I wasn't a drinker or a smoker, so I had nothing to worry about. There was no need to make a fuss of her simply doing her job.

When I was done, I capped the cup and handed it to her. She left me to clean myself up before I joined her back in the office.

"So, Alayah, how's it been going since our last meeting?"

"Good."

"How's the job?"

"No problems. I completed my training, so I'm on my own now."

"How do you feel having so much responsibility?"

"Needed. Useful. Someone's needed me my whole life. Before, it was my little sisters. In prison, I did the girls' hair. I don't think my aunt and uncle need me around, but they want me there, and that makes me feel good."

Ms. Vera smiled. "It makes a difference. A lot of people come home from prison to nothing—no job, no money, no family. It's so easy to end up back there when you feel like you're all alone. You're lucky to have people who love and care about you. I can't say the same for a lot of my clients."

She scribbled on her notepad momentarily before looking back up at me.

"Have you had any more trouble from the Wests?"

I shook my head. "No. I haven't seen anybody else, and according to my aunt, the social media post was removed."

"Good. You let me know if there are any more issues."

"Yes, ma'am."

"Any other news?"

I smiled. "I spoke with my sisters."

She gave me an empathetic look. "That's great, Alayah. I know how important that is for you. What about your mom?"

"There's no salvaging that relationship, Ms. Vera. She doesn't even want me to see them."

"You have to be careful, sweetheart. One call to the police, and she can ruin your parole."

"I know. I just…I miss them so much. They're older now, and they should have the right to decide if they want to see me or not."

"They should, but she's their legal guardian. Ultimately, she has the final say so. You have to respect that. It's different if you see them alone in public and you three have a conversation. She can't ban you from public spaces, but you can't just go to the house— you went to the house, didn't you?"

I hung my head, knowing that my face had given me away. "Yes."

"Alayah, do not go back over there. The last thing you need is to be enticed into a fight and someone to call the police. You'll be back in a cell before morning."

"I won't go back, but I won't stay away from my sisters. If they want to see me, I'm going to see them. I've lost too much time with them already."

She sighed. "I get it. You helped raised them. You took care of them. They're your babies, but ultimately, they're hers. She has a say in who they are around. I encourage you to proceed with caution or have a conversation with her."

"There is no talking to that woman. If I could talk to her, I wouldn't be sitting here with you. She hates me. She's always hated me, and she's never failed to let me know that."

She offered me a sympathetic look followed by a sigh. "I understand. Just be careful, okay?"

I nodded. We talked for a while longer before she dismissed me. I left the office with my mood slightly deflated. As I took the elevator down to the lobby, I took some deep breaths to calm my nerves as I recited my affirmations.

I am resilient and can overcome any obstacle.

I am becoming the best version of myself.

I deserve success and happiness.

I am in control of my thoughts and emotions.

I choose peace and tranquility in my life.

I am deserving of respect and kindness.

With a deep breath, I stepped off the elevator and made my way through the front then out to the street. Uncle Clive's shop was only about a fifteen-minute walk from here, so I made strides toward my destination.

When I walked in, Londyn was talking to a customer. I spoke and kept it moving to the time clock before heading back to the break room to put my things in my locker. After slipping my phone in my pocket, I closed the locker and damn near jumped out of my skin when I came face-to-face with Londyn and her wide smile.

"Don't do that! You almost gave me a heart attack!"

"My bad, boo. Sooo…"

"So what?"

"Oh, come on. Don't make me beg. What happened last night? You just ditched me for that man. See, this friendship is starting off all wrong."

"You left me with him to go suck face with that guy."

She laughed. "Okay. Maybe I started it. I was coming back, though."

I playfully rolled my eyes. "Sure, you were. Did you leave with him?"

She smiled as she looped her arm through mine and began walking back in the direction of my office.

"Friend, I'm not gonna lie. I hadn't seen him in a while, and I needed some dick. But we aren't talking about me. We are talking about you and that man candy you left with. Is he the reason you're late to work?"

"No, Londyn. I had a meeting with my parole officer this morning. I made it home before my curfew last night."

"So what did y'all do?"

I took a seat at my desk, and she took one across from me.

"We were talking about me missing out on a lot of life, and I said something about wanting to live on the wild side for a moment to feel normal." I held out my arm. "He took me to get a tattoo."

She gasped dramatically. "*Oooo,* that's cute and befitting. Did he get one?"

I nodded. "He added this same one to his chest piece."

"Okay for the matching tattoos! Oh, so you got to see him in all his glory."

I blushed, and it caused an even more dramatic gasp from her.

"Oh, my God! You liked it, didn't you?"

"I…Okay, first, let me say he has a very nice body. I don't know, Londyn. This is new to me. I've never had a desire for anyone. Him admitting he had a crush on me in high school, then seeing him like that...I don't know."

"So you've never been with anyone else?"

I shook my head. "No. That man ruined me before I could even think about boys like that. I kept my head down and in the books. I didn't talk to boys. I didn't look at them. Killian and I became friends through working on a class project. We started studying together, and it kind of just went from there. He never gave me special attention or anything like that. He was just a nice boy."

"It's okay to be attracted to him, love. It's normal."

"For you. For me it's...it's scary. I don't want to be vulnerable with him. We aren't even on that level. I mean, it's not like he said he *still* likes me."

"Baby, I guarantee he still likes you. Take it from me, men don't look at you the way he does if there weren't some sort of feelings there. I watched him watching you last night. Sure, he was engaged in conversation, but that man was always checking to see if you were comfortable."

Had I missed that? I thought back to the tattoo parlor when his friend tried to hug me, and Killian immediately held out a hand to stop him. It was like a natural reflex for him.

"So you feel safe with him around?" Londyn asked.

I nodded. "Next to my uncle, he's the only man I've ever been comfortable around."

"That speaks volumes. Girl, that might just be your husband."

I sat back in my chair, looking at her like she was crazy.

"Londyn, I've never had a boyfriend, and you're talking about a husband. Please be for real."

She laughed. "I am. You never know."

"*I* know. What do I know about dating? About men? What if...what if he wants to have sex with me? I don't know if I'm ready for that. I don't know what to do besides just lay there." I buried my face in my hands. "God, this is so embarrassing."

Londyn got up from her seat and came to sit on the corner of my desk. She pulled my hands away from my face and tilted my head so my eyes would meet hers.

"There is nothing for you to be embarrassed about. Your innocence was stolen from you, Alayah. You didn't have the same experience as most women. It's okay to be nervous or scared to enter new territory, especially with a man. You have to learn to trust yourself, then trust yourself with him. Take your time. Build your friendship with him. If and when you're ready for more, make that known. There's no need to rush into anything you aren't a hundred percent ready for."

I sighed. She was right, and I was overthinking this. My best option was to go with the flow. She may have thought that Killian still had feelings for me, but until he actually voiced it, there was nothing else for me to do.

CHAPTER 16

Killian

"UNCLE KILLIAN, I'M hungry," Ellie complained.

I peered over my laptop at the little pigtailed beauty looking at me with a pout. I was working from home today, and Ellie was out of school due to a teacher workday. Since my sister and brother in-law had to work and my parents were on a trip visiting my grandparents, I volunteered to watch my niece.

It was clear that I wasn't going to get much work done. Ellie was an active child and required a lot of attention. Since I was childless, there was only so much to keep her busy at my house before she looked to me for entertainment. She'd stopped me three times already. The first time, she wanted to play hide-and-seek.

The game didn't last long because baby girl was a giggler and gave herself away. The second time, she wanted me to color with her. The third time she wanted me to watch her favorite show with her. Of course, all those times, I was a sucker and gave in. Now she was hungry.

I closed my laptop and placed it on the coffee table. "What would you like to eat, baby?"

She tapped her chin as though she was thinking seriously about her answer. She gasped when it finally hit her.

"I want a cheeseburger kid's meal."

"All right. Go put on your shoes, and let me go grab my keys."

"Okay!"

She ran over to the front door and plopped down beside where her shoes were. I stood and went to grab my keys from the kitchen counter. Looking at the clock on the stove, I saw that it was almost noon. I knew we'd be passing the mechanic shop to go to the burger spot Ellie loved, so I pulled out my phone to call Alayah.

"Hello?"

"Hey. What time are you taking lunch?" I asked.

"*Um*…in a few."

"How long do you have?"

"An hour. Why?"

"I'm on uncle duty today. Some little person isn't letting me get any work done, and now she's hungry. We're about to go get some food. You wanna ride with us?"

She was silent for a moment too long, which made me pull the phone from my ear to see if she was still on the line.

"Layah."

"I'm here."

"You coming?"

"Is your sister okay with this—me being around her child?"

I didn't even think about that, but I knew Bridget would be fine.

"She won't mind."

"Have you asked her?"

"Would you like me to call her?"

"I'd feel better if you did."

"Hold on." I clicked over and dialed Bridget's number.

"Killian, you better not be calling to complain about the child you spoiled," she answered.

I chuckled. "First of all, I didn't spoil her."

"Keep telling yourself that. What do you want?"

"Ellie and I are going out for lunch. I invited Alayah—"

Bridget laughed. "Killian, don't be using my baby as your wingwoman. You can't pull her on your own, little brother?"

"You get on my nerves."

"But you love me. It's fine. You can take her. Maybe Ellie will give her a little love. I know you said she's been missing her little sisters."

"She has. And you know Ellie loves to make a new friend."

"That she does. Have fun. I'm sure I'll hear all about it when I pick her up."

"I'm sure you will. Love you, sis."

"Love you, too."

I clicked back over to Alayah. "Hello?"

"I'm here. What did she say?"

"Well, after she accused me of using my niece as my wingwoman, she said it was okay to—"

"Uncle Killian, come on!" Ellie yelled. "I'm starving."

"I'm coming, lil' girl." I chuckled. "As you can see, she's impatient. We'll see you in about fifteen minutes, okay?"

"Okay."

I hung up and shoved the phone into my pocket as I left the kitchen. When I entered the living room, Ellie was standing by the door with her little arms crossed.

"You took forever," she complained.

I playfully mushed her head before opening the door. "You can't be rushing people when you can't drive yourself."

"I can drive."

"Your little pink convertible doesn't count. Come on here, girl. We have to pick up a friend."

That started a whole round of questions as we made our way to the car. She wanted to know who we were picking up and why they couldn't drive themselves. When I told her Alayah's name, she asked if she was my girlfriend, if she had any kids, and if I was going to marry her. The questions continued the whole fifteen-minute drive. When we pulled up to the shop and Alayah walked out, Ellie gasped.

"Uncle Killian! She's so pretty!"

I smiled. "Ain't she?"

"She looks like Moana."

I chuckled. I could see where she would think that. Alayah's curls were wild, free, and blowing in the wind today. I got out of the car and went around to open her door. She smiled as she approached me.

"Hey," she said.

"Hey, beautiful." I leaned in and kissed her cheek, noticing the redness in her face when I pulled back. "I hope you're as hungry as Ellie."

I opened the door, and she climbed in. Rounding the car, I hopped in the driver's side.

"Ellie, this is my friend Alayah."

Ellie was looking at her wide eyed with a smile. "Hi," she said excitedly.

Alayah matched her smile as she extended her hand. "Hi, Ellie. It's so nice to meet you."

"You're so pretty. You look like Moana. She's my favorite Disney princess."

"Well, thank you. I've never seen *Moana*."

Ellie gasped. "No way! It's only the best movie ever. Uncle Killian, you have to show her the movie."

I chuckled as I pulled out of the parking lot. "Who said she wants to watch all that singing, Ellie?"

She scoffed. "That's the best part. Can you play a song for her?"

I sighed. "Which song, baby girl."

"'You're Welcome.'"

I searched my music because of course I had the soundtrack for her. As soon as the music started, she started singing and dancing in her booster seat.

"I'm sorry about this," I whispered to Alayah.

She giggled. "It's fine. Adrienne and Amiyah had me watching Disney movies when they were little."

"Are you listening, Ms. Alayah?" Ellie questioned.

"I'm listening."

The ride to the burger spot was filled with Ellie singing along. I knew I was going to hear this song in my sleep because she would most definitely want to watch the movie once we got home.

When we pulled into the parking lot of Burger Bliss, Alayah looked around like she was expecting someone.

"You good?" I asked.

"Adrienne works here."

"Do you wanna go somewhere else?"

"No. She and I are good."

That was news to me.

"I'll tell you about it later," she said, noticing the look on my face.

I nodded. Unlocking the door, I got out and went to open her door before getting Ellie out. With her balanced on my hip, we walked inside. As we approached the counter, I recognized Adrienne right away. I hadn't seen her since she was a kid, and now, she was a miniature version of her sister at her age. When she noticed Alayah, she smiled wide.

"You came back," she said, leaning across the counter to hug her sister.

"I told you I would."

It did my heart good to see them share a moment. I knew how important reconnecting with her sisters was. Adrienne looked at me and squinted.

"Don't I know you?" she asked. "I never forget a face."

"I'm Killian. Your sister and I used to study together at your house."

"That's right. You would cook sometimes so she could help us with homework."

"That was me. This is my niece, Ellie. Say hi, Ellie."

"Hi. You look like Ms. Alayah."

Adrienne giggled. "Well, she's my sister."

Ellie looked between the two of them. Reaching out, she touched both of their cheeks. "You have matching freckers."

"Freckles," I corrected.

"Freckles. Uncle Killian, why don't I have freckles? I want some."

"Some people are just born with them. Now, tell her what you want to eat."

She rambled off her order and kept asking questions as Alayah and I ordered our own food. There was never a dull moment with this child.

"I'm going on lunch in a second, so I'll bring the food to you," Adrienne said.

"Thank you."

After grabbing our drinks, we went to find a seat, making ourselves comfortable in a booth. Ellie claimed the spot next to Alayah.

"I'm glad to see you two reconnected," I said.

"Me, too. I still haven't had one-on-one time with them, but at least I know they're open to rebuilding our relationship. I know it won't be easy for obvious reasons, but whatever strife comes behind it is worth it. I miss them so much."

I reached out and grabbed her hand. "I know, love. I have faith it will all work out."

Ellie looked between us curiously. "Uncle Killian, I thought you said she wasn't your girlfriend."

"She's not."

"So why are you holding her hand?" She gasped. "Do you like her?" she whispered loudly.

"You know, Ellie, you are just as nosy as your mama."

"My mommy is not nosy...What's *nosy* mean?"

"You ask a lot of questions."

"Well, how am I supposed to know stuff I don't know if I don't ask?"

Alayah laughed. "She has a point, Killian."

I shook my head as Adrienne approached the table with our tray of food. She placed it in the middle of the table and took a seat.

"Let me see your phone," she said, holding out her hand.

Alayah dug into her purse and produced the phone, handing it to her. Her sister typed on it for minute before handing it back.

"I put my number in there and sent Miyah yours. I'm gonna create a group chat."

"Kennedy doesn't check your phone?"

"Of course she does. That's why we have two phones. Miyah gave you her second line, just like I did."

I chuckled and shook my head. "You're a sneaky one, huh?"

"If you had to live with that woman, you'd be sneaky, too. She's not gonna keep me away from my sister."

Alayah had a worried look on her face. When Adrienne noticed it, she wrapped her arms around her and kissed her cheek. That made her smile a little. I couldn't imagine not being able to see Bridget. Sure, she worked my nerves growing up, but we had always been pretty close. If I couldn't have that, it would break my heart.

After distributing the food, we dug in, making small talk. Ellie was busy enjoying her burger and coloring in the little activity book that came with her kid's meal.

"Where is Miyah?" Alayah asked.

"We had a teacher workday today, so she's with her little friends. I can call her right quick."

She picked up her phone and tapped the screen. A few seconds later, the sound of playful laughter could be heard as Amiyah answered the video call.

"Hey, sissy. What's up?"

"Look who's here."

She turned the camera so Amiyah could see Alayah. The happiest squeal came from her.

"Layah! I miss you!"

Alayah swiped a tear from her eye. "I miss you, too, baby."

"Why haven't you texted me?"

"I'm sorry. I just didn't want to get you in trouble. Your sneaky sister here informed me that y'all have two phones."

She giggled. "We do. Wait. How long are you gonna be there? I'm coming right now. Please wait for me."

Alayah looked over at me.

"We can wait," I said.

"*Oooo!* Who is that? Do you have a boyfriend?"

Alayah laughed. "He's a friend. You met him when you were younger, but I'm not sure if you would remember him."

"Oh. Well, I'm leaving the park now. It's right around the corner."

"We'll see you in a minute," Adrienne said.

They disconnected the call, and I could see the excitement in Alayah's face. I loved that she was gonna be able to see both of her sisters at the same time. I just prayed no drama followed.

It wasn't long before Amiyah was running up to the table. She damn near dragged Adrienne out of the booth so she could get to Alayah to hug her. It was the sweetest reunion. Alayah reintroduced us. She didn't remember me, but it was okay. I got the feeling Amiyah never met a stranger. She had the bubbliest personality, and I could tell she was friendly. Ellie was intrigued by the three of them to say the least.

"She has freckers, too!" she exclaimed, pointing to the speckles that littered Amiyah's nose and cheeks. "Uncle Killian, I really want some now."

I chuckled. "Well, baby girl, I don't know what to tell you. I can't just get a marker and put freckles on you."

She giggled. "I never seen brown girls with freckers. Only—" She looked around, then whispered, "white girls."

That made the sisters laugh.

"Freckles can show up on anyone. It's just more visible on people with lighter skin."

"*Awww*, man."

She was really disappointed about that. I could already see me getting a call from my sister later telling me she asked her how she could get the freckles she admired.

We stayed at Burger Bliss through the rest of Adrienne's lunch break. We only had a few minutes left to spare before I had to get Alayah back to work. It was bittersweet when they all had to part ways. The little sisters hugged their big sister with tears in their eyes, and she cradled them in her arms with so much love. I watched as she gently wiped the tears from their eyes and kissed their foreheads.

"It won't always be like this," she promised. "One day, we won't have to sneak to have a relationship. I promise, I won't ever leave you again. Nothing but death will keep me from you. I love you both so much."

"We love you, too."

They shared another hug.

"How about a picture?" I suggested, extending my hand for Alayah's phone.

She handed it over with no hesitation. With her in the middle and her sisters on either side, I snapped the picture of the three of them and handed the phone back to her. She gave a teary smile as she looked at it. They shared one final hug before we all went our separate ways.

In the car, Alayah was quiet as she stared at the picture. Suddenly, her head dropped, and her shoulders began to shake. Tears streamed down her face as she cried softly.

"Ms. Alayah, what's wrong?" Ellie asked in a tiny voice. "You're crying. Are you sad?"

Alayah sniffled. "No, baby. These are happy tears. I haven't seen my sisters in a long time. I'm just happy I got to spend time with them."

"Why don't you just invite them to your house?"

If only she knew it wasn't that simple.

"Maybe one day," Alayah answered.

She wiped her face clean and relaxed into the seat. Reaching over, she grabbed my hand.

"Thank you."

"For what? I didn't do anything."

"You invited me to lunch, and I got to see my babies. Even if it wasn't intentional, I appreciate that."

"Well, even if it wasn't intentional, seeing you smile made it worth it."

She blushed as I squeezed her hand. Lifting it to my lips, I kissed her knuckles. Much to my surprise, she didn't release my hand until we got to the shop. Turning to the back, she reached for Ellie.

"It was so nice to meet you, Ellie. I hope I can see you again."

"Me, too! We can watch *Moana* together."

She giggled. "I'd love that."

I got out of the car and went to open the passenger door. Alayah stepped out, and I closed it. She stood there for a moment, seemingly hesitating. She trembled slightly as she raised her arms and slid them around my waist before resting her head against my chest. The trembling didn't subside until I returned the embrace. A breath expelled from her lips as she relaxed in my arms.

This was different. She'd held my hand twice since being home—once during her tattoo and just now in the car. We hadn't shared an embrace. Even when I walked her to the door the other night, she'd only faintly touched my arm as she said good night. This was nice.

I gently cupped the back of her head and placed a kiss to her temple. She slowly pulled away, peering up at me with a red face.

"I'm sorry. I just…I needed that."

"It's no problem," I said, palming her cheek. "I don't mind hugging you when you need it."

She blushed a little harder. "I'd better get back inside. Thank you for lunch."

"No problem. Have a good day, Alayah."

"You, too."

I watched as she disappeared into the building. From my peripheral, I felt someone watching me. I turned my head to see Londyn with a big grin.

"I saw that," she yelled, laughing as she headed back inside.

All I could do was smile as I got back in the car. In my rearview, Ellie was grinning just as hard.

"What are you grinning at?" I asked.

"Uncle Killian has a girlfriend," she said, sounding like her damn mama.

She made kissing noises at me, followed by her high-pitched giggles. I shook my head as I put the car in drive.

CHAPTER 17

Alayah

THE WEEK HAD gone by, and surprisingly, I was in a great mood for most of it.

Being able to spend a little time with my sisters gave me joy like no other. True to her word, Adrienne created a group chat with the three of us. All week long, we'd been texting back and forth. It was nice being able to talk to them, even though it was a risk of Kennedy finding out. Aunt Penny and Uncle Clive cautioned me to be careful.

I tried to tell myself that, but my brain never failed to reason with me that I had a right to have a relationship with my siblings in spite of our mother's wishes. Yes, I did something horrible, but horrible things had been done to me, too. Horrible things would have been done to them as well if I hadn't done what I did. In my mind, we'd suffered enough, and I wasn't going to suffer anymore.

It was Saturday morning, and I didn't have any plans other than lounging around the house. I'd slept in a little later, then woke up and did my journaling. I'd gotten up to take my shower and dress for the day before cleaning my bedroom and putting in a load of laundry. Currently, I was laid out across my bed reading a book and texting Killian.

When his name had popped up on my screen earlier, I couldn't help but to smile. I felt myself becoming more and more vulnerable with him. The hug we'd shared after our lunch with his niece gave me so much comfort. It took me back to all the times when he'd hugged me in the past. The embrace was familiar. It was warm and firm, yet so soothing. I remembered his scent and somehow, even his heartbeat.

The sound of footsteps approaching my door caused me to look up from my book. There stood Aunt Penny with a smile.

"Hey, auntie. What's up?"

"I'm about to go meet up with a girlfriend of mine, but I wanted to let you know you have a surprise."

My brows furrowed. "A surprise?"

She stepped aside, and in walked my sisters. They both pounced on me on the bed just like they used to when they were little any time they came in my room when I was laying down. Aunt Penny laughed as she left us be.

"What are y'all doing here?" I exclaimed through my own laughter.

"We were bored," Amiyah answered.

"Kennedy is out with her little boyfriend, and I didn't have to work, so we decided to come see you," Adrienne added.

I couldn't contain my happiness as I smothered both their faces with kisses like I did when they were kids.

"Why are you in here reading?" Miyah asked, picking up my book. "I thought you'd be with *your* little boyfriend."

"Killian is not my boyfriend," I defended. "He's just a friend."

"That's what your mouth says. I saw the way he looked at you at Burger Bliss. I don't really remember him from when you were in school, but you must have liked him to bring him to the house."

"We studied together."

"And what are you doing together now?" Adrienne asked. "Casual lunch dates with his niece?"

They both made playful dreamy eyes and kissy faces toward me before bursting into laughter.

I rolled my eyes and mushed their foreheads. "Whatever."

Miyah poked my side. "We're just joking. You do look cute together, though. Hopefully he's not just playing the nice-guy role."

"He's not. He's always been very nice and sweet." I looked between them. "Do either of you have boyfriends?"

Miyah shook her head. "No. The guys at our school are only after one thing. I'm saving myself until marriage."

Adrienne waved her off. "Speak for yourself."

My head snapped around. "Are you having sex?"

"Not at the moment, but I have—"

"Adrienne!"

"What! I used protection. I know not to bring Kennedy any babies. I'd be stuck with her forever if I did that."

"You're still too young to be out here having sex. It's not just babies you have to worry about. There are STDs, and condoms break all the time."

She sighed. "I hear you. I'm not dealing with anybody right now. I'm just trying to stack my money and finish high school so I can get out of here. Are you gonna visit me?"

"I'm on parole. I can't leave the state without permission."

"Oh. How long does that last?"

"Three years."

"You have to stay out of trouble for three years?" Adrienne asked.

"Yes. No trouble, no drugs or alcohol—"

"You can't drink?" she exclaimed.

"I know you aren't drinking, too, Adrienne."

She looked away. "I've had a few."

I grabbed her chin and made her look me in the eyes. "Listen to me: You have to stop trying to live fast and grow up faster. There is nothing but trouble in that lifestyle, and it's so easy to find. You're seventeen, Adrienne. You know when I had my first sip of alcohol? I was fourteen. Rodney made me drink a whole cup of moonshine, and when I was drunk and passed out, he came into my room and violated me. I don't want that to be you. You have to be mindful of what you put in your body because you never know who is waiting for your inhibitions to be low enough to take advantage of you. Do you get that?"

She looked at me, teary eyed. "Yes."

"That goes for you, too, Miyah," I said, cupping her chin as well. "I don't want either of you to find yourself in my shoes. You can be a victim, and the world will still see you as the perpetrator. If I hadn't gotten parole, I would have spent thirty years of my life in prison for defending myself. Women don't have the luxury of saying no and that being enough. They will *always* blame us— it's the way we dress, the way we look, the natural curves of our bodies. You can cover up or bare it all, and men will still say you asked for it. The last thing you need to be out here doing is putting yourselves in positions where you can't say no."

They both nodded. I wasn't trying to mother them. I was simply speaking from my own experience and the horror stories my old cell mates shared with me. We were born with two things already working against us: being black and being women.

"I have something for y'all," I said, standing from the bed.

I went into my closet and pulled down my keepsake box. Taking it back in the room, I placed it on the bed and pulled off the lid. On top of everything in the box were two stacks of bound letters that I'd written to each of them over the years. Stamped on the front in bright red letters was the phrase *Return to Sender*.

Even when they were returned, I kept writing, hoping that one of them would get the mail before Kennedy.

I handed each of them their stack. "I told you, I never forgot about you. I don't know how much of a difference these letters will make now, but I wanted you to have them."

They reached out with trembling hands and took them from me. Miyah sniffled.

"Mama kept telling us we had to forget about you," she said faintly. "We weren't allowed to say your name in the house. For the longest time, she wouldn't let us come over here because she knew Aunt Penny and Uncle Clive were in contact with you. She kept saying y'all were trying to turn us against her."

I shook my head. "I would never try to turn y'all against her. I just…I believe in my heart that she knew what was happening to me, and she did nothing to stop it."

Adrienne looked away, and the expression on her face told me she knew something.

"What?" I asked.

"Nothing, just…I remember her asking me once if Rodney ever touched me. It was right after you…right after he died. I remember waking up to her standing over me one night, and it scared the shit out of me. She asked me over and over if anything happened. I kept saying no, and she kept asking to the point where she was digging her nails into my arms and shaking me like I was lying." She shook her head.

Part of me was worried that something *had* actually happened to them, and they just didn't remember. The thought terrified me. What if I'd been too late? What if they were carrying around repressed memories? Could it be the reason Adrienne was acting out?

If it ever came to pass that Rodney had touched them, too, I would kill my mother with my bare hands. She'd let a predator into our home, the place we were supposed to be the safest, and he'd ruined us.

I wrapped my arms around both of my sisters and held them close to me. If I could help it, no one would ever hurt them. That was a hill I was willing to die on.

After an emotional spiel in my bedroom, my sisters took turns reading each and every letter I'd written. I tried to keep things positive with telling them about my day or how proud I was of their accomplishments. I ended every letter with how much I loved and missed them.

A lot of tears were shed in that room.

Uncle Clive came in to see what all the fuss was about and found us huddled up together crying. Once I assured him that these were cleansing tears, he left the room, but came back shortly with three bowls of ice cream. He was such a great uncle. Even with me pushing almost thirty, sweets always made me feel better.

We ventured out to the big front porch to get some fresh air and began reminiscing about all the fun we'd had here. Like me, this was the one place they could just be kids. They didn't have to worry about being yelled at or talked crazy to. They simply got to be free.

We were so engrossed in conversation that we weren't paying attention to our surroundings until Kennedy's car pulled to a screeching halt in front of the house.

"Shit," Adrienne said, standing.

Amiyah and I did the same. As our mother stalked up the front steps, I could practically see the steam coming from her ears.

"Mommy, we can explain—" Miyah started.

"Shut the hell up, Amiyah," Kennedy yelled.

"How did you even know we were here?" Adrienne spat.

"I can always find you. Believe that." She stormed up the front steps and came straight into my face. "Didn't I tell you to stay away from my children?"

Adrienne sprang into action, putting her body between us.

"Ma, you need to leave."

Kennedy shoved a finger in her face. "You need to move before I drag you down these front steps. You aren't even supposed to be here."

"What's going on here?" Uncle Clive asked, stepping onto the front porch. He slid Adrienne to the side and took her place in front of me. Kennedy poked his chest with her pointy nail.

"Didn't I tell you and my sister my kids weren't allowed over as long as the bitch was here?"

"She is your daughter, Kennedy. Don't disrespect her like that."

She scoffed. "Disrespect? You wanna talk about disrespect. None of you have respected my wishes when it came to her. She is dead to me. You hear me? Dead. That means she's dead to every single one of you, too."

Uncle Clive shook his head. "I'll be damned if I turn my back on this child. Now, I get that you don't want them around her, but they're her sisters, Kennedy. They're my nieces, and if they want to come over here, I'm not going to turn them away when they come to my door."

"Clive, until you produce a child, you don't get a say in anything dealing with these two. You and Penny want Alayah so bad? Keep her. Just keep that murdering whore away from my children." She grabbed Adrienne and Amiyah by the arms and snatched them to her. "What did I tell you? Huh? Didn't I tell you not to come over here? You think you can just do whatever you want, no matter what I say?"

Adrienne snatched away from her. "You can't tell me what to do, Kennedy. She's my sister, and you can't keep me away from her."

"Like hell I can't. You live under my roof—"

"Then maybe I won't live under your roof anymore! Anyplace is better than being with you."

When Kennedy drew back and slapped her, I sprang forward and stood between them.

"What do you wanna do, bitch?" Kennedy asked, squaring up at me. "I told you what would happen the next time I caught you anywhere near my kids."

"I don't wanna fight you, Kennedy, but you aren't gonna be putting your hands on her."

"Who's gonna stop me? You? What, you're gonna put me in the grave, too? I would love to see you try that shit. You'll be back in lockup before you can blink."

"You would love to see me locked up again, wouldn't you? Tell me the real reason you went out of your way to make me look like the aggressor. You painted this false narrative of me and ran with it. I'm your daughter, Kennedy. Even if you can't stand the sight of me, some motherly part of you should have had my back. You should have believed me. You should have known what that man was doing to me."

"He never touched you," she screamed.

"Yes he did. I tried to tell you, and you wouldn't listen to me. Why would I lie about something like that? That bastard came into my room at night for years, and plenty of times while you were in the house. How could you *not* have known? Where did you think he was going when he snuck out of bed and was gone for too long? How could you miss the way he looked at me—the way he made me uncomfortable when he touched me? My God, Kennedy. You didn't even know that that man got me pregnant."

"You're nothing but a liar."

She slapped me so hard that I tasted the blood as it pooled in my mouth. Adrienne and Amiyah gasped. I could see the vein in Uncle Clive's neck straining as he yelled at her, but I couldn't hear what he was saying. Anger flooded my core as I touched my lip. The sight of the bright red blood on my fingers only fueled that anger.

Kennedy was yelling back at my uncle, and the girls were trying to pull her away. When she slapped him, too, something in me snapped. I drew back and reached around him, slapping her so hard that she almost took a tumble down the front steps. If Adrienne and Miyah hadn't caught her, she would have hit the ground. The passenger-side door of her car opened, and a tall, dark-skinned man got out, briskly making his way to us.

When Kennedy realized that I'd hit her, she tried to get at me.

"You're going to jail, bitch. You wanna put your hands on me?"

The unknown man grabbed her around the waist, holding her back.

"Baby, come get in the car," he tried to reason.

I shook my head. He'd sat there the whole time watching this madness unfold and done nothing.

"Let me go, Anthony."

"You're making a scene. I told you not to come over here. You could have handled this in the privacy of your home."

He snatched her back, towering over her as he spoke lowly to her. She kept looking around him at me. The snapping of his fingers seemed to make her focus her attention on him.

"Go get your ass in the car," he finally said, loud enough for us to hear.

Kennedy looked between the two of us. If she happened to make it past him and get to me, there was no telling what would happen. Finally, she retreated.

"Adrienne! Amiyah! Get your asses home right now!"

She stormed over to the passenger side and got in, slamming the door behind her. The man I now knew as Anthony turned to us with an awkward smile.

"I'm sorry about that, folks. I tried to reason with her."

"Just take her and get off my property," Uncle Clive said.

He nodded. "Come on, girls," he said to my sisters.

They looked at each other, then at me. As bad as I wanted to keep them here, I knew I couldn't. Kennedy would surely call the police to have them forcibly removed. I made my way down the steps and over to them. Gently, I pulled them into my arms and hugged them tightly.

"Go home," I whispered. "If she touches you, you call the police. You understand me?"

They nodded, tears flowing down their cheeks.

"Don't cry," I said, my own tears threatening to fall. "Everything will be okay. I love you both."

"We love you, too."

We shared another hug before Kennedy rolled down the window and screamed for them to go home again. I finally released them and went back to stand next to Uncle Clive. As I watched them climb into their car, my shoulders shook with emotion. He pulled me into his chest, and the moment his arms enclosed around me, I broke.

I told my sisters everything would be okay, but would it really?

CHAPTER 18

Killian

I **SAT AT** my desk looking over this mountain of a file for an upcoming court case. I'd been swamped for days now. It seemed like the peaceful weekend I had was nothing more than a setup. Just when I thought the week might be smooth sailing, I thought wrong. I'd been buried in paperwork since I'd gotten here this morning. I hadn't had time to eat or go to the bathroom yet because I was so swamped. With the way things were looking, I wouldn't be eating lunch either.

The sound of knocking on my door didn't bother me as much as I thought it would. I set my pen down, welcoming the reprieve.

"Come in."

Leaning back in my chair, I waited to see who would walk in. Much to my surprise, it was Alayah. I wasn't expecting her. She had grown slightly cold over the last couple of days. I felt like something had happened and she wasn't telling me what it was. Every time I saw her face, she looked so sad and withdrawn. Today was no different.

I stood from my seat and went to greet her.

"Hey, Layah," I said, reaching for her.

She pulled away slightly. "Hey, Killian."

"What are you doing here?"

"I need your help."

I nodded and led her over to a chair. She took a seat, and I reclaimed mine.

"What's wrong?"

Digging in her purse, she pulled out a folded piece of paper and handed it to me. My brows furrowed as I took and read it.

"A restraining order?"

"Apparently, I'm not safe for my sisters to be around, and I'm a bad influence. She'll stop at nothing to keep me away from them, Killian."

"What brought this about?"

She sighed. "The girls came to see me over the weekend. I didn't ask them to. They decided to surprise me, and there was no way I was going to tell them they had to leave. Adrienne said Kennedy was out with her boyfriend, but somehow, she tracked them to the house. She showed up and showed her ass with all that yelling and cursing. She threatened my sisters, slapped me, and when she slapped my uncle, I lost it and slapped her back."

"Shit."

"I need my sisters out of that house. I haven't heard from them in days, Killian. I know if I go over there, it's going to be a brawl, and I can't go back to jail. They need me."

She dropped her head in her hands and began to cry. I stood from my seat and went around to comfort her. I hated that she was going through this. All she wanted was a relationship with her sisters, and their mother was making it difficult at every turn. If it had been noted in the conditions of her parole, that would have been different. Alayah wasn't a danger to Adrienne, Amiyah, or anyone else for that matter.

"What am I gonna do, Killian? What if the judge sides with her?"

"Well, more than likely, this will be a family-court issue. We're gonna need a list of solid character witnesses. It would also be helpful if we had someone who can attest to how she treats the girls—like a neighbor or someone who's seen it first-hand."

"I'm sure someone in that neighborhood has heard or seen something."

"I think Erica would be a great help on this. I can help in the background, but I'd better serve you as a character witness."

She sniffled and nodded. "Is she here?"

"Let me call her."

I turned my desk phone around and called down to Erica's office. She answered on the second ring, and I asked her to come down the hall. She agreed, asking me to give her a few minutes. While we waited, I grabbed some tissue to wipe the tears from Alayah's face and a bottle of water for her to drink. Her hands were trembling as she twisted the top off and took a sip.

"We're gonna figure this out," I assured her.

There was a knock on my door before it opened and Erica walked in.

"Alayah? What are you doing here?"

I handed her the petition for the restraining order, and she read over it as I explained what led to the motion being filed.

"I figured this was gonna happen." Erica sighed as she took a seat next to Alayah. "We—"

"I want guardianship of my sisters—at least until both of them reach eighteen. That's only a few months for Adrienne, and she'll be off to college. Miyah still has two years before she graduates, but I can do this."

"Alayah, you're on parole. You're still trying to get yourself together. Are you sure you want to add on taking in two teenagers? You'd have to get your own place, a license, and transportation.

If this becomes permanent, they have to have health care, food, clothes, insurance… There's a lot you have to prepare for, honey."

"I can do it. I've been learning to drive, and I'm getting better at it. I'll get a car. I'll take on a second job if I have to. Please, Erica. I don't feel like they are safe with Kennedy. I haven't heard from them in a week, and I can't go over there. She isn't going to let my aunt or uncle in. Please! You have to do something; you have to help me."

There was desperation in her voice. Erica looked from Alayah to me then sighed.

"Okay. We can start with a wellness check. My husband is an officer. I can get him to do it. Once we see what he finds, we can move from there. We're gonna have to get on this quickly before the hearing. The more we get to prove her unfit the better. This can get very ugly, Alayah. Your past is gonna come up, and you may have to relive that trauma again in the public eye. Are you prepared for that?"

Alayah nodded. "For my sisters, I have to be ready."

"Should your request be declined, are your aunt and uncle prepared to step up?"

"Without a doubt."

Erica gave her a tight-lipped smile. "I'll make the call."

She stood and walked to the door.

"Wait," Alayah called. "I need to know how much this is going to cost me."

"Don't worry about that."

"Erica, I have to pay you."

"I believe in you, and because I believe in you, I'm not worried about you paying me. There are too many red flags when it comes to your mother, Alayah. Somebody has to knock her down a few notches. I'll be in touch."

She left us with a smile as she walked out of the office. Alayah buried her head in her hands and sighed heavily.

"Jesus be a fence," she muttered.

I pulled her to her feet and wrapped my arms around her in a warm embrace. For the longest time, we stood there with me rocking her from side to side in a soothing manner. Silence stood between us, but the surrounding emotion was so loud. She expelled a deep breath.

"I'm sorry for just popping up like this. I didn't know who else to turn to for something like this."

"It's not a problem. I can see how much strife this is causing you."

She peered up at me. "It's more depressing than being in prison. I couldn't do anything behind bars, and now it feels like I can't do anything on the outside. I feel like I've failed them all over again."

I cupped her face. "You didn't fail them, baby. You did the most selfless thing you could have done. You sacrificed your freedom. If that ain't an act of love, I don't know what is. Things will work out the way they're supposed to."

"I really hope so, Killian."

"Believe that." I kissed her forehead and wiped the tears from her cheeks. "Dry your eyes. You're getting these freckers all wet," I said, mimicking Ellie.

A faint smile appeared on her lips. For a moment, we stared into each other's eyes. Her piercing brown orbs were filled with a mixture of pain and hope. Then she did something I wasn't expecting. She stood on her toes and pressed her lips to mine. For a second, I pulled back, searching her face. There was no sign that she regretted the brief action.

Again, she stood on her toes and kissed me softly. The gentle pecks soon turned to her sucking on my bottom lip before migrating into her tongue caressing mine. She wrapped her arms around my neck and deepened the kiss. My arms enclosed her, holding her as close to my body as I possibly could. Moments passed, and we were still caught up in the intense lip lock.

Kissing her was everything I imagined it would be. Her lips were soft and juicy. Her breath was minty fresh, and the feeling of her body against me filled my core with every ounce of attraction I'd tried to suppress. The moment she pulled away, I instantly missed her.

"I have to get back to work," she said faintly.

I nodded. "Do you need a ride?"

"No. Londyn is waiting downstairs."

"Okay. Call me later?"

"I will."

She grabbed her things before leaving my office. I stared after her long after she was gone. One of these days, when this was all over, she was going to be mine.

CHAPTER 19

Alayah

I SAT ACROSS from my parole officer who had a slight frown on her face. When I called a few days ago to notify her of the pending court date for the restraining order, she was already well aware. She was out of town at the time, but as soon as she got back, she had me come in.

"What is this, Alayah? A restraining order?"

"My mother doesn't want me to see my sisters."

"And you went over there anyway?"

I gave her a quick rundown of the events that transpired, and she listened attentively while also shaking her head.

"They came to surprise me at my aunt and uncle's. I couldn't turn them away, Ms. Vera. Do you know what it feels like to be separated from the people you love most?"

"No, I don't." She sighed. "I've been in this business a long time, Alayah. One thing I can tell you is that the road to hell is paved with good intentions. People want to do the right thing but end up going about it the wrong way. I know you love your sisters. I know you miss them, but sweetheart, you are creating more problems for yourself."

"I will take the consequences of that. You don't know Kennedy Chambers. You don't know the things she's said, done, and let happen. She's not a good mother."

"She has to be somewhat decent to still have custody of those kids."

"They are afraid of her! Miyah doesn't want to upset her, and Adrienne knows how far to push it before the backlash. She did something to them. I know it...I feel it. Call it intuition or whatever, but I know she did. I won't stop until I know they're safe. That's why I had my lawyer do a wellness check."

"This is gonna get ugly."

"It should have gotten ugly a long time ago. I kept quiet about the extreme verbal abuse I suffered from that woman for years. She's never treated me like her daughter, and now that she knows my sisters and I are rebuilding our relationship, she's gonna do whatever she can to sabotage that."

"This isn't a good look for you. I know not seeing your sisters wasn't in the conditions of your parole, but she could very well press assault charges."

"She can't press charges on me without implicating her—"

"She's not the one on parole. Do you want to go back to jail?"

I sighed and shook my head.

"Good. If she's granted the restraining order, follow it. If not, you still need to follow her rules. At the end of the day, she is the mother, and those girls are in her care. Adrienne will be eighteen soon. She can do what she wants then, but until both of them are of age, Kennedy is their legal authority. I know that's not what you want to hear. I know this doesn't feel fair, but it's the reality of it."

I didn't say anything in response. I knew she was right, but my heart wouldn't hear it.

"Can I go now?" I asked.

"We have a few more things to discuss, and I need a urine sample." She reached into the desk drawer and placed a cup in front of me. "Let's get this over with."

I sighed heavily as I snatched the cup up and went to the bathroom with her on my heels. Once the sample was collected, we talked for a little while longer before she gave me permission to leave. Begrudgingly, I left the office and took the elevator ride back down to the first floor. I couldn't even say that I was disappointed with the way this visit went because it went exactly how I expected.

As bad as I hoped Erica's friend from CPS found something to incriminate Kennedy, I also hoped that she didn't. I didn't want to believe that Kennedy would hurt my sisters, but I also couldn't put anything past her. She had shown her hand way too many times for me to believe that ten years had changed anything.

Her social media presence alone said that. I'd created a fake account to keep tabs on her. Since her page wasn't private, I could see everything. She told strangers way too much of her business. She had posts showcasing the things her boyfriend brought her, the five-star dinners he took her to, or the lavish vacations she went on. Nowhere in those pictures were my sisters. My guess, while she was out living her best life, they were left to fend for themselves.

The last couple of weeks, she'd made several posts about me, my aunt and uncle, and my sisters.

With Adrienne and Amiyah, she mostly posted about raising unruly teenagers who didn't listen and thought they were grown. With Aunt Penny and Uncle Clive, she ranted and raved about them being unloyal and backstabbing her. Then there was me. She posted my mugshot several times, calling me a murderer, a whore, and just plain evil. She posted a picture of her bruised face from where I slapped her. While she didn't say I did it, the caption read, *A bitch thought she had me. Face still pretty.*

I shook my head at every post. The woman was forty-four years old and still playing these games. She didn't take accountability. She didn't listen to shit. If it wasn't what she wanted to hear, she got loud and defensive. I remembered the one time I tried to be brave enough to tell her what was happening to me.

I was fifteen at the time. She was in the kitchen, packing her lunch for work. The girls were upstairs sleeping, and Rodney hadn't gotten there yet. I'd come down to get a drink of water before going to bed. Nervously, I stood in the entryway of the kitchen twiddling my thumbs as I watched her.

"Either come get what you came to get or take your ass upstairs, Alayah," she said, not bothering to look up at me.

"Ma…can I talk to you?"

"What is it now? Don't ask me for any money because I don't have any for you."

"It's not money."

She looked up from the sandwich she was making. "What do you want? I know you want something."

"I don't want anything. I…I need to tell you something."

She sighed as she placed her hand on her hip. "What? Out with it."

I slowly walked over to her with my head down. "It's Rodney."

"What about Rodney?"

"I don't like him, Ma. He makes me uncomfortable."

"Uncomfortable how, Alayah? The man is always nice to you. Always buying you and your sisters shit. Having nice things makes you uncomfortable?"

"It's not that. It's…he looks at me like—"

"Stop, because I know you aren't implying what I think you're implying. Look at you, Alayah. Now look at me. Why would he look at you any kind of way when he has me? You're seeing shit that ain't there, and I'm about to help you see clearly. What you better do is stick to these

little nappy-headed boys around here. You wanna be fast, you better be fast with them. All I know is you better not bring me any babies."

"But, Ma—"

"Alayah! You listen, and you listen good. Rodney looks at you like a daughter. That's it, and that's all. He does more than your stupid-ass daddy has ever done for you. When is the last time you saw him? Exactly. Never. While he's off living his best life, I'm stuck with you. You should be grateful that somebody wants to take care of you. Now, I don't wanna hear another word about this, do you understand me? Get out of my face and go to bed."

She'd turned me around and shoved me away before going back to making her sandwich. I'd gone upstairs and cried my eyes out. There had rarely been a time where I felt like she cared about me, but that night solidified it. To be dismissed like that when I was crying out for help broke my heart.

I knew she said something to him because I woke up to him covering my mouth with his hand. I tried to scream, but he clamped it tighter.

"Shut up," he seethed. "You tried to tell your mama our little secret, pretty girl? Why would you do that?"

He removed his hand, waiting for me to respond.

"You—You hurt me. You won't stop hurting me."

"So you were just gonna tell your mama, huh? You think she would believe you over me? Kennedy loves me. She's never gonna find another nigga like me that will do what I do for her with three kids by three different men."

"Then I'll tell somebody who will believe me."

"No, you won't. You know why? Because you're gonna act like we're one big happy family. If you tell anybody, I'll make good on my promise. You remember that promise, Alayah?"

I remembered the promise well. He reminded me of it often. He didn't have to say it again for me to know to keep my mouth shut. I never uttered a word about it to my mother or anyone else again.

I shook those dreadful thoughts from my head. I already wasn't in the best headspace. I hadn't had a nightmare in a while, and I didn't want to start them up again by allowing thoughts of him to invade my mind.

I arrived at work about twenty minutes later. Sitting pretty on my desk was a bouquet of white roses with a card sticking out the top. The corners of my mouth turned up for the first time in days as I walked over to them. Plucking the card from the insert, I pulled it from the envelope and read it. The message was simple, yet sweet.

Just because, Killian.

I leaned in and sniffed the roses. It was very thoughtful of him to send them. There had been a shift between us the last couple of days. Since our kiss, things took on a more intimate feeling. Every night this week, he'd stopped by to check on me. While he was free to come inside, we would sit in his car in front of the house for hours.

Sometimes we talked. Other times we sat listening to music. Each time, however, the first thing out of his mouth was *How is your mental?* Sometimes that opened the floodgates for tears; other times, it led to a cleansing conversation. I could purge my feelings to him and not feel like a burden. Sometimes people only wanted you to listen to their problems, but they weren't willing to listen to yours in return.

Killian had always been easy to talk to. He'd always have an encouraging word or do something to make me smile. He'd never known that seeing him was the highlight of many of my low days. Without even meaning to, his friendship kept me afloat in times where I was about to tip over the edge.

In my world full of pain and dark, gloomy days, he'd been sunshine.

CHAPTER 20

Killian

"COME IN!"

I looked up from my computer to see Erica stepping into my office with a solemn look. As someone who was usually smiling, I knew that meant she wasn't coming to tell me good news. I turned away from the computer as she closed the door and took a seat in front of my desk.

"Bad news?" I asked.

"If bad news could be good, that's what this is."

My brows furrowed. "What do you mean?"

"So, the wellness check was completed."

"And? What did they find?"

She sighed. "Well, when Malcolm got there this morning, a neighbor was outside—you know, one of those nosy old ladies that sees a lot but says nothing. This time, she had a lot to say. My husband asked her if she'd seen or heard anything out of the ordinary lately. She said the same day Kennedy pulled up to the Easton home, she came home in a fit. She could hear her yelling at the girls, and they were arguing. She said she didn't think anything of it because she was always arguing with Adrienne."

I nodded. "Alayah told me her aunt says she's the defiant one."

"Well, apparently, this wasn't just an argument or her not listening. When Malcolm knocked on the door, he found the girls were home by themselves. Nothing wrong with that. They are old enough to be home alone. The unsettling thing were the bruises."

"Bruises?"

"Particularly on Adrienne. They were all over her arms, legs, and face. He said it looked like the poor child had been to battle. When he asked her what happened, she said she got jumped at school. He said she was still visibly shaken up by it, and he had to coax the truth out of her. She and Kennedy fought that day—not argued, fought, Killian. When Amiyah tried to break it up, she got hit in the process.

"They haven't been to school in a week because they're waiting on the bruises on their faces to heal. Kennedy told the school they both had COVID. That's why Malcolm went to the house. He went to the school first. She took the battery out of Adrienne's car and removed everything from their room. They are sleeping on a blow-up mattress, Killian. Right now, she's of town with her boyfriend because she needed to get away from them. She left them with no phones, and there is barely any food in the house. Adrienne says she's hit them before, but it's never been this bad. She's punishing them."

I was disgusted, and it only got worse when she showed me the pictures of the bruises, their rooms, and the nearly bare cabinets, fridge, and freezer.

"CPS is involved," Erica told me. "Right now, they've been taken to the hospital to be checked out. After that, CPS will take over."

"Has anybody told Alayah or the Eastons?"

"Alayah and Mr. Easton are at work, but I called Mrs. Easton. She was so upset, Killian. She kept saying they should have never let the girls leave with her. I've filed a petition for an emergency removal on the Eastons' behalf. Of course, the girls want to go with them, but Kennedy is going to fight that tooth and nail with Alayah being there."

I nodded as I stood from my chair. "I need to go see her. She's going to be a mess when she finds out."

"They should be home now. Mrs. Easton said she would call."

I started gathering my things, but I realized Erica was still sitting there watching me.

"Was there something else?"

"Killian, are you and Alayah a thing?"

I sighed. "I don't know what we are right now. What I do know is that I care for her as much as I did all those years ago. I don't want to rush her into anything."

She smiled softly. "Well, I know you will take good care of her. You're a good man, Killian."

She left me to my packing. Once I gathered everything, I had to sit down for a moment. This shit was crazy. I would have been willing to bet money that this wasn't the first instance of Kennedy putting her hands on her kids. She probably never hit them in the face where it would be visible. To know that she was right was going to relieve yet devastate Alayah.

I made it to my car in record time and left the office, headed for the Easton home. As I turned onto their road, I could see Alayah walking bristly toward the bus stop with angry tears streaming down her face. Pulling over to the curb, I got out and jogged behind her.

"Alayah!" I managed to get in front of her, slowing her strides. "Where are you going?"

"To find my sisters. My aunt and uncle said I need to wait, but I can't, Killian. She beat them, then took a fucking vacation with her boyfriend! That's why I didn't want them to go with her. This is why I wanted them out of that house!"

Her hands went to the sides of her head, and she began pacing. Tears streamed down her cheeks as she attempted to get control of her breathing.

"This is my fault. It's all my fault. If I had left them alone, none of this would have happened!"

She dropped to the ground, crying profusely. I took a seat beside her and pulled her into my arms. I was sure we looked crazy sitting on the concrete, but it didn't matter. Gently, I rocked her from side to side.

"You can't blame yourself, Layah," I said softly. "This isn't the first time it's happened. It just hasn't been this bad. She's going to be arrested for sure. If we can't get justice for you, we can get justice for your sisters."

She sniffled as her tears began to subside. "She has to be held accountable, Killian. She can't get away with this."

"She won't. Right now, I need you to get in the car and let me take you home. There's nothing you can do until the emergency hearing. Just pray that the judge will grant your aunt and uncle temporary custody."

"What if they don't?"

"Then, unfortunately, the girls would go into the system until they can find proper placement."

She shook her head. "No. We can't let them do that. What if they split them up?"

"Erica is gonna do everything in her power to make sure they stay together and come home with family. You can't stress yourself with this. I know that's easier said than done."

I climbed to my feet, then pulled her upright. She allowed me to lead her to the car and put her in the front seat. I climbed in, and we took the short drive back to the Easton residence. Mrs. Penny met us at the front door.

"Thank you for bringing her back," she said as I guided Alayah inside.

"No problem."

She embraced her tightly and kissed her cheek. "Why don't you go lay down for a bit? I know this is a lot on your mental right now."

Alayah nodded. "I might do that." She looked back at me. "Do you have to go back to work right now?" she asked faintly.

"Not right away."

"Can you stay with me a little while?"

I looked to Mrs. Penny for permission. I didn't want to be disrespectful.

She smiled softly. "It's okay, baby. I've already peeped what's brewing here. Go on."

She waved us toward the hall. Alayah grabbed my hand and led me to her bedroom. The moment we walked in, I said to myself that the space fit her. She kicked off her shoes and climbed on her bed to lay down. For a moment, she just looked at me before speaking.

"Can you lay with me?" she asked faintly.

I nodded slowly. After kicking off my shoes, I laid on the bed facing her. There was an ample amount of space between us. For the longest time, she stared at me, and I stared at her. She looked to be having a mental battle with herself. I reached out and grabbed her hand.

"Can I ask you for something?" she whispered.

"Anything?"

"Can I cuddle with you? I just...I feel safe in your arms."

I didn't say anything. Instead, I inched closer to her and opened my arms. Even though it was her request, she hesitated for a moment before sliding into my space. She curled into me, then rested her head on my chest and threw her arm around me.

I closed my arms around her, pulling her in close. She expelled a relaxed sigh.

"Better?" I asked.

She nodded. A brief silence fell upon the room. The only thing that could be heard was the sound of breath leaving our bodies.

"What if I've ruined their lives?" she asked.

"You haven't. You've brought light to an ongoing situation. Something had to be done or it probably would have kept happening until they were old enough to leave and never come back. You trusted your gut, and you went through the proper channels to get help. That's all you could have done. Right now, you just have to trust that the law will do the right thing."

She scoffed. "How do you trust a system that failed you?"

I didn't have an answer for that. She had every right to be concerned, and I couldn't tell her otherwise. The system could be finicky. There were people who cared more about lining their pockets than serving justice. It wasn't unfounded to learn about officials who purposely pad sentences or corrupt officers to terrorize the people they were supposed to protect. It was a broken system, but there were so many people trying to fix it and be better. I prayed this wasn't one of those things that got swept under the rug.

CHAPTER 21

Alayah

A WEEK LATER

I NERVOUSLY SAT in the courtroom behind my aunt, uncle, Erica, and Mary Proctor, the DCFS worker assigned to my sisters' case. Killian sat next to me on one side, holding my hand for comfort. On the other side was Ms. Vera. She came to ensure that I didn't do anything to put myself at risk. My leg bounced anxiously as we waited for the judge. Kennedy hadn't been brought in yet, but it was my understanding that she'd been arrested as soon as she touched down at the airport.

I felt a slight relief when Erica called with the update. Of course, she was livid. She claimed that Adrienne attacked her, and she defended herself. It was just like her to shift the blame to somebody else.

"Are they gonna start soon?" I whispered to Killian.

"They should."

Just then, the side door opened, and Kennedy was escorted in, chained in handcuffs. Her eyes landed on us, and the scowl on her face deepened. She was seated next to her lawyer, and behind her were her boyfriend and surprisingly, Mrs. West. I was confused as to what she was doing here. The relationship between my mother and Mrs. West's son ended ten years ago. Why would she stand beside her along with her new man?

The doors to the judge's chambers opened, and out walked an older woman who was introduced as Judge Bishop. Everyone stood and waited for her to be seated before reclaiming our seats.

"Court is now in session. It's my understanding that this is for the emergency removal of Adrienne and Amiyah Chambers from the home they share with their mother, Kennedy Chambers. I see we have representatives from DCFS present. Who do we have here today?"

My mother's lawyer stood. "Your Honor, I'm Penelope James, representing Kennedy Chambers."

Erica stood next. "Erica Sawyer, representing Clive and Penny Easton. With me is Mary Proctor, the case manager assigned to Adrienne and Amiyah."

The judged nodded. "Thank you. Mrs. Sawyer, please present the reasons for this emergency removal request."

"You Honor, Mrs. Chambers showed up at the Easton residence to claim her daughters who were visiting with their sister and her oldest daughter, who's seated behind me."

She motioned to me, and Kennedy sprang to her feet.

"Your Honor, I specifically told her and my children to stay away from each other. I don't want them around—"

Judge Bishop cut her off. "Ms. James, I implore you to remind your client not to speak until spoken to."

"Yes, Your Honor."

She guided Kennedy back into her seat, whispering softly to her. The judge motioned for Erica to continue.

"As I was saying, she came to claim her daughters. During that time, Ms. Chambers was very verbally and physically aggressive toward Mr. Easton and her oldest daughter. She slapped both of them and made threats toward her other two children. She forced them to leave with her. Their sister, expressing genuine concern for their well-being, requested a wellness check when she didn't hear from the girls in over a week.

"An officer was first sent to the school, where it was discovered that neither of them had been in attendance for the entire week. He was told they were at home with COVID. The officer then went to the Chambers family's residence. The problem was the disturbing conditions he found them in. Do I have permission to approach the bench?"

The judge nodded. Erica picked up an envelope and made her way to the front.

"Exhibit A. These are photos taken by the officer of the bruises on both girls."

She handed over the photos and made her way back to the table as the judge looked them over. I hadn't seen the photos, but the look on her face told me they were bad.

"In addition, Ms. Chambers further punished her daughters by removing all personal belongings from their bedroom, leaving them with only a blow-up mattress—no pillows, no blankets. Just the mattress. She took away any device that could be used to call for help should the need arise. She also took the battery out of Adrienne's car to ensure they wouldn't leave. While she left town to go on vacation with her boyfriend, the girls were left with no food. She scared them to the point where they hadn't left the house in days.

"My clients are petitioning for temporary custody—at least until both girls are of age. Mrs. Easton is Ms. Chambers' older sister. Adrienne and Amiyah know and love their aunt and uncle. They are ready and willing to take the girls home today."

Judge Bishop nodded. "Thank you. Ms. James, does your client wish to respond to these allegations?"

"Yes, Your Honor. My client maintains that she does not abuse her children. The incident in question stems from a highly emotional incident. Ms. Chambers has expressed time and time again that she doesn't want her daughters around their sister, a convicted felon. She had every right to be concerned for their safety."

Erica stood. "Your Honor, I've also represented the eldest Chambers sister in her fight to freedom. Yes, she was convicted, but the circumstances were extremely sensitive. She served ten years in prison for the death of the man who molested and raped her for years. That man happened to be her mother's boyfriend at the time. Clearly, she has a history of poor decision making when it comes to her children and their safety."

"Rodney never touched her," Mrs. West yelled.

Judge Bishop banged the gavel. "Order. Ma'am, who are you?"

"Marjorie West. Rodney West was my son. She killed him in cold blood."

The judge shook her head. "While I sympathize with your loss, Mrs. West, this isn't about you—"

"You Honor, you can't let those children live in a house with a murderer. They were in the home when she did it. Do you know how traumatizing that would be?"

I was about to stand when both Ms. Vera and Killian grabbed my hands. Forced to relax in my seat, I took several deep breaths. She wanted to talk about trauma like her son hadn't scared me for life.

Judge Bishop sighed. "I will address these concerns later. Mrs. West, sit down. One more outburst, and you'll be the one sitting behind bars. Ms. James, please continue."

"Thank you, Your Honor. As I was saying, Ms. Chambers and her daughters were both very upset with the circumstances surrounding their visit with their sister. It was made very clear that she didn't wish them to have any contact. My client maintains that things got heated at home. Both she and her daughters exchanged licks, and she feels very bad about that. She has every right to be concerned about who her children are around, even if it's their sibling."

Erica shook her head. "With all due respect, your honor, Ms. Chambers wasn't concerned when her eldest daughter tried to tell her what her boyfriend had been doing to her. She served ten years when she shouldn't have served a day. If the woman would protect a rapist, surely, she would lie to protect herself. According to her daughters, this isn't the first, second, or even third instance of this occurring.

"She's just never left bruises to this extent. Sure, she was upset. I'll give her that. However, it doesn't erase the fact that she bruised them so badly that they had to miss school to avoid circumstances just like this. It doesn't excuse the extreme stripping of their possessions and leaving them for days with no food and no way to contact anybody if there was an emergency. That, Your Honor, is abuse and neglect.

"The girls are old enough to speak for themselves. I have here a sworn statement from each of them, detailing things that have gone on in that house." She picked up the papers and walked them over to the judge. "They are not safe, Your Honor. They should be with people who love, care for, and respect them."

Judge Bishop nodded as she looked back to Ms. James. "Do you have anything else, Ms. James? Nothing you produce will make this look any better for your client."

Ms. James shook her head. "Nothing else, Your Honor."

Kennedy's head snapped toward her. "Nothing else? Do something. That's what you were hired for. I did not abuse my children. They attacked me, and I defended myself. Don't you see what's happening here? This is nothing but the influence of that murdering bitch. She will stop at nothing to turn everybody against me and ruin my life."

That started Mrs. West up again, too. The courtroom was filled with nothing but yelling and cursing directed toward me. I sat quietly, squeezing the hell out of Killian's hand. I wasn't afraid, but the anger I felt was enough to have me leaping over the railing that separated us and wrapping my hands around Kennedy's neck.

Judge Bishop slammed the gavel. "That's enough. Remove both of these women from my courtroom and lock them up."

We all watched as the two of them were escorted out, kicking and screaming. Kennedy's boyfriend shook his head as he left the courtroom, too. Once it was quiet, the judge spoke again.

"Given the severity of the allegations and the evidence presented, I'm inclined to grant the emergency removal. The problem here is the mother's concern about placement."

I couldn't take it anymore. I stood from my seat, against Ms. Vera and Killian's attempts to make me sit down.

"May I have permission to speak, Your Honor?"

She looked at me for a moment then motioned for me to continue.

"Your Honor, I would never hurt my sisters. I love them. I helped raise them from the time they were babies until my incarceration. Yes, I was convicted of manslaughter. I served my time, and I was a model inmate. My mother intentionally severed the relationship with my sisters. For ten years, she refused every phone call and every letter I wrote to them.

"When she learned I would be released, she forbid me to try and repair the relationship she severed. Under normal circumstances, I could understand her reasoning, but this isn't normal. I take full responsibility in the part I played in ending a man's life, but I don't regret it because I finally saved myself from years of abuse that I fully believe my mother knew was happening. I saved my sisters from the same fate.

"I have been on the straight and narrow since I came home on parole, and I am not a danger to my sisters. If it would help bring them home faster, I will leave my aunt and uncle's home and find somewhere else to live."

Several gasps went up around the small space. I could hear everyone talking to me, but I kept my gaze locked on the judge.

"You said you're on parole. That means you've been given an approved residence. You'd have to go through the parole board or your parole officer to get a change approved, and this is a time-sensitive matter."

Ms. Vera stood. "Your Honor, my name is Vera Washington. I'm Ms. Chambers's appointed parole officer. She's been a model parolee, and I know how much this means to her. If she can find adequate placement, I will sign off on it."

"That's all fine and dandy, Ms. Washington, but—"

"She can stay with me."

My head snapped in Killian's direction. He stood from his seat. The judge squinted.

"Is that you, Mr. Lake?"

"Yes, ma'am. I'd like to offer my home to Ms. Chambers. I've known her since we were kids. I'm willing to accept responsibility for her. I'll make sure she stays on the right path. I'll ensure she gets to and from work and adheres to the terms of her parole."

"And I'll check in with her twice a week," Ms. Vera added. "We are currently on an every-other-week schedule, but I'm willing to amend that if it helps with this process."

Judge Bishop was quiet for a moment, I guess assessing the option. She scribbled something down, then nodded.

"Given the circumstances, I will agree to releasing Adrienne and Amiyah into the custody of their aunt and uncle following Ms. Chambers' departure from the home."

"Thank you, Your Honor," I said. "May I ask a question?"

"Go ahead."

"Will I be able to see them? My mother has petitioned to have me restrained from seeing my sisters."

Erica interjected. "Your honor, I filed an emergency motion to dismiss the restraining order yesterday, given the circumstances, and it was accepted."

That made my heart flutter. She hadn't told me that piece of information yet. Erica reached into her briefcase and produced a document.

"I also filed a request for visitation on Ms. Chambers' behalf."

The bailiff came over to retrieve the paperwork and took it to the judge. Silence ensued as she read over it. I watched as she picked up her pen and scribbled something down.

The judge nodded. "I will allow supervised visits on the weekends. Ms. Chambers, your aunt, uncle, or Mr. Lake need to be present. You can see them today, but you must vacate the home before your curfew."

It wasn't what I hoped for, but I would take it. "Thank you."

She slammed the gavel. "This hearing is adjourned."

She left the courtroom, and we all filed out in silence. Maybe this wasn't the turnout we expected, but at least the girls would be with family, and Kennedy would soon get exactly what she deserved.

CHAPTER 22

Killian

"**IS THAT THE** last of it?" I asked, setting the box in the back of my car.

Alayah nodded sadly.

She was happy with the judge's ruling that her sisters could live with her aunt and uncle, but also sad that she was leaving. Right after we left court, I took her to grab boxes to pack up her things and to make a copy of my house key for her. Before we could go back to the Eastons', we had to make a stop at my place so Vera could check it out for approval.

She'd given me a short list of things that needed to be resolved by the time she visited again next week. I assured her it was no problem, and it would be done. We'd been diligently packing up Alayah's belongings and the ton of books her aunt had purchased for her. Since they only had a three-bedroom, one of the girls would be taking her room.

I closed the trunk and walked over to where she stood on the bottom step of the front porch and grabbed her hands.

"I know this isn't how you pictured things going, but it's better than nothing."

"I know," she said faintly. "I promise I'll be a good houseguest. You don't have to worry about me making a mess, and I'll cook. If you want me to pay—"

I placed a finger to her lips to silence her. "Let me stop you while you're ahead. You don't have to pay me for anything. I know what I signed up for, and I trust you."

"I appreciate you, Killian. I was prepared to go find an apartment or something."

"You can stay as long as you'd like. If and when you're ready to be on your own, I'll help you find a place."

"Thank you for being a friend."

I chuckled. "Have you been watching *The Golden Girls?*"

It took a second for her to catch on to the correlation. She playfully slapped my chest before wrapping her arms around my neck and hugging me tightly. When she pulled away, she palmed my face and pressed her soft lips to mine. The kiss we shared was slow and sweet. We'd shared a few kisses now, and I'd grown to love the feeling of her lips against mine.

It always took me by surprise when she made the first move. On the plus side, it was a good thing she allowed herself that vulnerability. Many victims of assault never reached a level of comfort where they can be physically vulnerable with another person. As much as I loved kissing her, I wanted her to have control and freewill over her desires. That wasn't to say that I would never kiss her first, but right now, she deserved to have the choice.

Our lips parted at the sound of a car pulling into the driveway. Upon further inspection, I realized that it was Ms. Proctor, the DCFS worker. Alayah broke away from me and ran down the driveway. Her sisters hopped out and ran into her arms. The bruises on their faces were still visible as well as the many on Adrienne's arms.

I'd read the statements Erica provided the judge. She'd detailed how her mother hit her repeatedly with a closed fist or how she pulled her hair out at the root. I could only imagine what was going through her mind at that time. To watch the woman who birthed her beat her like a stranger on the street, it would forever live in her mind.

As I watched them, it was like they were those five- and seven-year-old little girls again. They clung to her as she hugged them and kissed the tops of their heads.

"I got you. I got you," she said repeatedly. She looked up at the Ms. Proctor. "Thank you."

The woman smiled. "I can tell you genuinely care for them."

"They are my babies. I'd do anything for them."

She nodded and went to the trunk to grab their things. I made my way down to the car to help her as Mr. and Mrs. Easton came out of the house. The five of them gathered, sharing hugs and kisses, and we hauled the bags inside.

"I think they will do just fine here," she said.

"They will," I assured her. "If there is nothing else that woman loves, she loves her sisters. They need each other."

She nodded in agreement. We headed back outside where she spoke to the family for a few minutes before heading to her car. Everyone made their way inside the house. Mrs. Easton had prepared a quick dinner of chicken alfredo, garlic bread, and corn on the cob. We all gathered around the table to eat. Alayah sat next to me, smiling as she looked at her sisters who sat across from us.

"I'm so happy you're here," she said, clasping her hands over her heart.

"We're happy we get to be with you," Amiyah admitted.

The smile on Alayah's face slowly receded. "Ms. Proctor didn't tell you?" she asked.

"Tell us what?"

"The condition of you staying here is me leaving."

Amiyah's eyes widened. "But...But why? Why do you have to leave?"

"There were concerns of my influence over you. I'll be staying with Killian and visiting you on the weekends."

"That's bullshit!" Adrienne exclaimed.

Alayah's head snapped in her direction. "Watch your mouth, Adrienne."

She hung her head. "I'm sorry. I'm just upset."

"I know this isn't what we pictured, but it's better than nothing. Baby steps. It won't always be like this."

Adrienne nodded. "When do you have to leave?"

"My things are in the car."

Adrienne and Amiyah's gazes drifted over to me.

"Promise us you're gonna take care of my sister," Adrienne said. "Promise you won't hurt her or take advantage of her. And don't be one of those controlling men that keeps her away from us."

I extended my hand to her. "I promise. I'll do everything in my power to make sure the three of you never have to go through that again."

She looked at my hand then back up at me. Slowly she reached out to shake it with Amiyah doing the same. That seemed to be good enough for them—at least for now.

After eating dinner, Alayah and I had to leave since it was getting close to her curfew. Her goodbyes with her sisters were sad, but I promised I'd make sure she came over this weekend. The drive to my house took about twenty minutes. Once we got there, we unloaded her belongings, and I showed her around the house.

I'd purchased a one-story, four-bedroom, three-bath home three years ago in a neighborhood not too far from my parents. My sister actually lived three houses down. It was safe to say we never strayed too far away from home or each other.

"You have a nice home," Alayah said as we turned down the hall to the bedrooms.

"Thank you."

"Why so big when it's just you?"

"I bought it with a family in mind. I wanna get married one day. Of course, I'd have to actually be dating to do that," I added with a chuckle. "For now, I use one of the extra rooms as my office. Then there's the official guest room and Ellie's room."

"She has a room here?"

"She insisted on it. She was only two when I bought the house, but when I gave my family a tour, she walked in that room and said 'Mine'. I think it was the pink walls."

"That's cute. You must have her often."

"As often as I can. They actually live three houses down. Sometimes my sister will stand in the driveway and let her walk down here. It's nothing to hear her little taps on the door at any given time. I'm sure she'll make her way over sometime this week. At least you'll have another friend."

She giggled. "She's adorable, so I don't mind having a little friend. Can I ask you something?"

"Sure."

"How are you going to explain me living here to your family?"

"What do you mean explain? I don't have to explain anything to them about my choices. I'm not in any danger here."

"It just…it might get awkward."

"Listen, my family really minds their own business for the most part when it comes to my love life. As long as I'm safe, secure, and happy, they will be okay. Besides, Ellie has already run back and told them you were my girlfriend."

Alayah laughed. "She did what?"

"The day of our lunch. My parents called to check in, and she had to tell them all about her day, including meeting Uncle Killian's girlfriend. It was the first thing she said when my sister walked in the door, too."

"That's funny. I can almost hear her cute little voice."

"I hear her voice in my sleep sometimes." I shook my head. "This is where you'll be sleeping," I said, opening the door to the guest room.

The room was almost as spacious as my master and shared a Jack and Jill bathroom with the room I'd set up for Ellie. My mother had picked out all the furniture in here and decorated the space. In the middle of the floor was a black tufted platform bed with black nightstands with gold accents on either side. Each of them held a gold lamp with a black shade. Gold mirrors hung behind each nightstand, and a large gold-framed picture was centered above the bed.

The bedding was white with black, white, and gold accent pillows. A fifty-inch TV was mounted to the wall directly across from the bed with a fireplace beneath it. The room had a huge walk-in closet and a bay window she could sit in. It was very cozy and had yet to be used.

"This is beautiful," Alayah said, looking around.

"Thank you."

"Did you decorate?"

I snorted. "God, no. This is all my mother."

"She has great taste."

"She has expensive taste."

She giggled. "Well, I love it. I can see my bookshelf right there," she said, pointing at the wall.

"I guess we do have to find somewhere to put your books since you made me do all that heavy lifting."

"You lifted it with no problem. Think of it as a workout."

"I work out enough. You see these guns?" I flexed a muscle, causing her to blush.

"Yeah…I see."

"I'm gonna go grab some hangers from my closet in case you wanted to unpack anything tonight."

"Thank you."

I left her with a smile as I headed for my bedroom. Inside, I went to the closet, pulling down any unused hangers I could find before taking them back to the guest room. Alayah had busied herself with putting the clothes from her suitcase into drawers. I placed the hangers in the closet and headed back to the door.

"I'm gonna go take a shower and get ready to lay down. If you need me, you know where to find me."

"Okay."

"If you need towels or washcloths, they're in the cabinet in the bathroom."

"Thank you."

I gave her a slight smile. As I went leave the room, she called my name. "Killian?"

"Yeah?"

She placed the shirt in her hand on the bed and slowly walked over to me. She rested her hands on my chest and leaned in to kiss me.

"Good night."

"Good night, love."

Our gazes lingered for a moment before she went back to unpacking. I closed the door and retreated to my room.

CHAPTER 23

Alayah

"**H**AVE A GOOD day at work," Killian said as he pulled up in front of the shop.

"You, too."

I leaned over and pecked his lips, a habit I'd become too comfortable with. We hadn't discussed what was going on between us, but there was definitely something brewing. The first time I'd kissed him in his office, I'd had to work up the nerve to do so.

My attraction to him was becoming overbearing, and I didn't know what to do with myself. Every time I looked at him, my face flushed. I wasn't used to my heart racing because of a man. Every time we touched, I wanted the feeling to last a little longer. Every time we kissed, I felt a warmth spread through my body that was foreign to me.

He was the calm.

The voice of reason.

He was peace like I'd never known.

I got out of the car, and the first person I saw was Londyn. She stood with her hands on her hips and a smirk on her face.

"Good morning, Londyn," I said, with a smirk of my own.

"Don't good morning me, heifer," she exclaimed, playfully mushing me. "What was that?"

I giggled. "I don't know what you're talking about," I said, walking up ahead of her. She quickly followed me into the building.

"Oh! So you're just gon' insult my intelligence and my eyesight like I didn't just see you kiss that man? Ms. I'm Not Looking for a Man is out here kissing fine-ass lawyers who drop her off to work. Did you spend the night over there? Oh my God! You did! Did you…you know? I bet you did. You look like you're in too good a mood, and only good dick can do that."

"Londyn, why do you ask me questions if you insist on answering them yourself?"

She laughed. "You know my mouth works faster than my brain sometimes, girl. I get overstimulated. I'll be quiet. What's up?"

I sighed as I sat at my desk and motioned for her to sit as well. She quickly copped a seat and crossed her legs. I took a deep breath and gave her the rundown of everything that had transpired over the last couple of days. She went through a range of facial expressions but ended up with a smile.

"You know you could have called me," she said. "I would have been there to support you."

"I didn't want to burden you, Londyn."

She scoffed. "If we're gonna be besties, you have to understand that your burdens are my burdens."

"I'm sorry. I've never really had a female best friend before. I've always just kind of kept to myself."

"I get that. This is a new life for you, so I won't take offense, but you have to start showing me some love."

"How about I take you to lunch, wherever you want? I mean you'd have to drive, but I'll pay."

"I'll take you up on that." She leaned forward in her chair with a grin on her face. "So…when are you going to tell that man you love him?"

"Say what now? I never said I love him."

"Maybe not, but it's written all over your face, boo. You might not realize it now, but you will. I'll be here to say I told you so." She stood and walked to the door that led to the back. "Oh, and I want a fish sandwich for lunch. Be ready at one, and you're driving. We really have to get you that license now."

She blew me a kiss before heading to the back. I shook my head as I relaxed into my chair. Her words echoed in my head. Did I love Killian? What did that look like? It was sad that as a woman approaching her thirties, I'd never known love outside of family and friendly relationships.

I'd missed out on so much of life and experiences. I didn't know intimacy with a man that wasn't filled with trauma. What the hell would I do if he touched me? How would I react? How would my body react? I wasn't sure what to do with this influx of unfamiliar emotions I was feeling.

"Good morning, baby girl," Uncle Clive spoke, breaking my thoughts.

I looked up to see him coming through the back door.

"Hey, Uncle Clive."

I stood and went to hug him. He kissed my forehead before stepping back to look at me with a smile.

"I missed riding to work with you this morning," he said.

"Right. No morning coffee stops. Did the girls sleep okay?"

"They slept well. I could hear them snoring through the walls," he added with a chuckle. "How was your first night with Killian?"

"It was fine. His home is beautiful."

"Are you comfortable there? He make you feel welcomed?"

"I'm comfortable, and yes, he did."

"You let me know if I need to make other arrangements for you. I mean it. The first time he gives you the wrong vibe—"

"Uncle Clive, I promise Killian is a good person. I've known him since school, and he's always been super nice to me. He's a great friend."

"We kiss our friends?"

I blushed, and it caused him to chuckle. "You saw that?"

"I did. But before I saw that, I saw you sitting in that man's car in front of the house for hours the other week. You don't even do that with Londyn, and I know you like her, even if it was forced."

I giggled. "I like him. I just…I'm afraid to say anything. I don't know how to handle men, Uncle Clive. The closest thing to a man I know is you."

He laughed out loud. "The closest thing! Damn, baby girl. I at least thought I was a whole man."

"I'm sorry. Wrong choice of words."

"I know what you mean. Let me tell you this: When a man is worthy of you, he will make it easy for you to handle him because he will handle you with love, care, and respect. You won't have to worry about who you are with him or who you need to be. There's no censorship or guilt about being vulnerable. You simply get to be you." He cupped my chin and smiled. "You deserve that. If that happens to be with that young man, your aunt and I will support you."

"Thank you, Uncle Clive, not just for being the best uncle, but the best father figure. I love you, and I'm so grateful for you."

"I love you, too. Penny and I never got to have our own children, but you and your sisters have always held a special place in our hearts. We've got all our girls now—maybe not under the same roof, but we've got you."

We shared another hug. God truly blessed me with him and Aunt Penny. Without them, I had no idea where I would be. I would have had nothing to come home to, no *home* to come home to. Prison would have been my home for the next twenty years. I owed them my life.

I wandered around the empty house, giving myself a solo tour. Londyn had dropped me off about twenty minutes ago since Killian was still at work. It was so quiet—too quiet. After ten years of constant noise, when it got too quiet, it made me anxious.

I decided to hook my phone up to the Bluetooth surround sound. As the smooth sounds of "Brown Eyes" by Destiny's Child blared through the speakers, I rummaged through the kitchen looking for something to cook for dinner. I wanted to earn my keep around here. If the man wasn't going to let me pay him for rent, the least I could do was make sure he had a hot meal when he walked through the door.

I found some pork chops unthawing in the fridge and decided to smother them along with some mashed potatoes and steamed broccoli. I sang along to the music as I moved around the kitchen. While I wasn't the best singer, it reminded me of all the times I cooked dinner for my sisters, and they would be right there singing and dancing along with me.

I was miserable and still found a way to make the smallest things enjoyable for them. The song transitioned into "Chills" by Fatty Koo, and my singing got louder. I was so into the song that I didn't hear the footsteps behind me until someone started singing along.

My head whipped around, and I was staring in the face of a woman who resembled Killian. As I looked closer, I recognized her from the pictures in his home as his sister. She smiled and laughed as she approached me.

"You were getting it in here, girl," she said as I turned the music down. "I didn't mean to scare you. We were on a walk, and

Ellie had to use the bathroom. She knew you were here, and she just had to stop to see you, so I let myself in. I'm Bridget, Killian's sister."

"Alayah. Killian's…friend."

"I know who you are. My little brother used to talk about you all the time."

"He did?"

"Girl, he had the biggest crush on you. I heard your name so much, I think he said it in his sleep."

I blushed. Before I could respond, Ellie came running around the corner.

"I washed my hands, Mommy!" she said, raising her little hands for her mom to see. When she looked over and saw me, a big smile broke out on her face. "Ms. Alayah!"

She ran over to me with her arms out. I didn't hesitate to scoop her up for a hug.

"Hi," I said, smiling at her.

"Where have you been!"

"I had some family issues to take care of, Ellie."

"Are they okay?"

I nodded. "Everything is okay now. Thank you for asking."

"Mommy, this is Uncle Killian's girlfriend," she whispered loudly as she pointed at me. "The one with the freckers."

Bridget laughed. "I know, baby."

"We're not—"

"Girl, if you aren't, you will be. He told me you were here, and I just wanted to introduce myself. I'm sure we'll be seeing a lot of each other, so don't be a stranger. Maybe we can get together for a drink sometime. Don't worry, I have perfected the art of mocktails. It won't get you drunk, but it still tastes good."

I smiled. "That would be nice. Killian told me you live three houses down."

"Yes."

"Would you like to stay for dinner?"

"My dinner is in the crockpot. I just wanted to officially introduce myself to you. We can plan something for another day. You're more than welcome to come to Sunday dinner with our family. Your little friend there has already told my parents you're Killian's girlfriend."

"But she is, Mommy. I saw him kiss her."

"It was a forehead kiss," I explained.

"It was still a kiss," Ellie said matter of factly.

I giggled. "I guess you're right. "

"Uncle Killian told my mommy you live here now. Does that mean I get to come over and play with you?"

"I would love to play with you. You still owe me a movie date."

"Yes! Mommy, doesn't she look like Moana? Look at all her hair." She fluffed the mass of curls on my head.

"You know what, you do," Bridget agreed. "Anyway, I'm not gonna hold you up. We just wanted to say hi. Come on, Ellie. Daddy should be home."

Ellie wrapped her little arms around my neck and squeezed. When she pulled away, she kissed my cheek.

"See you later, Ms. Alayah."

"See you later, baby."

I placed her on her feet, and she ran to her mother. They headed for the front door, and as soon as they got to it, it opened. Killian walked in and grabbed up Ellie, tossing her in the air. She erupted in a fit of giggles as he smothered her face with kisses. I smiled as I watched the interaction. I knew he loved that little girl like she was his own. He and his sister spoke for a few minutes before she and Ellie left to go home.

He kicked off his shoes and set his things down before making his way into the kitchen to greet me.

"Hey, love," he said, kissing my cheek.

"Hey."

"You have it smelling good in here."

"Thank you. I just wanted to show my appreciation for you letting me stay here."

"Baby, I told you, I don't need any thanks. I will take a plate of whatever you're cooking though. My mouth is watering."

I giggled as I opened the fridge and grabbed him a beer. "How was your day?"

"It was decent. I had court this morning. I finally got this client's charges dropped, and I'm glad to be done with it. She omitted so many things that she was about to send herself to prison. Anyway, I don't want to bore you with work. I see you had visitors. I should have warned you she was coming to be nosy."

"She was nice, and Ellie was Ellie. The food will be done soon if you want to change into something comfortable."

"Thank you, baby."

He went to walk off, but I grabbed his arm and pulled him back. He stepped into my space, lowering his gaze to me.

"What is it?" he asked.

"Don't make me ask."

"Nah, baby. Use your words. I want your consent."

I never imagined that asking for consent could be so sexy. I swallowed hard as I peered up at him.

"I want a kiss."

He smirked as he wrapped his arm around my waist and pulled me into him. Cupping my chin, he lowered his lips to mine, kissing me softly and slowly. His tongue slipped into my mouth, and his free hand moved to the nape of my neck. I felt his fingers thread through my hair, giving it a soft pull. A moan slipped from my lips, catching me by surprise.

I pulled away from him, attempting to control my hormones. I turned back to the stove, completely flustered.

"You good?" he asked, touching the small of my back.

"Mmm-hmm," was all I could offer.

I heard him chuckle as he left the kitchen. Closing my eyes, I inhaled deeply.

"Calm down, girl," I told myself. "You don't even know if you're ready for all that yet."

Even as I said the words, I wasn't sure if I believed them. I hadn't been touched in ten years, not by me...not by anyone. I didn't know the first thing about real pleasure. Did I really want to go experimenting? Londyn's voice entered my head.

"You better play with yourself like a DJ scratching a record in the club."

I giggled to myself. Maybe I needed to test those waters to see if I even had a sex drive.

CHAPTER 24

Killian

I STEPPED OUT of the shower and grabbed my towel.

After drying my body, I wrapped it around my waist and headed into my bedroom. I grabbed a pair of boxers, shorts, and a t-shirt and tossed them on the bed. I didn't want to keep Alayah waiting, so I made haste in moisturizing my skin. I took my skin care seriously as a man. No woman could ever say I was ashy, smelled, or had crusty ass feet.

Once I was dressed, I headed back to the kitchen to find that Alayah had set the table for us. She sat waiting patiently for me to join her. The spread she prepared looked and smelled amazing. I remembered watching her cook dinner for her sisters. She'd always find ways to make the food appealing to them, like making mashed potato mountains with broccoli trees and gravy rivers.

I remembered thinking she would make a great mother one day. The thought crossed my mind whether she even wanted children now. The image of a little mini us ran through my mind briefly. I could see a beautiful little girl with freckles and a head full of curls who looked just like her. Then I saw a little boy with every bit of my likeness.

It made me smile.

I joined Alayah at the table and reached for her hands to bless the food. Once I was done, we dug in. The pork chop was so tender and flavorful. The mashed potatoes were creamy, and the broccoli was cooked just right.

"You put your foot in this," I said, swallowing.

"Thank you. It's just a little something. I wanted to be useful. You won't let me pay you."

"Alayah, you don't have to be useful. While you're here, this is your home. I want you to be comfortable. Don't feel like you have to make homecooked meals all the time, even though I could get used to this," I added with a chuckle.

"I'll try to remember that this is home." She giggled softly. "I bet you didn't think we'd end up here from a study session."

"I didn't. But the best things are unexpected."

She smiled. "They are."

Our gazes locked for a moment. She chewed slowly as she watched me.

"Something on your mind?" I asked.

"A lot is on my mind."

"Like?"

She shook her head. "I'd rather not say."

I decided not to press her. We continued to eat, mostly in silence. When we were done, I helped her clear the table and do the dishes before she retreated to her room to shower. I settled on the couch in the dark to watch a little TV before I went to lay down for the night. It wasn't long before I heard the sounds of Alayah's feet on the hardwood floor.

Looking over my shoulder, my eyes widened as she came around the corner in a short pajama set. My mouth watered at the sight of those thick, luscious thighs on full display. She rounded the couch, and my eyes drifted to the plump roundness of her ass.

Shit!

She took a seat on the other end of the couch and tucked her feet under her. I flipped through the channels until I came upon *The Best Man.*

"I love this one," she said faintly.

"You know they made a limited series after the second one."

"They did? I'll have to catch up."

"Maybe after your movie date with Ellie, we can have a movie date of our own."

She smiled. "I'd like that."

"I have this projector and a screen I set up for her in the backyard from time to time. She loves watching movies on it."

"I love how thoughtful you are with her. You're gonna make a great dad one day."

"I hope so. I mean, my dad is pretty great, so I have some big shoes to fill."

"How many kids do you want?"

"Maybe two—a boy and a girl. Honestly, I just want them to be healthy. I'll love whatever I get." I looked over at her. "Do you want kids? You ever thought about that, considering...you know?"

She looked down at her fingers, plucking at her nails. "Once upon a time, I wanted a family. I told myself if I ever had children that I would be nothing like my mother, and their father would be nothing like mine, whoever he is. My babies would be loved and respected."

She said that with conviction, and I could tell that she meant it.

"They would be lucky children to have you as a mom. Watching you care for your sisters then and now, Mama Bear would be nothing to play with."

She giggled. "I wouldn't. There are very few things that take me out of character, but my kids most definitely will."

"I'm glad to see you have hope for the future."

"I've been thinking a lot about my future lately. I think I want to open a natural hair salon. I'm thankful to Uncle Clive for this job, but for the first time, I have a chance to have something of my own. I have to make that work for me."

"I got you. Whatever you need to get that up and running, I'll help with. If you need somebody to sweep those little beady beads off the floor, I can do that, too."

She laughed out loud. "I appreciate that. I do want to take an apprenticeship or something, just so I can learn a little more first."

"I like the way you think. There's always room for improvement."

A satisfied smile played on her face. She scooted a little closer to me, pausing for a moment before resting her head on my shoulder. She slid her arm around mine, then laced our fingers. I placed a kiss to her forehead as we settled back into the movie. Aside from the audio, it was quiet and still.

That was until the flashback of Harper and Mia making love. Alayah sat up, squirming slightly. Her eyes averted from the TV, and she looked over at me. When I caught her staring, she abruptly looked away.

Again, I asked, "Something on your mind?"

"Can I ask you something?"

"Anything."

"It's personal."

"Ask your question, love."

"When…When's the last time you've been with a woman?"

"Oh, well it's been a while—like eight months or so."

"Have you had a lot of partners?"

"I can't say that I have. Five at best."

"Would you say you satisfied them?"

I chuckled. "I haven't had any complaints if that's what you're asking. Why so curious?"

She gave me a look. "I've never…I've never been with anyone willingly. I never had a traditional first time, and I don't…you know."

"Masturbate?"

"Yes. I've never had the desire until recently. I don't know if I'm ready to have the full experience." She took a deep breath. "What I'm trying to say is I want to experience something pleasurable. I don't trust any other man to take care of me the way I think you would take care of me, Killian. I feel like you would respect my body and not make things as awkward as I probably will."

She hesitated for a moment, before throwing caution to the wind and straddling my lap. Those enticing brown orbs peered down at me as she raked her nails through my beard.

"Do you want me, Killian?" she asked.

I nodded. "Yes."

"You have my consent."

I stilled in my seat. Did she just give me permission to pleasure her?

"Are you sure?"

She nodded. "I'm sure."

I reached for the remote and turned the TV off. With her secured in my arms, I stood from the couch and carried her down the hall to my bedroom. Inside, I placed her in the middle of the bed. Stepping back, I pulled off my shirt. Her eyes perused my tattooed chest. Reaching up, she traced the outline of the matching tattoo I'd gotten with her.

Taking her hand, I kissed her fingers before leaning in to kiss her lips. My hands rested on her thighs, then moved up her sides and under her shirt. She trembled slightly.

"I can stop," I said softly.

She shook her head. "I'm okay."

I lifted the shirt over her head and pulled it off, tossing it behind me. Staring back at me was the most beautiful set of full breasts with perfect Hershey-kissed nipples. I eased her down onto her back and took the first nipple into my mouth. She gasped.

Closing my eyes, I sucked and savored the taste of her as I alternated between the hardened buds.

"K–Killian…" she whimpered.

As I continued to suck her nipples, I trailed my fingers up her thighs. A slight tremble shook her. Slipping my hand into her shorts, I was surprised to find the insides of her thighs coated in her essence.

"Can I touch you?" I asked.

"Y–Yes!"

I wasted no time cupping her mound in my hand. My middle and ring finger dipped into her wetness and circled her clit. Another gasp expelled from her, followed by a moan.

"Oooo!"

That was possibly the sweetest sound to grace my ears. I strummed her clit a little faster, causing her back to arch from the bed. The pleasure written on her face was undeniable. She deserved this, and I was more than willing to bring her to her first bout of real ecstasy.

"Can I taste you, baby?" I whispered against her lips.

She nodded. "Yes."

I pulled my hand away long enough to maneuver her shorts down over her hips and pull them off. She was soaking wet at this point. The aroma of her sweet arousal permeated my nostrils and made my mouth water. I dropped to my knees in front of her and draped her legs over my shoulders.

Her swollen clit peeked out at me, beckoning my face to the sweet spot between her thighs. Closing my eyes, I wrapped my lips around the sensitive bundle of nerves. Her legs immediately began to tremble. She gasped repeatedly as I kissed and sucked her clit.

"K–Killian. Oh my God…"

I moaned into her, and the vibrations had her legs clamping around my head. Reaching up, I toyed with her equally sensitive nipple while enjoying my meal.

"Oh my God," she cried out.

"I'm gonna penetrate you, okay? Just relax. I'll be gentle."

She looked down at me and nodded slowly. When I eased the first finger in, she tensed slightly.

"Relax," I coached. "Look at me, baby."

Her gaze fell to mine as I slowly eased the finger in and out of her.

"You're doing so good, love. Keep breathing…deep breaths."

As she took another deep breath, I slid the second finger in.

"Good girl. That's it. Tell me how it feels."

"It…shit. It feels so good."

"Don't you deserve to feel good, Layah?"

"Yes… Killian, please. I'm gonna—"

"You can hold it," I said, strumming her clit with my thumb. "It's so much better when you hold it. Squeeze."

Her walls contracted around my fingers, and another audible cry came from her. At this point, her head thrashed about wildly against the bed. Her hands gripped the comforter, and her toes curled next to my ears. Bated breaths filled the air surrounding us. I latched on to her clit once more as I continued to glide my fingers in and out of her wetness with skilled precision.

The moment I tapped against her G-spot, her body went into a fit of uncontrollable spasms. She gasped repeatedly, attempting to steal back every breath I'd stolen and then some. With a final stroke of my fingers, her essence coated my hand and ran down my wrist. Her breath caught in her throat as she rode the magical wave of her first orgasm. I pulled my mouth away so I could watch her writhe before me.

She was cumming, and I was still stroking her middle. Those thick thighs trembled, and it was a pleasure to watch her come down from the high. She laid there, panting heavily, tears streaming down the sides of her face. I pulled my fingers away and licked her essence from them. I had to savor every drop of her sweetness as I possibly could.

When she finally returned to a normal state, she sat up and looked at me with drunken eyes.

I smirked. "Are you good?"

She nodded. "I need a nap."

I chuckled. "Let me clean you up, and we can go to bed."

I stood and went to grab a warm washcloth. After cleaning her up, I tossed it into the laundry bin then helped her redress. Pulling back the covers, I tucked her safely under before joining her. She snuggled close to me and rested her head on my chest.

There was no talking about what she'd just experienced.

No checking her mental level.

None of that.

Within a minute, she was down for the count with a smile on her pretty face.

CHAPTER 25

Alayah

"**OKAY. I HAVE** to say something," Londyn said as we sat in the break room having lunch.

She'd cooked last night and brought me a serving, so we didn't go out for lunch today. I looked up from the bowl of chicken and fried rice to find her watching me.

"What is it, Londyn?"

"You're glowing—like radiating. Either you're pregnant, which I know ain't the case, or you got some. Spill the tea, bitch. Did something happen with that fine-ass lawyer?"

I immediately felt my cheeks redden. Every time Killian ran across my mind today, I found myself smiling for no reason. His mouth did more than affirm and encourage me. Last night, I reached heights in pleasure that I never thought possible. I'd had no inkling of a sex drive in so long. To find myself sexually attracted to him was one thing, but to give myself to him was another.

I never imagined being so bold in asking for what I wanted. Maybe Londyn had rubbed off on me. Hearing the words leave my lips had me looking at myself like, *Did I really just ask that?* He didn't disappoint. I loved that he was gentle and reassuring.

"Hello. Earth to Alayah," Londyn said, waving a hand in my face. "Look at you over there daydreaming."

I covered my face and gave a girlish giggle. "Yes. Something happened."

"Something like?"

"We didn't have sex, but he did…you know." I gestured suggestively.

Her eyes widened, and a grin broke out on her face. "Was it good?"

"Well, I don't have anything to compare it to, but it was great. He was so gentle with me, Londyn. He took care of me and respected my body."

Londyn poked out her lip. "I love that for you, babe. I've never dealt with all you've been through, but I know how special it makes the moment when the man is thoughtful." She gave an excited little clap. "I'm so happy for you. Soon, we can compare sexcapades."

I had to laugh. "Girl, I'm not sure I want to know what goes on in your bedroom. You might scare me."

She gasped. "How dare you!"

"I'm just saying. Your level of freak nasty would put me to shame."

She flipped her head. "Well, you know, I've been at this a long time, baby. I've got skills for days. I'll put this thang in a man's lap and have him falling in love." She stuck out her tongue and twerked in her seat.

I shook my head. "You are wild."

"You love me though. You won't say it, but I know you do."

"I do love you, girl. You're solid, and I appreciate that."

She smiled as she slid her chair over and hugged me. "I love you, too, boo. We have a driving lesson after work tomorrow. You've been doing so good. I think you'll be ready in another month or two. Then we have to get you your first big-girl ride. My brother works at a dealership, so I'm sure I can get you the hookup. Just ignore him, though. He likes to get under my skin by flirting with my friends. Pain in my ass. Being the big sister is so ghetto sometimes."

I giggled. "I'm finding that out. Adrienne has quite the mouth on her. She curses, and I know it's largely in part to the way Kennedy spoke to them. Every time I talk to her, I have to get on her about her language."

"You're such a mom."

"I mean, I was their second mother for the first part of their lives, and my job isn't done now. Even if I never get custody, I want to be in a position to take care of them if they ever need anything from me, you know?"

"I get it. I'm the oldest of eight kids, so big sis gets called for everything. Like, baby, call your mama. That lady gave birth to you, not me. Guess who ends up doing it anyway?"

I laughed. "I'm sure they love you for it."

"They better. They know how I'm coming about them. I will smile in my mugshot. *Ooop!* Sorry, girl."

I waved her off. "You're fine."

"Speaking of mugshot. I looked yours up. I see why you were Prison Bae."

I rolled my eyes and stood to throw away my trash. "Bye, Londyn."

Her laughter echoed behind me. "You know you're fine, girl. Walk away slow so I can see all that booty meat."

I couldn't help but laugh at her. If she did nothing else, she boosted my confidence.

I headed back to my office. There were only a few minutes left on my break, and I wanted to call and check on my sisters. With all the bruises and emotional scars they still had, the school had allowed them to work from home so they didn't fall behind. My aunt was on top of their studies, making sure they got everything turned in on time. Sliding behind my desk, I grabbed my phone and called Adrienne and Miyah on a video call. Thankfully my aunt had gotten them both new phones on the family plan.

"Hey, sissy," Amiyah answered with a smile.

"Hey, Lay," Adrienne said.

"Hey. I just wanted to check on you guys. Do you need anything?"

As I stared at their beautiful faces, it saddened me to see them with bruises. I could tell they were healing and could probably be covered with makeup at this point, but still. It was like looking into the faces of my children, and it hurt my heart.

"We're okay," Adrienne answered. "We grabbed what we could when we left. Eventually, we'll go back to the house to get the rest of our things."

"I don't wanna go back there," Miyah voiced.

I sighed. "I know, baby. This will all be over soon."

"I need my car," Adrienne said. "I pay the car note and insurance on that. It's mine, and she had no right to take my battery out."

"I'll ask Killian to pick up a battery on his way home, and we'll go get your car on Saturday. Do you have the keys?"

"Yes. But hold on. Let's not skip on the part about Killian. Is that your boyfriend now?"

"We're... I don't know what to call us, to be honest. I like him. He likes me."

"Awwww!" they cooed, causing me to roll my eyes.

"Don't start."

"What?" Adrienne exclaimed. "There's nothing wrong with having a boyfriend, Layah. I mean, you've never had one, have you?"

"No, I haven't."

"And he seems like a good catch. He's nice, good with kids, he has a good job, and I know he has good benefits. Plus, he's fine—like really fine."

"Watch it."

"I'm just giving credit where credit is due, big sis. He clearly adores you, and we saw you two kissing on the front porch. That didn't look very friendly to me."

Miyah laughed. "It was friendly enough."

"You two are just full of laughs today, huh? I hope you know your schoolwork like you know how to joke."

Miyah laughed harder. "That's the most momlike thing you've ever said. Yeah, you're getting older."

"I'm not even thirty yet!"

"You're close enough," Adrienne said.

"I'm about to hang up on y'all."

Even if they were low-key trying to roast me, I was so happy to have moments like this. They could flame me, and I would take it all in good stride.

"My lunch break is over, but I'll call you tonight. I love you guys."

"We love you, too."

We blew each other kisses before disconnecting the call. I settled into my chair with a smile. At least in some aspects of my life, things were finally feeling normal.

Much to my surprise, when I walked out of work with Londyn trailing me, I saw Killian waiting beside his car. A smile crept across my face at the sight of him. He looked so handsome in his tailored suit. It hugged his biceps in ways that made me jealous. If I was sitting on a jury while he was in court, I don't think I'd be able to listen to a thing he said because I wouldn't be able to take my eyes off him.

"I guess you don't need me to take you home since your boo is here," Londyn jested.

"I guess not."

"See how you didn't deny that? You know what's up." She playfully slapped my arm before pulling me in for a hug. "I'll see you, boo."

"See you."

She walked off toward her truck, and I headed over to my ride. Killian pushed off from his car as I approached him.

"Hey, beautiful," he said, reaching for me.

"Hey, you."

I went into his arms and tilted my head for a kiss. He pressed those lips I'd grown to love so much against mine, and I melted right there. Thinking about what his mouth had done to me last might made me moan. He pulled away with a smirk.

"It's like that?" he asked with a chuckle.

I blushed. "I like kissing you, okay? What are you doing here? I thought you would still be at work."

"I didn't have much else on my plate after court, so I left a little early. I wanted to take you to dinner."

I looked down at my outfit, thankful that I'd put a little effort into my appearance today. I would have hated to sit across from him in my normal attire of jeans and a t-shirt while he was in a suit. Today, I'd worn a red-and-white floral blouse with pair of black high waisted, flare-leg trousers, and flats.

"You tired of my cooking already?" I jested.

"Never. I thought it would be nice to take my lady out for dinner."

I blushed. "Your lady?"

"Well, maybe not officially. I want you, Alayah. I'm willing to wait until you're fully ready, but I need you to know that. Do you have a problem with being my lady?"

I shook my head. "No, but when did you decide this?"

He stepped back and took my hands. "I told you I had feelings for you back in high school. I never acted on them because I didn't feel like it was a right time back then. Being around you since you've been home has proven to me that those feelings never went away. It took me a while to realize that you are the reason I chose a career as a lawyer.

"Every time I step into a courtroom, I fight for people whose voices have been taken from them and they can't fight for themselves. I wish I would have spoken up about the things I suspected were going on with you. I wish I could have done something to help you back then—an anonymous call or something…"

I placed a finger to his lips. "You couldn't have helped me. I was so afraid that I probably would have lied to avoid the backlash. When you're terrified of someone, you do anything to keep them satisfied so things don't get worse, Killian. That was me, just trying to survive until I could better my situation. That's no guilt for you to hold." I cupped his face and pecked his lips. "You were exactly what I needed when I needed you, and I don't take that for granted."

Wrapping my arms around him, I hugged him tightly. He buried his face between my neck and shoulder as he hugged me back.

"I'm so happy that you're home, baby," he whispered.

Pulling away, he kissed me with so much passion and desire. It wasn't until the sound of someone clearing their throat behind us that we parted. I looked back to see my uncle.

"Hey, Uncle Clive," I said, turning around to face him.

"Baby girl. Mr. Lake."

"Mr. Easton." Killian extended his hand to shake his. "How are you, sir?"

"I'm well." He pointed between us. "Is this officially a thing?"

"We're still working on it, Uncle Clive."

"I see. Well, do me a favor, son."

"What's that?" Killian asked.

"Try not to tongue my niece down in front of me. She may be grown, but she's still my baby."

Killian chuckled. "My apologies, sir. I couldn't help myself."

"*Umm-hmm.* I'll see y'all on Saturday." He kissed my cheek. "Love you, baby girl."

"I love you, too."

He walked away, and I turned back to Killian.

"You ready to eat?" he asked.

"I'm ready."

CHAPTER 26

Killian

"KILLIAN!"

I looked up from the coffee I was pouring to see Erica rushing toward me in the break room. I'd just gotten to work and had enough time to put my things down and grab a hot cup of Joe before she rushed me.

"What's up?" I asked.

"Put the coffee down and come to my office. You have to hear this."

I really needed this cup of coffee. After Alayah and I got home last night, we'd showered and cuddled in my bed. Cuddling turned into kissing, and before I knew it, I was face deep between her thighs again and again. I'd quickly come to realize the taste of her was a favorite of mine.

The great part about that was she seemed to love looking down at the top of my head as much as I liked having it positioned between her thighs. I indulged in her twice last night and this morning before I dropped her off to work.

"Killian, did you hear me?" Erica asked.

"My bad. Just give me a second. I'm coming."

"Hurry up," she yelled over her shoulder as she walked out.

I turned back to my coffee and quickly added my cream and sugar. After giving it a stir, I left the break room and headed for Erica. When I walked in, it looked like tornado had hit her office. Files and papers were all over the place. She was sifting through them like a madwoman.

"What happened in here?" I asked.

"Close the door."

I did as she asked then took a seat while she gathered some papers.

"You are not going to believe what I found," she said, huffing as she took a seat behind her desk. "Killian, when I say I've been working my ass off on Alayah's case, I've been working my ass off. Rodney West's family may have money but they are full of bullshit and corrupt individuals. The lawyer who served as the family's counsel, a cousin. Two of his family members served on the jury—all different last names, so nobody made the connection.

"They played like they didn't know each other so well. The fucking judge… Killian, the judge was his Rodney's step-grandfather. The Mr. West we saw in the courthouse is not his father. His father died when Rodney was twelve. His mother married that man when he was fifteen and gave her children his last name. The judge was never married to Mr. West's mother. He's his lovechild outside of his marriage."

"Hold on. You're giving me a shitload of information."

"It gets worse. The officer that got to the scene first, another cousin. Killian, they had to have been feeding each other information." She handed me the stack of papers in her hand.

"What's this?"

"Rodney West's juvenile records…unsealed."

"How did you get this?"

"I filed a motion to unseal his records after the Eastons retained me. When they first came to me last year and told me the story, I asked them for some time to do my own research to ensure I could help. When I dug into Rodney, I found a few different petty charges on him, nothing to make me raise an eyebrow. Then I saw he had sealed juvenile records. You know when you file a motion to unseal them, you can see the dates since it's in the process of becoming a public record.

"His juvi record dates back to age thirteen. In that file is a record of him being a peeping Tom, and there are several allegations of him touching girls inappropriately, but somehow, the charges were dropped. I went through every name on that list and spoke to them personally. These are their written statements." She handed me more papers. "When I told them about Alayah, they all had the same look of guilt on their faces. You know why? All six girls—now adult women—were paid for their silence by the judge."

It was like my brain was on overload from all the information she'd just thrown at me. This was a game changer. Every person involved could be brought up on charges of obstructing justice.

"They knew what he was doing?" I asked in disbelief.

Erica nodded. "They did. I can only imagine the conversations that took place in that household. They knew he was a sick individual and left him to prey on innocent girls all for the sake of keeping up their image. I'm going after everybody that helped cover this shit up. Someway, somehow, Kennedy is going down for this, too."

"The tapes. Alayah kept mentioning tapes."

Erica shook her head. "The tapes might be a lost cause. They searched every inch of the Chamberses' house, his place, and his parents' place and found no trace of the tapes. It's like they just disappeared."

"They have to be somewhere. She wouldn't just pull a story like that out of her ass. We know sexual deviants sometimes keep trophies of their victims like underwear, hair clippings, and whatnot. If he had those tapes, he kept them somewhere where he could watch them—admire what he'd done. He wouldn't be able to help himself not to."

Erica thought for a moment. "How often was he at that house when you went over there?"

"Every time I was there, he was there. I remember her telling me he spent the night four maybe five times a week."

"They have to be there."

"And just how do you suppose we get a warrant for that? You're bringing evidence against a judge, Erica. Nobody is gonna wanna touch that shit."

"The Wests aren't the only people with connections, honey. It might take me some time, but I'm gonna get it."

I took a long sip of my coffee. "Do we tell Alayah?"

"Well, she asked me to let it go, so technically, I'm not operating as her lawyer right now. Once I get everything I need, I'll present it to her. I need your help, Killian. You can work off the books, but I need you behind the scenes. Somebody has to help me put this whole thing together. I want her conviction overturned and her off parole. She deserves to be completely free."

"Whatever you need, I got you."

"Alright, lover boy."

I tried to hide my grin. "Whatever."

"Don't deny it. You've had this glow to you since she moved in. I love to see it. You just keep her happy, and we won't have any problems. I want to see my girl flourish."

"So do I. My goal with Alayah is to keep her happy."

"Good. Because I like you and all, but if you break her heart after all this, we will have beef forever."

I chuckled. "I don't want any smoke."

"I'm glad we're on the same page. Now, I hope you have your thinking cap on because we have a lot of work to do."

I took another long sip of my coffee and placed it on the desk. "Let's get to it."

It was Saturday, and Alayah and I were headed to the Eastons so she could spend time with her sisters. We'd stopped to get the battery for Adrienne's car before making our way over. They all decided that they wanted to get out of the house. Of all things, the girls decided that they wanted to go to an indoor zip-lining and obstacle course spot downtown. I bought the tickets last night, and even though I wasn't the biggest fan of flying across a rope suspended in the air, I would indulge to make them happy.

Later, Kadeem, his family, my sister, brother in-law, niece, and my parents were coming over to the house to grill and eat. I'd invited the Eastons to come along as well. I figured it would be good to get everybody together so they could start getting used to one another. Letting Alayah go wasn't in the cards. She had very little family, and I wanted my family to become hers, too.

We pulled up to the house around ten, and the girls came out with smiles on their faces. I could tell they were wearing makeup because the bruises on their faces weren't there. They climbed in the backseat and reached over to hug their sister before buckling themselves in.

"Don't you two look happy," I said as I pulled onto the street.

"Well, you'd be happy, too, if you didn't have to look at this ugly bruise today," Adrienne said. "Aunt Penny did a great job covering it up."

"Bruises and all, you're both still as pretty as you've always been," Alayah said. "It's nice to see you without it though. Y'all ready for this zip line and obstacle course?"

Miyah nodded. "Are you gonna participate, Mr. Lake?"

"Please, call me Killian. And yes, against my better judgment, I'm gonna get up there."

"Don't tell me you're afraid of heights," Adrienne said. "A big man like you?"

I chuckled. "I feel safer on the ground."

"Don't worry. I'm sure my sister will nurse you back to health if you fall. I mean, aren't girlfriends supposed to take care of their boyfriends?"

Alayah rolled her eyes. "I see what you did there. Mind your business."

"Come on, Layah. You have to give us something. I need to know if Mr. Lawyer Man here is as good a boyfriend as he is a friend." She tapped my shoulder. "You better treat my sister like a queen. She's been through enough."

"I hear you, Adrienne," I answered. "I assure both of you that Alayah is safe and well taken care of with me. I love your sister very much."

The two of them squealed in delight while Alayah stared at me with wide eyes. I didn't mean to say that out loud, but once the words left my mouth, I felt like a weight had been lifted from my shoulders. I loved Alayah Chambers. I think I'd always loved her. I just never got the chance to love her out loud. Now that I had the opportunity, it was all gas, no brakes.

Alayah sat quietly for the duration of the ride while her sisters chattered away in the backseat. I could tell she was still processing what I'd said. I didn't need her to say it back—I just needed her to know.

When we pulled into the parking lot of Urban Indoor Adventures, the girls filed out of the car. Alayah sat there for a moment before turning to me.

"You love me, Killian?" she asked, barely above a whisper.

I nodded. "I love you. Every part of you—whole, broken, and healing."

Tears slipped from her eyes as she stared at me. "You mean that?"

"Of course I mean it." I took off my seatbelt and leaned over into her space. "I want you—all of you—whenever you are ready for me. When you feel like you can't love yourself, I'll love you enough for the both of us. I'll remind you of your worth when that little voice in your head is being cruel. I choose you. I choose you through your laughter and your tears, through your triumphs and struggles.

"I see you, baby. You are invaluable, Alayah, and you deserve the kind of love that you've poured into others. I know you carry burdens from your past. You have deep wounds that are healing but may never completely heal—all that trauma, all that pain has made you strong, resilient, and incredibly brave, even if it was intended to break you. You've weathered storms that would have broken a weaker person, and you've broken through those barriers with a heart still capable of kindness and love. How could I not love you?"

"Killian," she whimpered. She cupped my face and kissed me softly. "I love you, too."

We shared another kiss, this one passionate and filled with the love we'd just professed. It was crazy how much of a difference those three little words had already made.

The incessant tapping on the window finally forced our lips apart. We looked up to see Adrienne standing in front of the car with her hands on her hips.

"I know y'all are in love and everything, but y'all can do all that later. Come on!"

Alayah and I looked at each other and shook our heads.

"Teenagers," she mumbled. "Let's get out of here before I have to tell Miss Thang about herself."

I chuckled as I opened the car door. "Let's go."

CHAPTER 27
Alayah

HE LOVED ME.

I couldn't pretend like I wasn't floating on cloud nine right now. The confession had me stuck on stupid, then to have him explain it to me... I was a mess. I must have dipped into the bathroom at Urban Indoor Adventures three times to cry my eyes out. Being loved by my sisters, my aunt, and uncle was one thing.

To be loved by Killian was another.

I'd sworn off men. I told myself I didn't want or need them. Life as a lonely cat lady wouldn't be so bad. Then here came Killian Lake—once my only real friend and now my lover. When I first ran into him at the grocery store, I was angry. We'd been close, and the fact that he never wrote me or anything hurt my heart when I first went in.

Then I had to remember that we were kids. He had his entire life ahead of him. He had plans for college and a career that didn't include me and my thirty-year sentence. I hadn't even thought about what school had been like for him after my arrest. I could only imagine the number of questions and whispers that went on behind his back.

Kids could be messy as hell. Everyone knew we were friends. They saw us sitting together at lunch. We had the same study hall.

We sat next to each other in class. We were always together, so by my assumption, he had to have faced some backlash for being friends with me—a murderer.

Even after all these years, he still found his way back to me. I'd never imagined seeing him in that courtroom at my parole hearing would lead to that man telling me he loved me.

As I stood at the bottom of the zip line waiting for him to come down, all I could do was smile and laugh. He *really* didn't like heights and had insisted on going last.

"Come on, Killian," Adrienne yelled. "Don't be a chicken."

Miyah started making chicken noises, and Adrienne joined in.

"Y'all are really funny," he yelled. "Let's see how you get home."

The two of them reeled in their laughter, but continued to snicker as they watched him. The instructor seemed to be giving him an encouraging word, but he wasn't going for it.

"You got this, baby," I yelled, surprising myself.

"Look at her hyping her man up," Adrienne whispered loudly to Amiyah.

"Y'all are about to get on my nerves," I said.

They both laughed as they wrapped their arms around me.

"Come on, sissy," Adrienne jested. "We have a lot of years to make up for with being the annoying little sisters. But for real, we love to see you happy. If he's gonna be our brother-in-law, he has to get used to the teasing. It just means we like him."

"Y'all really like him?" I asked.

Amiyah nodded. "We do. Every time we see you with him, you're smiling. That's a big improvement to when we first saw you. You looked…well, you looked dead inside."

I felt dead inside when I first came home. Sure, I was free, but parts of me still felt caged and broken. I felt like I got out and had nothing to live for. Yes, I wanted to live, but I was just existing. I didn't feel like that anymore.

"Miyah is right," Adrienne agreed. "Also, I don't think I ever apologized for how I treated you when you came to the house."

"You don't have to—"

"Yes, I do. You were more of a mother to us than Kennedy ever was, Alayah. Things were so different without you around. We had to grow up fast. It was like our childhood ended when you went away. I was so angry because you weren't around to protect us. I feel like if you'd been there, you would have stepped in when Kennedy did the most. She would have left us alone.

"Then I realized she only left us alone because *you* took care of us. She would call us out of our name or hit us and take away our things. Now I realize you probably went through that, too, on top of being assaulted by that nasty ass…that perverted man. What I'm trying to say is my anger was misdirected, and I'm sorry. I love you."

I smiled softly. Leaning in, I kissed her cheek. "I love you, too. All is forgiven. We're just gonna focus on the future."

She nodded, then looked up at Killian. "You won't have much of a future if he stays up there any longer. Come on, Killian. Hey, give him a push!"

"They can't push him," I exclaimed. "Babe! You have to come down at some point."

"This ain't that point," he yelled back.

I palmed my face. "I'll be right back."

I made my way back across the room and climbed up to the platform he stood on with the instructor.

"Killian Lake," I said, my hands on my hips, "are you really that nervous?"

"Listen, I had a bad experience in collage, okay? Following my friends had me hiking across a rope bridge. Even though I had a harness on, I lost my footing and fell over the side. I was halfway to the other side hanging upside down for like fifteen minutes. My whole life flashed before my eyes, baby."

I didn't mean to laugh, but the look on his face was funny.

He kissed his teeth. "See, you and your sisters are gonna be walking home."

"*Awww,* baby." I cupped his face and pecked his lips. "How about I go down with you?"

He peered around me at the instructor. "Can she do that?"

"Sure. We have a tandem zip line that allows two people to go at once."

"Why didn't you say that before?"

"I didn't think you'd be up here this long."

Killian gave him a side eye as the instructor grabbed the equipment to hook me onto him. Once we were all set, I wrapped my arms around him.

"On three, we go. One…two…"

Before I got to three, I pushed off from the ledge, sending us sliding down the line with him cursing the whole way as my sisters cheered us on. As someone who was usually cool, calm, and collected, it was funny to see him out of character. Once we were on the ground and unhooked, he turned to Adrienne and Amiyah.

"The next time y'all pick an activity for us, pick something less traumatizing."

They both laughed as they gave him sisterly hugs.

"Poor lil' tink tink," Adrienne jested, causing him to playfully mush her forehead.

"Please tell me y'all have had your fix of this and we can move on to the obstacle course."

"Come on, Courage the Cowardly Dog."

"I foresee a future of me and you tussling, lil' girl."

"You get harassed by association. Accept and embrace that."

I smiled and shook my head at their bantering, but honestly, I loved that they could get along. The three of them held weight in my heart, and if they could love each other, that would do me all the good in the world.

The obstacle course was just as funny as the zip-lining experience. Killian and my sisters really sounded like siblings with their back-and-forth banter. We had such a good time, and I couldn't wait for more days like this.

Currently, we were on our way to my childhood home to put the battery in Adrienne's car. It was like a cloud of gloom spread over us as we pulled into the yard. Kennedy was being held without bail, so we didn't have to worry about her coming out to act a fool.

"We're gonna grab a few things while you put the battery in," Adrienne said, taking off the car key.

Killian nodded as he took the key from her and got out of the car. "Are you good?" he asked, looking back at me.

"I'm good. I'll just wait here."

"Okay." He leaned back in the car and pecked my lips before closing the door.

I sat there, staring at the house as my sisters went inside. Memories began to flood my mind of the time I spent here—the things I endured. Part of me felt bitter. Why me? Why did I have to suffer at the hands of a woman who should have loved me? Why would she allow a man who wasn't our father to stay with us overnight while she wasn't in the house?

As I sat there brewing in my thoughts, my limbs somehow took on a mind of their own. I opened the car door and got out. I could hear Killian calling my name as I made my way up the front steps, but I couldn't answer him.

Trembling fingers reached for the knob and turned it to push the door open. I stood in the entryway looking around the place. Kennedy had upgraded the furniture, but all I could see was the living room as I remembered it. Absentmindedly, I walked through the house until I came to *that* door. My old bedroom. The place where my nightmares were real.

Turning the knob, I slowly opened the door and stepped inside. While the room was now filled with my sisters' taken possessions, all I could see was my old bedroom.

The iron-framed bed against the wall where my nightmares began.

The mismatched desk where I used to study.

The beanbag chair in the corner where I used to read.

Then I saw the blood…there was so much blood. I could hear myself pleading with Rodney to stop because he was hurting me. I saw the fear in my own eyes as I frantically grabbed those scissors and stabbed him repeatedly. Every time my hand came down, my body shuddered.

I couldn't breathe. My hand flew to my chest, clutching my shirt. Why was this shirt so tight?

"I–I can't breathe… I can't breathe!"

I could hear my sisters behind me, but I couldn't answer them. Adrienne screamed for Killian, and the next thing I felt was his strong arms around me pulling me out of the room. With my back against the wall, he cupped my face and spoke to me.

"Breathe, baby. Deep breaths. Follow me."

He began deep breathing, mimicking what I needed to do. Closing my eyes, I listened to the sound of his voice and followed along. After a few minutes, my lungs recovered, and I could breathe again. Opening my eyes, I found the three of them looking at me with worried expressions.

"Are you okay?" Killian asked.

I nodded. I hadn't had a panic attack in years, and that one felt like it would take me out. Much to my surprise, he picked me up and carried me back outside to the car.

"Why would you go in there, baby?" he asked, voice full of concern. "I was calling you."

"I'm sorry. I just…I couldn't stop myself from going in. It's been so long, I didn't think it would do me like that."

"I get that, but don't relive that trauma if you can avoid it. You're in a good place. I don't want you undoing all the work you've done on yourself. You've worked too hard to come out of a dark place. Don't give those demons your energy."

I sighed. "I hear you."

He cupped my chin and pecked my lips. "I'll be done in a second, and we can get out of here."

I nodded. He closed the door, leaving me there with my thoughts. It wasn't long before the girls were filing out of the house with trash bags of what I assumed were clothes and shoes. Killian grabbed the bags and placed them in Adrienne's trunk. They went back inside once more and returned with their laptops and tablets then came over to me. They opened the passenger door, leaning in to hug and kiss me.

I smiled faintly. "I'll see you at Killian's."

They nodded and closed the door. Once everyone was in their respective cars, we left. Killian reached over and grabbed my hand.

"I know your heart is heavy right now, but we're about to be around the people that love us. No matter how much was taken from you, you're gonna get that back tenfold. You're in a position to win in every season, baby. Nobody will take another thing from you if I can help it. I've got you."

As we pulled to a stop sign, I leaned over to kiss him. I believed him when he said he had me. He'd followed through on every word he'd spoken since we'd reconnected, and I loved him for it. I didn't have experience with men, but I knew from my uncle that there was nothing like a man who tells you what he's going to do, then actually does that shit.

Putting the panic attack and helpless feelings out of my mind, I decided to focus on the good instead of the things that brought me down. Today had been a good day, and this evening would be better.

CHAPTER 28
Killian

ALAYAH'S SPIRITS HAD lifted by the time we got to my house. My parents were already there along with Bridget, Ellie, and Collin. Of course, they had made themselves comfortable in my home. The Eastons had pulled up not long after we made it, and Kadeem said he and the fam were on the way.

When I introduced Alayah to my parents, my father offered her a warm smile and a handshake while my mother pulled her in for a hug. She was acting like she'd never met her. Although Alayah had never been to my home in high school, my parents were very active and showed up to school events, so they had met her before.

"It's so nice see you, baby," my mama said, rocking her from side to side. "I'm happy you're home."

"Thank you, Mrs. Lake. It's good to be home."

Ellie slid her little body in between them and raised her arms for Alayah to pick her up. She smiled as she scooped her up in a hug.

"Hi, Ms. Alayah!"

"Hi, baby."

"We can watch our movie now."

Bridget shook her head. "Please go watch that movie with her. She will not stop talking about watching *Moana* with the real-life Moana."

Alayah giggled. "Can I help with anything first?" she asked my mother.

"No, baby. Bridget and I made all the sides earlier. We're just waiting on the meat to come off the grill. Go on in there with my grandbaby. She's been waiting on you."

"Okay, Ellie. Just let me shower and change clothes first."

"Okay. Hurry back."

"Mr. and Mrs. Easton, girls, make yourselves comfortable," I said. "I'm sure my mama will make you feel right at home. She has a way of doing that."

Mama playfully slapped my arm. "In not so many words, he's saying I invade his space."

"You do at times, but I love you, so I let it slide. I'll be back."

Alayah and I headed down the hall to the bedrooms. She dipped into hers, and I went into mine. After stripping down, I headed into the shower. Once the water was hot, I stepped inside. As the water ran down over my body, I heard the bathroom door open. When I looked back, Alayah was standing there clutching a towel around her with her hygiene products in her hands.

"Can I join you?" she asked.

Instead of answering, I opened the shower door to let her in. She dropped the towel, and my eyes trailed her beautiful frame. My baby was flawless. She stepped in and turned to face me. Slowly, she drank me in from head to toe. This was the first time she'd seen me fully naked.

Her eyes stopped at my groin area, widening as she took in my length.

"You want me to take *all* of that at some point?" she asked.

I chuckled. "I'll be gentle, and it's only if and when you want it."

Her gaze lowered again, and she swallowed hard.

"You've *um*...you've pleasured me. I think I should return the favor."

"Baby, you don't have to do that. I like pleasing you. I don't do it for anything in return."

She peered up at me. "Well, I don't know anything about oral pleasure, but I could give you something."

Before I could reiterate that she didn't have to, she took my dick in her soft hand and began to stroke it. I closed my eyes, and I inhaled deeply. I hadn't been with a woman in months and hadn't self-pleasured in about as long. Her gentle strokes slowly pulled a moan from me.

"Shit..."

I felt her soft lips against my neck, causing my head to drop back. She trailed kisses from my neck to my chest before gently grabbing my chin and pulling my lips to hers. As our lips and tongues intertwined, she continued to stroke my dick. The blood in my veins was rushing, and I knew it wouldn't be long before I erupted.

"I love you," she whispered against my lips.

"I love you, too, baby. So fucking much."

I turned her so her back was to my front. While she continued to stroke me, I reached around and parted her lower lips with one hand while the other toyed with her pebbled nipple. With the first swipe against her swollen clit, I found her soaking wet.

I pinched her nipple harder as I nuzzled my nose into her curls.

"Does pleasing me turn you on, Layah?" I asked.

Her response came out as a breathy "Yes."

I loved that she was discovering her sexual desires after years of abuse. Some people were never the same after that.

As I strummed her clit, I gently sank my teeth into her shoulder, causing a whimper to come from her.

"Killian..."

"You can take it," I whispered. "I feel you throbbing for me, baby. I love that shit."

She gasped as I bit harder and stroked her faster.

"Oh my God…"

"Right there…that's it, mama. You feel so good to me, Layah."

Her body trembled against mine. When her free hand gripped the hand I was stroking her with, I knew I had her. Her soft strokes to my dick became firmer as she bucked against my hand.

"Finish for me, love. I want to feel you all over these fingers."

That had her head dropping back and her mouth opening. Before she could cry out, I clamped a hand around her mouth. Muffled cries beat against my hand as she came against the other. The sweet sounds pushed my nut forward, shooting out of me and hitting the shower floor.

"Shit!"

Once she quieted down, I released her mouth, and an exasperated breath expelled from her lips. I chuckled as I pulled my fingers away and turned her to face me. She peered up at me in a drunken gaze as I painted those juicy lips with her essence before kissing it off.

When I pulled away, her eyes were still closed.

"Baby?" I called.

"Hmm?"

"You okay?"

She nodded. *"Mmm-hmm."*

I smirked. "Let's wash up and get out of here before they start gossiping."

By the time we returned to the front, Kadeem and his family had made it. I dapped him up and gave him a brotherly hug.

"What's up, bruh?" he said.

"Ain't nothing." I turned to greet his wife. "Hey, Kyah," I said, hugging her.

"Hey, Killian."

"Congratulations on the little one."

"Thank you."

I scooped Parker up to hug her. "Hey, lil' bit. How you doing?"

"I'm fine. Where's Ellie?"

"Dang, Parker. It's just forget me when you see your little friend, huh? You didn't even hug me back."

She giggled as she wrapped her arms around my neck. "Sorry, Uncle Killian."

I placed her on her feet. "Ellie should be in the den. She's about to watch a movie."

"What movie?"

"Moana."

Her eyes beamed with excitement because she loved that damn movie, too.

"Mommy, can I go?" she asked.

"Hold on," I said. "I want you to meet someone. Baby!"

"Baby?" Kyah echoed. "You have a girlfriend?"

"Something like that."

"When did this happen?" She smacked Kadeem's arm. "Why didn't you tell me?"

"Baby, I don't be in this man's business like that."

"Lies."

Alayah came out of the kitchen, her sundress swaying around her hips. I couldn't help but smile because she was looking radiant. Kadeem slapped my chest.

"Look at him grinning," he jested to Kyah.

Parker gasped. "Moana!"

Alayah came to my side, and I wrapped an arm around her.

"Baby, you already know Kadeem, but this is his wife, Kyah, and their daughter, Parker."

Alayah smiled. "Hi, Kadeem. It's nice to meet you, Kyah." She stooped to greet Parker who was giving her the same look Ellie did when she first met her. "Hi, Parker. It's nice to meet you, beautiful."

Parker covered her face and giggled. She then grabbed Layah's face and pressed her forehead to hers. Alayah smiled and looked up a little confused.

"It's the way Moana greets people," Kadeem explained.

"That is adorable," Alayah said, hand over her heart.

"It's adorable until she accidently headbutts you."

"I said I was sorry, Daddy!" Parker exclaimed.

He laughed. "I know, princess. Go on and find Ellie."

"Okay. Bye, Moana!"

She ran off toward the den, leaving us alone.

"It's good to see you home, Alayah," Kadeem said.

"It's good to be home."

"You went to school with them, too?" Kyah asked her.

"I did."

"*Awww!* So you two are high school sweethearts?"

"Not exactly," I answered. "I am sweet on her, though."

Alayah blushed, and Kadeem pretended to gag. "You're still lovesick, I see. Layah, I don't know how you missed the googly eyes this man made at you in high school. If I had to hear your name one more time, I was gonna hook y'all up my damn self."

I rolled my eyes. "I wasn't that bad, Kadeem."

"Bullshit."

"Baby, stop telling Killian's business," Kyah fussed. "He's glowing right now, so I take it all is well. That's all that matters." She winked at me.

I chuckled. "That's why I like you, Kyah."

"I know." She looped her arm through Alayah's. "Come on, girl. The two of them are about to go gossip."

"I kind of got dragged into watching *Moana* with Ellie so that's where I'm headed."

"Great. I can't escape that movie anywhere." Kyah sighed. "At least let me make a drink so I can stomach those two little girls singing at the top of their lungs."

She pulled Alayah toward the kitchen. Kadeem chuckled as they walked off.

"What's funny?" I asked.

"You really are glowing, my guy. That's a fresh *I'm in love* type of glow."

"I *am* in love, man. Real bad."

"I knew it was coming. Does she love you back is the question."

"She does."

He smiled. "I'm happy for you, man. You two deserve the happy ending you were robbed of. I fully believe that if she hadn't been locked up, you would have finally made her yours."

"I might have worked up the nerve."

"Hey, she's yours now—unofficially."

We slapped hands again before heading toward the back deck where my dad, Collin, and Mr. Easton were. As we passed the den, I could see Ellie and Parker practicing the island dance from the movie. They were already getting into character. Adrienne and Amiyah were gyrating right along with them.

As we passed through the kitchen, my mama and Mrs. Easton were in deep conversation while Kyah and Bridget made themselves a drink. The two of them and Alayah were talking like old friends. Maybe they would eventually become friends. I knew she had Londyn, but hey, the more the merrier.

Outside, the men huddled around the grill. Pops looked back at me and smirked.

"It took you long enough to come outside," he said.

"I don't know what you're implying, old man."

He shook his head. "Sure you don't. Everything good? Y'all had fun today?"

"Man, I spent hours being clowned by three different women. The girls wanted to go indoor zip-lining, and you know how I feel about heights after that traumatic experience."

Kadeem laughed. "I know you aren't still going on about that hike, Killian."

"I almost died."

"You're being dramatic as hell. We weren't even that far off the ground."

"Tell that to my head, neck, and spine if I'd fallen headfirst. I don't care what you say, I prefer solid ground."

"They didn't hassle you too bad, did they?" Mr. Easton asked.

"Sir, they almost had to walk home."

The men laughed.

"Nah, but seriously though. They had fun, mostly at my expense. I loved seeing them so happy together."

He nodded. "They deserve these moments. Too many have been stolen from them. I'm just glad I'm still here to witness it."

A round of "Amens" went up around the space.

"So how has it been having a houseguest?" Collin asked.

The rest of the men looked at one another and grinned as they waited for my response.

"It's been nice," I answered. "After being here by myself for so long, it's nice to come home to someone. Even better, it's someone I care for deeply."

"You know, my baby is convinced she's gonna have a new auntie," Collin said. "She's already talking about matching Halloween costumes with you two."

Kadeem playfully nudged me. "I don't think Killian has enough muscles to be the Maui character."

"He definitely doesn't have the hair for it," my pops jested.

"What y'all aren't gonna do is stand in my yard insulting me. If my niece wants me to be Maui, then I'll be Maui."

"That's why she's spoiled now," Collin said. "I don't know what she's gonna do when you have your own kids."

"Run my pockets still. One of these days I'll tell her no."

Mr. Easton chuckled. "Son, take it from a man that's been married a long time: You never say no."

Then men nodded in agreement.

"It only gets worse when you have daughters," Kadeem said. "Don't let Kyah and Parker get to giving me those sad faces. I just hand over my bank card and accept defeat."

"So you're a sucker is what I'm hearing," I joked.

"I'm a man who knows how to pick my battles." He slapped my shoulder. "I can always take you to the beauty supply store and get you a thirty-inch body wave."

I jerked away from him. "You're lucky I respect my elders, or I would have choice words for you."

We all laughed at that one. It felt good to gather with my people. It let me know that I worked too much and needed to take more time for things like this. Work would always be there, but people were leaving this earth every day. Time waited for no one, and I wanted to enjoy whatever time I had left with the people I loved most.

CHAPTER 29

Alayah

I SMILED AS I watched Ellie and Parker sing along to the movie like they hadn't seen it a million times. I didn't see the comparison of me to Moana, but I guess it could be the hair and our similar complexions. Either way, I was flattered they thought I looked like a Disney princess.

Currently, they were perched on my sisters' laps. They'd both quickly taken to Adrienne and Amiyah. I guess it was that fascination with teenaged girls. When we first settled into the den, they were playing in my sisters' hair and tracing their freckles, trying to figure out how to get some of their own.

Watching them made me wonder how Adrienne and Amiyah would be if I ever had kids. Miyah for sure would be the pushover auntie. I could see her never saying no and letting them run amuck. Adrienne would be the cool aunt, the one they could call if they were ever in trouble and didn't want me to know.

"Looks like our girls made friends," Kyah said to Bridget.

Bridget laughed. "When have you ever known Ellie not to make a friend? Alayah has been her friend in her head since she met her."

I giggled. "She's a sweetheart."

"She can be a little sour patch at times. Are you prepared for sleepovers? You see she has a whole bedroom here."

"I did see that when he gave me a tour of the house. And yes, I'm prepared. I'll do my best to keep her entertained."

"So, Alayah," Kyah said, sipping her mocktail, "you went to school with my husband and Killian. Was he really a ho back then?"

I covered my mouth to stifle my laugh. "He, *uh*…he was very friendly with the ladies. I don't remember him ever *not* having a girlfriend. When Killian told me he got married, I was shocked. What did you do to that man?"

Kyah smirked. "I let him know I was the best thing to happen to him and he'd never get another me. He fell in line when he saw I wasn't down for playing games. Trust me, honey, if a man wants to, he will."

"Oh, she knows that," Bridget chimed in. "I've never seen my little brother like this. I mean he was never for the streets. He's always been respectful and loving, but girl, him with you. No questions asked, he just does it."

I blushed. "Killian is a wonderful man. I was lucky to have him as a friend and even luckier that our friendship blossomed into a love I never imagined."

"Wait! So he's told you he loves you?" Bridget asked.

I nodded. "He has, and I love him, too. I don't think there was any way I couldn't love him. He's been so kind and patient with me—so supportive and understanding. I feel so much peace with this man."

They looked at each other with their bottom lips poked out.

"I love that for you, babes," Bridget said. "My brother is a good man. I know you two will be happy. Hopefully, I can get some nieces and nephews out of the deal. I'm ready to return the spoiling he's done to my child. Just know when you say no, TiTi Bridget is gonna say yes."

I rolled my eyes. "Well, TiTi, your brother and I would have to be doing something for you to get nieces and nephews."

"Wait," she whispered. "Y'all haven't…you know?"

"We haven't taken it that far. Between y'all and me, I'm dying to know what it's like with him. I'm just…I'm afraid. We've done things. He's given me control over my desires and asks for my consent, but taking it all the way? I'm afraid I'm just gonna lay there or my mind will revert back to the trauma."

Kyah's brows furrowed. "Trauma? Were you assaulted?"

"Kadeem didn't tell you?"

"Tell me what?"

"I *um*…I spent ten years in prison for offing the man that raped and molested me for three years."

"What? Oh my God!"

I quietly gave her a summary of my history. As I spoke, tears filled her pretty brown eyes.

She reached out and grabbed my hand. "How are you surviving right now, honey?"

"My family and that man outside. If it weren't for them and my lawyer fighting to get me out, I'd be spending another twenty years behind bars."

"That is asinine. Thirty years for getting rid of trash? And your mama? I'm pregnant, but I have some homegirls for her. You just say the word."

I shook my head. "She's not worth it. Karma will take care of her."

She kissed her teeth. "Karma can always use a little help. Don't let the cute face fool you. I used to get down with the best of them, and I still have friends in the gutter. I'm talking brass knuckles, razor in the mouth carrying gutter."

Bridget slapped her arm. "Kyah, you're gonna scare the girl."

I giggled. "Trust me, I've seen a lot on the inside. There isn't much that scares me. It's just the mental aspects that still get to me from time to time. I don't want to be in the middle of something intimate and have a panic attack."

"Does he talk you through it?" Kyah asked lowly.

"Talk me through it?"

"Through the process, your orgasm."

"I don't think I want to know that," Bridget said, grinning. "That's my little brother."

Kyah rolled her eyes. "You know that man has been out here slanging penis before, Bridget." She looked to me for confirmation. "Well?"

"He does."

"Then you'll be fine, girl. A man who talks you through it take cues from your body. They listen and pay attention. Sex with them isn't just for their pleasure. It's for yours, too. Whatever negative headspace you find yourself in, he'll bring you out of it. You just have to trust him. Given that you've already trusted him with your...you know. I'd say you have nothing to worry about. If you're ready, initiate and let him take the lead. *Only* if you're ready."

I nodded as I thought about what she said. Was I ready? Really ready? The last couple days of exploring with him had been wonderful. It was a shame at my big age that I was just learning my body. Sex and lovemaking were supposed to be beautiful and exhilarating, yet for so long, I associated them with pain and displeasure.

It was traumatizing and dehumanizing for me.

I didn't get the chance to give my virginity to someone worthy. I didn't get to save myself for my husband or my first love. Maybe being intimate with Killian would give me part of what was stolen back. I mean, I knew it wouldn't make me a born-again virgin, but at least he could possibly turn something so ugly into something...magical.

The gathering had been well under way for a few hours now, and I had to say that I was enjoying myself. By the time the movie went off, everybody was ready to eat. We migrated outside to eat and enjoy one another's company. The sun had set, and Killian lit the tiki torches around the outdoor entertainment space.

While Adrienne and Amiyah entertained Ellie and Parker, the rest of us sat around talking and enjoying mocktails and beer. I sat next to Killian, leaning into him as he draped an arm around my shoulders. Every so often, he leaned in and kissed my temple or my cheek, and I would blush uncontrollably. I couldn't tell if this was just him or if it was the beer he'd consumed, but I was loving the affection.

"You two look absolutely happy together," Mrs. Lake noted with a smile.

"My girl has been blushing all night," Bridget added. "Then there's Killian, smiling like a fool. Just look at him."

"You are my biggest hater, you know that?" Killian said. "You and Kadeem."

Kadeem scoffed. "Why are you bringing me into this? I ain't even said nothing."

"You were thinking it."

"Oh, so you read minds now? You fell in love, and it gave you superpowers or something?"

Everybody laughed.

"No superpowers. I just know you," Killian answered. "Baby, you should have heard the way these men were on me earlier."

"We didn't say anything that wasn't true," Mr. Lake said. He looked down at his watch. "I think we better be heading on out. It's past our bedtime."

Most everyone agreed with him that it was time to go. We started moving to clean up and take things inside. Once the to-go plates were packed and all of the food was put in the fridge, everyone hugged us goodbye then made their way to their cars. Killian and I stood on the porch watching them.

He dropped his arm around my shoulders, and I wrapped mine around his waist. Once the last car had driven off into the distance, we headed back inside to lock up the house then made our way to his bedroom. As I watched him undress to get in the shower, my thoughts drifted back to earlier. I was so busy admiring his body, that I didn't realize he was staring at me.

"My eyes are up here, love," he jested.

My face reddened at being caught. "Sorry. I got distracted."

"Are you joining me in the shower this time?"

I slowly nodded and began to undress as he headed into the bathroom. Once I was fully disrobed, I followed him. He was already in the shower, standing under the waterfall. Again, I admired him. I loved every flex of his muscles. The cute little dimples of his ass. The tattoos etched into his skin. I found him simply breathtaking.

My gaze dropped to the appendage hanging heavily between his legs. His long, thick, and veiny member was a perfect work of art. Although I didn't have much to compare it to, his dick was the prettiest thing I'd ever seen. I thoroughly enjoyed stroking him to a release just a few hours ago. Looking at it now, it had me concluding that I wanted more. His mouth was amazing, and his fingers were magical, but that third leg was something to sing about.

I climbed into the shower with him. Comfortable silence fell between us as we cleansed ourselves of the day's events. Once we were done, he shut off the shower, and we got out to dry ourselves off. After brushing our teeth, we headed back into the bedroom. While he went to his dresser, I sat at the edge of his bed, trying to work up my nerve to ask for what I wanted.

Closing my eyes, I channeled all the advice I'd gotten from Londyn and Kyah. I said a prayer, which was wild considering what I was about to do.

"Baby?"

The sound of Killian's voice caused my eyes to open. I peered up at his handsome face.

"Everything okay?" he asked.

I nodded. "Yes."

"Something on your mind?"

Again, I nodded. "I *um*...I want you to make love to me."

His eyes widened. "Right now?"

"Yes."

"Are you sure you're ready for that, Alayah? I don't want you to feel obligated—"

I stood and dropped my towel as I stepped in front of him. "I don't feel obligated. I want you...I want to feel you." I slowly unwrapped the towel from his waist and dropped it to the floor. "And I want you to feel me."

He hesitated for a moment, searching my eyes as though he were looking for something that told him I didn't want this. He wouldn't find it. Cupping my face, he leaned forward and kissed me slow and passionately. My nipples brushed against the hard pecs of his chest, causing a tingle to flow through me.

He walked me backward to the bed. The next thing I felt was him lifting me from the floor and my legs being pulled around his torso. He climbed on the bed, his lips never parting from mine. As my back touched the mattress, I was met with the heavy weight of his body against mine. It was so soothing and comforting.

His lips traveled a path down to my neck. He stopped briefly to give each of my nipples special attention before continuing to kiss down my stomach until he got to the meeting of my thighs.

I shuddered as he kissed the insides before swiping his tongue through my slit to capture my clit.

"Killian…" I said in a breathy whisper. "Please."

He chuckled. "I'm just getting you ready for me, love," he said, easing two fingers into me.

My back arched from the bed as the combination of his lips and fingers sent me to new heights. My tunnel was already slick with desire, but the attention he gave her had her overflowing. I was on the brink of orgasm when he pulled his mouth and fingers away. Reaching into the nightstand, he pulled out a condom and tore it open. I watched as he rolled it down over his length.

Once it was on, he leaned in to kiss me again. The tip of his dick kissed my clit, causing me to moan loudly. He grabbed himself and slid the tip up and down my soaked slit.

"I'll ask again," he said softly as he pulled his lips away. "Are you sure?"

"Yes."

He positioned himself at my entrance, and I closed my eyes.

"Look at me," he commanded. I opened my eyes, and I found him staring at me with sincerity. "I don't want you going in your head. I want you to look at me as I fill you. There should be nothing clouding this moment right now, okay?"

I nodded nervously. He hovered over me and gave a slight push, causing me to tense a little.

"Relax," he said, peppering my face with kisses. "This may hurt a little, but I would never hurt you. Relax."

I took several deep breaths as he pushed into me. Inch by inch, my walls stretched to accommodate his sizable member.

"That's it," he praised. "You're doing so good, love."

His hips began to move as he slowly thrusted into me. Our gazes remained locked on each other. With every stroke, the tension released from my body, and pleasure soon replaced it.

"Killian…" I moaned his name as my nails sank into the flesh of his biceps.

"Shit, Layah!" He groaned loudly. "You feel so good, baby."

He draped my legs over his shoulders and sank deeper into me, causing me to gasp.

"Oh…oh my God!"

"Tell me how it feels."

"So good. Shit! So good!"

"You deserve to feel good. I want to give you nothing but love and pleasure."

His pace picked up, and for a second, I tensed again.

"Stay with me," he coached. He leaned in and kissed me. "There you go. Open up for me, mama. Play with your clit."

Blindly, I reached between us, locating the sensitive bundle of nerves. As my fingers circled it, the tension eased, and once again, all I felt was pleasure. My mouth opened, and a loud cry fell from my lips.

"*Oooo!*"

"Doesn't that feel good?" he asked, nipping at my nipples.

"Yes!"

I matched my strumming to his strokes. When he sped up, I sped up. When he slowed down, I slowed down. I was so wet that every thrust of his length could be heard over the sounds of me panting heavily. My legs trembled, and my toes curled.

"I…I feel it," I whispered breathlessly. "I'm gonna cum!"

The muscles of my stomach tightened. My clit throbbed beneath my essence-covered fingers.

"I'm gonna cum," I repeated.

Killian didn't miss a beat in removing my legs from his shoulders and wrapping them around his waist. I felt my upper body being lifted from the bed. Killian hugged me to his body as he continued to thrust into me. The combination of his strokes and the friction against my clit had me clinging to him for dear life. My eyes closed, and with a final deep stroke, my body exploded from the inside.

A string of curses left my lips, and I basked in the immense pleasure coursing through me. Tears streamed down my face, and my body trembled with excitement as he filled the condom with a loud grunt.

For a long moment, he just held me as I held him. When my back finally touched the bed, I felt him slide out of me. He disappeared from the bed and went into the bathroom. I could hear the water running as I lay there, trying to regain my senses. I never expected lovemaking to be so beautiful, yet so exhausting.

Killian returned from the bathroom, void of the condom, with a warm rag in his hand. He cleaned me up, then tossed the rag aside. Leaning over me, he pecked my lips.

"How are you?" he asked.

"Spent."

He chuckled. "You'll build stamina over time."

Pulling back the covers, he tucked me under then climbed in with me. I cuddled up next to him and rested my head on his chest.

"Thank you," I said faintly.

"For giving you some dick?"

I giggled. "No. For being the perfect do-over. I love you, Killian. Thank you for taking care of me."

He tilted my chin and kissed my lips. "I love you, too. I'll always take care of you."

"Let me catch my breath, and we can go again. You might have created a monster. You can't get rid of me now."

He laughed out loud. "I would never want to."

CHAPTER 30

Alayah

TWO WEEKS LATER

I STEPPED OFF the bus and started walking in the familiar direction of my aunt and uncle's. It was Saturday, and Killian had gone into the office for a few hours, leaving me to fend for myself. At first, I thought about taking the short walk down to Bridget's, but I didn't want to impose on her time. Deciding that I wanted to spend the day with my favorite people, I hopped on the bus and made my way over.

I'd been the happiest I'd ever been the last couple of weeks. It wasn't just because Killian was blowing my back out, although it added to my good mood. I was just…happy. When I told Londyn we'd finally taken things to the next level, she was ecstatic. We were in the break room eating lunch. It was only the two of us, and she was rambling about something when I randomly said it.

"Killian and I had sex."

She kept talking, and I thought she didn't hear me until she grew quiet.

"What did you say?"

"Killian and I had sex."

She squealed and stomped her feet. "Yes, bitch. I'm so damn happy for you. Just tell me, is he carrying around a big ol' donkey dick? That man walks like he has big dick energy."

I laughed. "It's quite impressive."

"Did you run? You look like a runner."

I scoffed! "No, I didn't run! Even if I wanted to, I couldn't. He held me so close to him that I didn't want to go anywhere."

She stuck out her lip. "Awwww, pooh! He made love to you."

I blushed. "It was so beautiful, Londyn. He was so gentle and attentive. It was exactly what I imagined my first time being like."

"I love that for you, baby." She reached over and hugged me. "Now you just have to learn how to ride. Men love that shit. You ride him like you're riding a prize-winning bull, and I bet you're gonna end up pregnant."

I rolled my eyes. "Nobody is trying to get pregnant right now. We're taking precautions."

"Good. 'Cause I'm not ready to be a godmother quite yet."

"Godmother?"

"Well what other bestie is going to be the godmother if not moi?"

I laughed. "I can't with you."

She'd occupied the rest of our lunch with asking me details and giving me an unsolicited sex talk. I can admit, I made mental notes of a few things. She had way more experience than I did, so I trusted she knew what she was talking about.

As I headed across the street to the house, I noticed that Adrienne's car wasn't there. I walked up the front steps and used my key to get in.

"Hello! Aunt Penny! Uncle Clive!"

"We're in the kitchen, baby girl," Uncle Clive yelled.

I made my way into the kitchen where they were settled at the table reading the newspaper and drinking coffee. I smiled as I hugged and kissed them.

"I've missed you guys," I said, taking a seat at the table.

Uncle Clive chuckled. "I see you five days a week and on Saturdays."

"I know, but I don't live here anymore. It's different."

"We miss having you here," Aunt Penny said. "It's not the same."

"Where are the girls?" I asked, picking up the sales papers.

"Adrienne wanted a drink from Coffee-ish, and Miyah rode with her. I think she said they were gonna stop by the house and get the rest of their clothes and whatever else they needed. With Kennedy being locked up, I'm sure it won't be long until the bank comes to claim the house."

I shook my head. "I wouldn't be sad if it burned to the ground."

And I wouldn't be. Terrible things happened in that house. It would be a miracle if the bank could get a return on it. That fact that Kennedy continued living there after everything that happened was proof that she was a twisted-ass individual.

According to Killian, she was being held in the protection unit at the same correctional facility I did my time in. I knew that population was segregated from the rest of the prisoners. If she ever made it to general population and they found out what she'd done, she wasn't going to survive. If by chance she did, she'd never be the same.

Killian also told me that Mrs. West was spending thirty days in county for contempt of court. I couldn't feel bad for that old bitch. She had no business at that custody hearing. What kind of character witness would she have been on Kennedy's behalf when she raised a rapist and a pedophile? She could go to hell.

I was so lost in the thoughts that I didn't realize I had zoned out until the front door swung open and Adrienne and Amiyah came running in with panicked looks on their faces. Uncle Clive,

Aunt Penny, and I jumped to our feet, all of us asking the same question.

"What's wrong?"

I noticed the box in Amiyah's hand. They both looked at me with sorrowed expressions.

"You need to call Killian," she whispered.

"Amiyah, what is that?" Uncle Clive asked.

She shook her head, tears streaming down her face as she looked at me, and that's when I knew exactly what it was.

The tapes.

An overwhelming urge to vomit quickly rose from my stomach and up my throat. I raced for the half bath down the hall, barely making it before I spewed my guts into the porcelain bowl. Over and over, I threw up everything I'd eaten. The thought of them seeing what was on those tapes had me heaving until I had nothing left to give.

Flushing the toilet, I collapsed on my knees with my head against the floor. Violent screams erupted from my burning throat as hot tears streamed down my face. My aunt came rushing into the bathroom. She paused momentarily before I heard her open a cabinet then turn on the water.

She knelt in front of me and lifted me from the floor to sit me on the edge of the tub. I sat there crying profusely.

"They saw the tapes. They saw what he did to me..."

She lifted my head to wipe my face with a warm rag. "I know it hurts, baby."

"I never wanted them to see me like that," I wailed, falling against her.

She wrapped her arms around me and held me tightly as she kissed my temple. Through my cries, I could hear her praying. I closed my eyes, just wanting to disappear. I almost would have preferred if the tapes were never found than to have my little sisters witness what happened. They would never unsee that shit.

"Stand up, baby," Aunt Penny said, easing me to my feet. "Killian is on his way, and he's bringing Erica with him. We're gonna go out there, and we're gonna handle this as a family. We're right here with you, baby. Come on."

I allowed her to guide me out of the bathroom and into the living room. As soon as I appeared, my sisters vacated the comfort of Uncle Clive's arms and ran to me, hugging me tightly. I fought back the returning tears to be strong for them.

Swallowing hard, I asked the question I'd been dying to know. "Where were they?"

They both pulled back and looked from each other to me. Miyah was the first to speak.

"I was in Mama's room looking for a suitcase. She had this old trunk in the closet, and I thought I could use it to put some stuff in. It was heavy, and I couldn't pull it, so I took the stuff out. When I lifted it from the spot, I noticed some loose floorboards. At first, I thought nothing of it until something told me to lift them up. That's when I found the box. I thought it was just a bunch of old DVDs or something, so I put one in and... I'm so sorry that happened to you, Alayah. All those tapes...God! I'm so sorry."

She ran off down the hall, crying profusely. Adrienne followed her. I felt the vile taste of vomit enter by throat again but forced it back down.

"She knew," I choked out. "She knew the truth all this time, and she protected him."

"Alayah—"

"No! I want her dead. She deserves to fucking rot right next to that nasty son of a bitch. I'm her daughter. Her fucking daughter. How could she let something like this keep going?"

I wanted to throw something. Bang my head against the wall. Anything to ease the blow of my suspicions being true. She knew those tapes would prove my story. She knew he had them, and she hid them.

I could feel a panic attack coming. Covering my ears, I began pacing like a madwoman, reciting my affirmations.

I am resilient and can overcome any obstacle.

I am becoming the best version of myself.

I deserve success and happiness.

I am in control of my thoughts and emotions.

I choose peace and tranquility in my life.

I am deserving of respect and kindness.

That shit wasn't working. Aunt Penny was trying to talk to me, but it was just making me angrier.

"Leave me alone," I screamed.

Anger surged through me at a level I'd never felt. It was overwhelming...consuming. I felt like I was back in that bedroom with those scissors in my hand. I could almost feel them imprinting my palm as I gripped them tightly.

I stopped pacing when I caught sight of a reflection in the mirror, only it wasn't mine. It was Rodney staring back at me. I could hear his voice in my head.

"Hey, pretty girl. I miss you."

I frantically shook my head as the image shifted from him to Kennedy. She wore the familiar scowl on her face. Her reflection said nothing. She just looked at me with disgust and hatred.

"How could you?" I whispered.

"Alayah," Aunt Penny tried.

"How could you?" I screamed.

As though the scissors were in my hand, I raised my arm and struck the mirror repeatedly, asking the same question.

"How could you? How could you?"

I felt a strong pair of arms around me, and my first instinct was to fight back. I thrashed about wildly, trying to break free. In my mind, I was back in that room, pinned to the bed, begging and pleading for mercy.

"Alayah, it's me," Killian yelled, putting me in a bear hug. "It's me, baby."

I caught sight of his reflection in what was left of the broken mirror. I looked down at my hands, finally realizing that they were cut and bloody. My blood was smeared all over Killian's shirt and arms from him trying to hold me back. He was breathing heavily as he held on to me.

"Killian, she knew…"

"I need you to calm down. We need to get you to a hospital so they can tend to your hands."

I shook my head as I went limp in his arms.

"I just wanna die. Please, just let me die."

That was the last thing I remembered before everything went black.

I felt the heat from the bright lights beating down on my face as I struggled to open my eyes. My head was pounding, and my body felt heavy as hell. My eyes finally opened, and I was met with a tiled ceiling. I could hear the monitor beeping next to me. Turning my head, I saw Killian next to me with his head resting on his arms, sleeping peacefully.

Across the room sat my aunt, uncle, and sisters, all sleeping as well. I went to reach for Killian to wake him up when I realized my hands were bandaged up to my arms.

"What the hell?" I mumbled.

Beside me, Killian stirred. He looked up at me and smiled softly. He stood and kissed my forehead.

"You're awake."

"What happened?"

"You *um*…you blacked out. Your aunt said you were talking to yourself in the mirror and then you started hitting it. I had to hold you down, and you were fighting hard to get free. You cut up your hands pretty bad."

Tears sprang to my eyes at the realization that I'd tried to fight him. How could I do that to him?

"I'm sorry—"

He shook his head. "No, baby. There's nothing to be sorry about. You had a moment."

"Did I hurt you?"

He chuckled. "Do I look hurt?"

I looked him over, finding him in perfect condition. I sighed heavily as I relaxed into the bed.

"Are they putting me on a seventy-two-hour hold?"

"No. I explained the circumstances. They do want to keep you overnight just for observation, and they recommended you speak to the psychiatrist. You have symptoms of PTSD, which is understandable. The doctor just wants to see if they can prescribe you something."

I nodded, tears streaming down my face. As he was talking, the memories of what happened came flooding back. I remembered my sisters walking in with that box and the looks on their faces. I never wanted them to see that side of my trauma. I suffered too long to keep it from them for them to see it live in living color.

"Should I wake them up?" Killian asked, following my gaze. "They're worried about you. You scared them, baby."

I shook my head. "I'm so fucked up, Killian," I whispered through my tears. "Maybe you should just get out of this while you can. I can find somewhere else to live—"

"No. We aren't doing that. You aren't running from me, and you're not finding somewhere else to live. Your home is with me now, Alayah. I love you. You understand that? I love you, and I'm here with you through everything. Get that negative thinking out of your head right now. When they release you, you're coming home with me, and we are gonna deal with this together."

"I don't deserve you."

"Yes, you do. You deserve me, you want me, and I want you. That's it, that's all. Do I make myself clear?"

All I could do was nod. He stood and kicked off his shoes. Putting down the railing, he climbed into bed with me and pulled me into his arms. After placing a kiss to my temple, he rested against the pillow.

"Get some sleep, love."

I closed my eyes and settled into the warmth of his body. Before long, I was out.

CHAPTER 31

Killian

I SAT IN the conference room waiting for Kennedy to be brought in.

It had been two weeks since Alayah was released from the hospital. She seemed to be in and out of a depressed state. The meds the psychiatrist had prescribed hadn't fully kicked in yet, so she was mostly moody. Mr. Easton had given her time off work to recover since she couldn't do much with her hands. That alone had her frustrated. She cried often, and when she wasn't crying, she was sleeping.

With sleep came the nightmares. The first one she had in bed with me scared the hell out of me. She woke up screaming and confused.

"No…no, stop! Please!"

"Alayah…Alayah, baby, wake up. You're having a nightmare."

I tried to shake her awake, and she woke up screaming and swinging. I wasn't quick enough with my movements, and she manage to get me in the jaw.

"Shit!"

"Killian? I'm so sorry. I'm sorry."

She broke into a fit of tears. I moved my mouth to make sure nothing was dislocated, and it wasn't. It just hurt like a bitch.

"Don't cry," I said, pulling her into my arms.

254

"I hate being like this," she wailed. "I don't want to keep hurting you."

"I think you need to talk to somebody, baby."

She nodded as she pulled away from me. She tossed back the covers and got out of bed.

"Where are you going?"

"To my room. I just…I think I need to sleep alone for a little bit."

"Layah…Layah, wait."

She ignored me as she left the room.

Since that night, she'd been sleeping in her room. That didn't stop me from waking up when she screamed. I always ran to check on her. Usually, the door was locked. She said she didn't want me to see her like that. I felt like she was reverting to who she was when we first got back in contact.

Knowing those tapes still existed was really doing a number on her. She'd agreed to talking to someone and had set up virtual meetings with a psychiatrist. I hoped that it would help. Honestly, she probably should have been seeing someone all along. As much as she wanted to live normally, her circumstances weren't normal at all.

Erica and I had sat in her office going through them. They were hard to stomach, but we had to get a timeline of the dates from the timestamps. It didn't help that we could hear everything. I couldn't get the sound of Rodney grunting and Alayah's whimpers out of my head. After we finished going through them, I'd gone to the bathroom and thrown up because I was disgusted.

With this evidence, the case Erica and I had been working on would be foolproof. We'd already filed an appeal of Alayah's conviction with the new evidence presented. I was sure it would take some time, but given everything we provided, there was no way we would be rejected.

The sound of Erica's voice broke my thoughts.

"You okay?" she asked.

"Yeah. Just in deep thought. I still can't believe this shit, Erica."

"I know, but justice will be served."

The door to the small room opened, and I looked up to see Kennedy walking in with a sour look. Her attorney walked in behind her and took a seat. Kennedy sat, and the guard handcuffed her to the table before leaving the room.

"The fuck are you doing here?" she spat.

"We have a matter to discuss, Ms. Chambers," Erica said. "I'm sure your attorney has had time to go over the additional pending charges you have."

Kennedy ignored her as she glared at me glaring at her.

"Don't I know you?" she asked, squinting at me.

"Alayah and I studied together at your home when we were in high school."

She smirked. "Yeah, that's right. You were always sniffing around her like you wanted something. Did you get it?"

I cleared my throat as I reached into my briefcase. "I'm not here to discuss my prior relationship with your daughter."

"Then how about we discuss the current one. You fucking her?"

"Kennedy," her lawyer said firmly. "This is a serious matter. I was trying to tell you—"

Erica interrupted her. "Wait. You haven't briefed her?"

"She wouldn't let me talk."

Erica shook her head. "Ms. Chambers, you're in deep shit. I just wanted to give you a heads-up that we will be filing additional charges against you for obstruction of justice and possession of child pornography."

"The hell are you talking about?" Kennedy yelled.

"The tapes, Ms. Chambers," Erica said calmly. "You know, the ones hidden under the floorboards in your closet?"

Kennedy's eyes widened slightly, but she quickly pulled it together. "I don't know what you're talking about."

Erica pulled a piece of paper from her own briefcase and slid it across the table.

"Really? Because this right here is from forensics. Along with Mr. West, they pulled your fingerprints off several of those DVDs."

"Again, I don't know what you're talking about."

Her lawyer turned to her. "Kennedy, you need to come clean if you knew about this. Lying on that stand is only going to make matters worse."

Kennedy's head jerked in her direction. "You need to do your fucking job. They can't stick me with this!"

"On the contrary, we can." I pulled out the thumb drive and my laptop. "You see, Ms. Chambers, when you have knowledge of criminal activity, you are just as guilty as the person committing the crime when you don't report it. In your case, you knew what Mr. West was doing to your daughter, and you did nothing to stop him."

I turned my computer around and pressed play. Her jaw visibly clenched as she watched Rodney assaulting her child. I made sure to turn the volume up so she was forced to listen to it.

"Turn it off," she said angrily.

I didn't move. As the video kept playing, she had to listen to Alayah plead for him to stop while he praised her for how good she was. On this particular tape he could be heard telling her how much better she felt than Kennedy herself.

"Turn it off," she screamed.

This time I stopped the tape.

"How many times have you watched this yourself?" I asked. "You didn't even flinch when you saw the content."

"Fuck you."

"Answer my question: How many times have you watched this? What part of this looks like a seventeen-year-old girl seducing a grown-ass man? You can't sit here and lie like you did at that trial and say she wanted this. She was begging and pleading for him to stop. She didn't want this at all."

"Get out."

Erica touched my arm. "Killian."

I ignored her. "You let your boyfriend rape your daughter over and over and over again, and you told yourself she asked for it. You told other people she asked for it. Look at her." I shoved the computer toward her. "Look at what you allowed to happen."

"You don't know anything!"

"The proof is right there." I tapped the screen. "These tapes were found in *your* bedroom tucked away beneath a trunk that sat on top of loose floorboards."

She laughed. "Where is the warrant? You had no right to go through my home. That will never stand up in court."

It was my turn to laugh. "Here's the thing about the law, Ms. Chambers. If evidence is turned over voluntarily, I don't need a warrant. The person who found and turned over these recordings did so of their own free will. They had a conscience. *That* will stand up in court."

Her eyes widened as I closed the laptop and placed it back in my briefcase.

"If I can help it, you're gonna rot in this place—and that's only if you survive. They aren't too nice to child abusers here."

"You can't prove that I knew what was on those tapes," Kennedy said.

I shook my head. "We both know you did."

Erica began packing up. "Just to be on the safe side, I've filed a motion to have you take a lie detector test."

Kennedy turned to her lawyer. "Do something, bitch!"

"There is nothing I can do, Ms. Chambers. The evidence is overwhelming at this point. We just have to go through the motions—"

Kennedy jumped up, causing the table to rattle from the force of her jerking at the handcuffs.

"You're good for nothing. Get the fuck out of my face. You're fired!" She turned to me and Erica as we stood to leave. "You are not gonna pin this on me. Do you hear me? Y'all and my whore bitch of a daughter can go to hell!"

Erica shook her head. "We'll see you in court, Ms. Chambers."

We left the room with her screaming at our backs. There was silence between us as Erica and I walked out to the parking lot. She stopped just shy of the car and turned to me.

"You almost lost it back there," she said.

"I know. I apologize."

She sighed. "It's over now. We won't see her again until court. Just don't lose it in there. I don't have the kind of pull to get you out of being held in contempt."

"I promise I'll keep it together."

"Good. You headed home?"

"Yeah. I need to check on Alayah."

"How's she doing?"

"She's...there."

She offered me a sympathetic smile. "Just keep taking care of her. I know things are hard for her right now, but there is light at the end of this dark tunnel. She has to keep her head up. We're gonna get them."

I prayed that she was right. Everybody involved in this mess needed to pay, and if I had anything to do with it, they would.

A WEEK LATER...

Today had been the longest day, and all I wanted was to go home, shower, eat, and relax. I felt like I'd been working around the clock, and my body was tired. My mind was exhausted. After that meeting with Kennedy, I decided it was best to take a step back from this case. I was emotionally invested and taking things way to personal…even if it was.

The woman I loved was hurting because of the sorry excuse she had for a mother.

I couldn't fix it. I couldn't ease her pain. I couldn't take it away. Listening to her scream at night broke my heart. Wiping away her tears only fueled the anger I felt. This world was already cruel enough. The last thing anybody should have to deal with was the level of cruelty she experienced from her own mother.

Since Alayah had basically locked herself in her room, I asked her aunt to come over during the day to check on her and make sure she was okay. It would kill me if she sought to end her pain by taking her life. I wanted to give her more credit than that as far as her strength, but her psyche was fragile right now. We couldn't take any chances.

When I got home, the house was quiet, but I could smell food cooking in the kitchen. Thinking that Alayah was up, I headed in that direction. I was surprised to find my sister at the stove.

"Hey, Bridget," I said, hugging her. "What are you doing here?"

"Ellie wanted to see Alayah. I figured she could use a visit from her bestie. They're taking a nap."

I nodded. "You didn't have to cook, you know."

"I know. But I also know things are hard right now. I just wanted to help where I could."

"Thanks, sis." I discarded my jacket and tie, then went to the fridge for a beer.

"How are you feeling, Killian?"

"Like she's pulling away from me, Bridget. I get it. It's one thing to suspect her mother knew. To have it confirmed that she had the tapes all along…that shit broke her heart. I'm sure some part of her was holding on to hope that Kennedy had some shred of decency. What kind of mother does what she did? I can't imagine Mom ever being like that."

"Some women aren't cut out to be mothers. I can't even say it's motherly instincts because I don't know what the issue is with her. My heart goes out to Alayah. I can only imagine what she's feeling."

I sighed heavily. "I'm gonna go check on her."

I placed my beer on the counter and headed down the hall to Alayah's room. The door was slightly ajar. I stepped in and smiled softly. Alayah was sleeping soundly with her head resting on Ellie's chest. My niece had her little arms wrapped tightly around her mass of curls like she was trying to protect her.

It was adorable.

Ellie loved her some Alayah, and I believed her little spirit offered Alayah some peace. I stood there for a moment watching them before I went over to the bed and sat down gently as not to wake them. Resting a hand on Alayah's leg and closing my eyes, I said a silent prayer.

Father God, I come to you a humble servant, asking you to heal all the broken parts of the woman I love. Her heart is heavy, and her mind is weary. Grant her the strength she needs in moments of weakness. Bestow upon her the courage in times of fear. Give her peace amid pain and suffering. I pray that Your restorative power flow through every cell of her body, every corner of her mind, and every depth of her spirit. These and all blessings I ask in Your name. Amen."

Standing from the bed, I made my way out of the room and down the hall to my bedroom to shower and change out of my work clothes. By the time I made it back into the kitchen, Erica was sitting at the island talking to Bridget.

"Hey. What are you doing here?"

"I come bearing good news. Where is Alayah?"

"She's in her room."

"Can you go get her?"

"I'll get her," Bridget said. "I feel like this is a private moment anyway. The food is done, so Ellie and I are gonna head on home." She came over to hug and kiss me. "Love you, little brother."

"Love you, too."

She disappeared down the hall, leaving me and Erica alone. I noted the smile on her face, realizing she really did have good news.

"We got them?" I asked quietly.

She nodded. "We got them. Warrants are being served as we speak. That discovery rule played a big part in this, Killian."

She was referring to the statute of limitations. With the discovery rule, the limitations begin when the offense was discovered instead of when it occurred. I would pay money to see the looks on these people's faces when the cops pulled up to their houses.

A few minutes passed before my sister was walking down the hall with Ellie and Alayah behind her. Ellie smiled as she ran over and jumped into my arms to say good night. She kissed my cheek before scrambling over to Alayah. She gave her a big hug, then followed her mom out of the house. Alayah made her way over and gave me a loose hug before pecking my lips. She still looked tired, but she was alert.

"Hey, Erica," she said faintly. "What are you doing here?"

"Why don't you have a seat, baby?"

I stood and pulled out a chair for her. She sighed as she took a seat. I took one as well.

"What's going on?" she asked.

Erica took her hands. "Killian and I have been working very hard on this case. There has been a ton of new evidence and discoveries that have taken place, Alayah. Several people involved in your case all had a personal connection to Rodney. The judge that presided over your trial, two jury members, and the officer that was first on the scene were all part of his extended family."

"W–What? How do you know that?"

"Extensive research, honey. I had to cash in a lot of favors, but it was worth it. It turns out, you weren't Rodney's first victim. There were six other girls—now adults—whose families were paid off by the judge to drop the charges. That man got away with being a predator for years because somebody was covering up for him. His mother and that whole family have been covering his ass since he was thirteen. It's all coming to light now.

"Warrants are being served. Kennedy is being brought up on additional charges of possessing child pornography and obstruction of justice. The best part of all this: Your conviction is being overturned. You're gonna be a free woman, Alayah."

Alayah's eyes widened. "O–Overturned?"

"Overturned. No retrials. No parole. You will have to go to court as part of the legal process, but you're free."

Alayah looked from Erica to me with tears streaming down her face. She began breathing heavily, clutching her chest.

"I'm free…I'm free. Oh God."

She broke into a full-blown cry. I wrapped my arms around her to keep her from slipping out of the chair and to the floor.

"You won, baby," I whispered, rocking her.

She'd won big. Erica and I had decided not to tell her about the request for restitution that we'd put in. More than likely, it would be granted. The system had failed her thanks to members of their own, and they needed to pay her for every year of freedom she'd lost. It would never make up for it, but it would be a hell of a start to a new life.

Alayah gathered herself together and sat up straight.

"Thank you," she said, reaching for Erica. "You never gave up on me, even when I told you to."

"I promised your aunt and uncle I would get justice for you. I always keep my word. Congratulations, love."

Alayah embraced her tightly before letting go and throwing herself into my arms. She cupped my face and kissed me passionately.

"Thank you," she whispered. "I love you so much, Killian. Thank you for seeing me."

"Always, baby. I told you, I got you. That's for life." I pecked her lips. "We have to celebrate."

"I have to call Aunt Penny and Uncle Clive and my sisters… and Londyn and—"

"Let's just call them all over. We have every reason to celebrate you."

"Please tell me you'll stay," Alayah said to Erica.

"I'll just have to call my husband."

"Invite him, too," I said.

"I'll just step outside and call him."

She stepped out the back door, phone in her hand. Alayah turned to me with a smile.

"How are you feeling?" I asked, pulling her into my chest.

"Like I can finally breathe again."

"Well take a long, deep breath. It's only up from here."

CHAPTER 32

Alayah

A MONTH LATER

I **WALKED OUT** of the courthouse with a smile on my face with the people who loved me at my side. Alayah Chambers was officially a free woman with a sizable restitution check. When Erica first began telling me what she and Killian had been up to, my first feeling was embarrassment about other people seeing those tapes. It was bad enough that my sisters saw them.

However, as I listened to her tell me the rest of the story, my heart began to fill with hope. When I learned of my impending freedom, it was like the weight of the world was lifted from my shoulders. It did my heart good to know that somebody was being held responsible for allowing a predator to run free for years.

When the story broke, the women who were paid off came forward. All of them had similar stories of how they no longer associated with their families because they took the money instead of fighting for justice. My heart went out to them. I knew what they were feeling all too well.

"How do you want to celebrate your first official day of freedom?" Killian asked, grabbing my hand.

I looked around at the smiling faces of my loved ones.

Aside from Killian, my aunt, uncle, and sisters were there along with his parents, sister, brother in-law, Ellie, and Londyn. I couldn't have made it this far without each of them in some way. They had been such a light in my life since the moment I'd touched civilian soil. It hadn't been easy. In fact, being outside the prison walls was harder than the ten years I spent inside.

My mental had been tested so many times.

The day I learned my sisters saw those tapes, I had a mental breakdown. It seemed like everything kept coming at me one instance right after another, and that was my breaking point. My therapist had been a Godsend. It helped that she was a survivor of assault herself. She understood me on a level that nobody else could.

In the month and a half of seeing her and being on my medication, I could already feel the changes. When I first got to prison, I spoke with the prison psychologist a few times the first couple of weeks. She wasn't helpful, and I wasn't making progress, so I refused to go back. The woman tried to make me feel guilty about what I'd done.

True, I took a life, but it was my last resort. Knowing now that I wasn't the first young girl to be Rodney's victim gave me even more reason to believe that I'd saved not only myself and my sisters from the same fate, but some other innocent little girl.

"I just want to go home," I finally answered. "All I need is to be surrounded by you all."

"We can throw some food on the grill," Mr. Lake suggested. "Whip up a few sides, turn on some music."

I smiled. "I'd like that."

"We can stop by the grocery store on the way to the house," Killian said.

I pulled away from him. "Actually, can I meet y'all at the house? There's something I need to do. If I don't do it now, I'm never going to do it."

He looked at me curiously. "What is it? Do you need me to come with you?"

"No, baby. This is something I need to do for myself. I'll meet you at home. I promise."

He nodded slowly. His home was officially my home these days. I mean, it had become my home when I moved in, but now it was my residence since we'd put an actual title on our relationship.

I was his lady, and he was my man...*my man.*

I loved being with him. I loved sleeping next to him and waking up to him. Killian gave me peace. He was one of my biggest supporters and my best friend. I knew that there was nothing in life I couldn't get through without him at my side.

Killian slid me the keys to his car. I'd officially gotten my license last week, thanks to Londyn. She'd taken the task of preparing me seriously and didn't slack off as my teacher. Even though she was extra as hell, I loved her for believing in me.

"Don't get in there driving like a bat out of hell," she warned me as I walked to the car.

I giggled. "That's you, not me. I'm a cautious driver. I love you guys. I'll see you soon."

I climbed in the car and cranked up. As I went to back out, there was a tap to the window. I looked up to see my sisters and Killian. Rolling the window down, I peered up at them.

"You're going to go see her, aren't you?" Adrienne asked, crossing her arms.

"I have to, Adrienne."

"No, you don't. She doesn't deserve anything from you, sissy."

"She's right," Miyah agreed. "As far as I'm concerned, she's dead to me."

I understood their pain. They were still angry with Kennedy about the way she did them. Our aunt and uncle were granted full guardianship over them now. They didn't even acknowledge Kennedy as their mother anymore.

"I understand, y'all. I really do. I just have things I need to say and answers I need to know before I can lay this whole thing to rest."

"And what if she doesn't give them to you?" Adrienne asked. "You'll be inflicting pain on yourself for nothing."

"She has nothing else to lose at this point by telling the truth. If she doesn't, I'll leave it alone. I promise."

They looked at each other, then at me and nodded. Both of them gave me a hug and kiss before rejoining our family. Killian stooped and leaned into the car.

"You know you don't have to do this alone, right?" he asked.

"I know, but I need to. I can handle it." I cupped his chin and pecked his lips. "I love you."

"I love you more. Hurry home. Don't make me have to come up there because I'll be rocking an orange suit if she steps out of line."

I rolled my eyes. "Orange isn't your color, babe. I'll be home within the hour."

He nodded and kissed me once more before stepping away. I backed out of the parking space and headed in the direction of the correctional facility. Truth be told, I was a little nervous about going to visit Kennedy. I'd asked Erica to get me on her visitation list, and she'd pulled some strings.

There was a lot I had to say to the woman who birthed me—a lot of answers I needed. Even if it hurt, I prayed she would do one decent thing in her life and be honest with me.

My life had been an emotional rollercoaster. While there were more highs than lows recently, the lows were pretty damn bad. I wasn't even on social media, yet I'd been the topic of conversation among the West family. They hated my guts for "ruining" their family like the family wasn't filled with people who aided in Rodney's deviant behavior. They covered up his shit for so long, it was no wonder he was so confident he would get away with it all.

Mrs. West was in the psych ward at a mental hospital. After the tape evidence came out, she lost it and tried to kill herself. My guess was she was trying to save face. She was playing crazy so she didn't have to own up to the part she'd played in her son's outcome. Her family claimed my release drove her insane. Bullshit. If she wanted to play crazy, she could sit in the psych ward until she died for all I cared.

The two family members that served on my jury were served with hefty fines. Unfortunately, the responding officer that fatal night didn't receive any punishment and neither did the lawyer. That outcome was somewhat expected, but it was still disappointing. Erica wanted to dig deeper into them, but I just wanted to let it go. I needed peace.... I deserved that much.

I pulled into the parking lot and got out of the car, voiding myself of anything that would be considered a weapon or contraband. As I looked up at the building with barbed-wire fences surrounding it, I couldn't believe I was back here. Ten years of my past resided within these walls. I told myself I'd never come back.

No matter how bad I missed my bunkies.

No matter how well I'd done inside.

Nothing would have ever made me come back. Now here I was.

I sat at the no-contact visitation center waiting on Kennedy to be brought in. My leg shook nervously. Erica had arranged this particular visit because there probably would have been two of us behind bars if this meeting had taken place face-to-face. Kennedy hated me, I hated her, and if I got my hands on her, there was no telling what I would have done.

I closed my eyes and took a deep breath as I waited. Reciting my affirmations and saying a prayer helped to calm my nerves a little. When I opened them, Kennedy was sitting in front of me with a stoic look. We stared at each other for the longest time until I picked up the phone. It was about fifteen painstaking seconds before she picked up hers, too.

"What are you doing here, and what do you want?" she asked.

"I need answers, Kennedy."

"I ain't got none for you."

"Don't give me that bullshit. After all you've done—after all you've let be done to me—you owe me answers."

"I don't owe you shit. I gave you life—"

"You made my life a living fucking hell," I snapped. "From the moment I came into this world, you have hated me. What did I ever do to you? Why didn't you just get an abortion if you didn't want me? You could have given me up or did anything besides keep me to treat me like shit."

"You think I wanted to keep you? I didn't. You are the bane of my existence, just like your damn daddy. He got me pregnant and disappeared. My parents *made* me have you. They forced me to give birth to a child I didn't want because they didn't believe in abortion or adoption. Your sisters chose you over me from the time they were born. I used to have to listen to them scream and cry at the top of their lungs. No matter what I did to soothe them, they just wouldn't shut up. The moment you spoke to them, all that hollering stopped. I was their mother. I gave birth to them, and they acted like they couldn't stand the sight of me when it came to you!

"My own sister chose you over me. She's always wanted you and your sisters because she can't have a kid of her own. Rodney chose you over me. I did everything to make that motherfucker happy, and he chose you…a fucking child. You ruined my life the day you were conceived. I hated you. I hated you, and I wanted you to suffer for making my life miserable."

I shook my head as tears streamed down my face. "You hated me enough to let your boyfriend rape me for three years?"

"I didn't...I didn't know at first."

"Did you know when I tried to tell you?"

She was quiet.

"Did you know?" I demanded.

"No."

"Then, when did you know, Kennedy?"

"It doesn't matter. I'm serving time for it."

"It doesn't matter? You failed the lie detector test. You knew about the tapes, Kennedy. You could have saved me from being in this place for ten years, and you didn't. I would have settled for you turning them over and pretending like you didn't know versus you lying to put me away. At least I would have had my freedom! For once in your life, tell the fucking truth!"

She stared at me with a blank expression. "I'll take that to my grave. You got what you wanted, didn't you?"

I scoffed. "Got what I wanted? What I wanted was a mother who gave a damn about me. I wanted a normal childhood. I wanted to not be raped repeatedly by a sick, perverted ass man who got me pregnant. You know what he told me when I miscarried? That we would be careful next time. He never planned to stop, and you weren't going to make him. How can you live with yourself? Do you sleep well at night knowing what you've done—how you've ruined my life?

"How can you sit here and look me in the face knowing that you eventually knew I was telling the truth and not feel a single ounce of remorse? Were you so desperate for a man to love you that you could overlook something so sick? Was your hate for me that strong?"

She just stared at me. I looked at her in disbelief. I wasn't sure why I was shocked. Kennedy Chambers didn't have a remorseful bone in her body. She would never own up to her wrongdoings. It would always be someone else's fault. I was fighting a lost cause.

"I don't even know why I'm here," I said, shaking my head. "Since I ruined your life, let me ruin it a little more: I won. My conviction was overturned, and my record will be expunged. My sisters and I now have a beautiful relationship, and you will never see them again. You're here, and I get to go home to my family and a man who loves more than I ever imagined.

"I have the brightest future ahead of me while you will spend the rest of your life in prison. All the hate in your heart for me ruined you. You can't blame that on anybody but yourself. I'm done being your punching bag. I'm done letting you, Rodney, or anybody break me. I may be bruised, but I am far from broken. You…don't…win. Have a nice life, bitch."

I hung up the phone and stood from the seat. As I walked away from the glass, I felt a sense of pride. I didn't get the closure I wanted, but I got what I needed. I had indeed won in more ways than I could ever imagine.

As I made my way to the door, I locked eyes with two familiar faces. CO Judy and Carissa. Both smiled when they saw me. Carissa mouthed something I couldn't hear to Judy who motioned for me to pick up the phone.

"My baby," Carissa exclaimed. "Oh, I miss you."

"I miss you, too, Riss. How are the girls?"

"Same shit, different day. You look so good, baby."

"Thank you. I'm fully free now, so I can come back to visit you."

"I saw the news. I'm so happy you finally got justice. But don't come back here, Alayah. Ain't nothing good inside these walls for you, baby. I miss you, and I love you, but I knew there was better for you on the outside."

"Carissa… I love you. You loved and protected me for ten years. How am I supposed to forget about you? Can I at least write you?"

She smiled. "I'll take a letter. I knew you would be fine. I finished raising you to be a tough cookie. I ain't your mama, but a little of me rubbed off on you. You are glowing right now. You got a man out there, don't you?"

Just as I went to answer, Kennedy was escorted past us. She glared at me, and I glared at her until she was gone. When my eyes landed on Carissa again, she gave me a knowing look.

"I got you, baby," she said.

"Riss—"

"I love you, Lay Lay."

"I love you, too."

She hung up the phone and looked to CO Judy who gave me a nod. I hung up the receiver and left the visitation center. Back in the car, I sat there for a moment, waiting on the tears to come again, but they never did. It was like my brain said, *Enough of that.*

No more tears.

No more worry.

No more pain.

It was time to move on with life. While so much had been taken from me, I'd gained so much in return. I couldn't afford to look back. I was leaving my past right here to rot with Kennedy because I had no room for it in the future I was trying to build.

With that thought, I cranked up and pulled out of the parking lot. There was a celebration happening, and I was the guest of honor. What better way to celebrate my freedom than to be surrounded by the very thing that got me through my toughest times—love.

EPILOGUE

Alayah

A YEAR AND A HALF LATER

"**S**HE'S HERE," I yelled from the front porch.

I was giddy with excitement as my sister came down the road. Adrienne been away at school for months now, and I was too excited to see my baby. The day she left for college was bittersweet for me. I felt like I had just gotten her back, then she was leaving.

While I was sad to see her go, I knew that it was time for her to go off into the world on her own. She'd gotten a full-ride scholarship to her dream school, and I would never hold her back from that. We made the most of our time together before she left and whenever she came home. Still, that was my baby, and I missed her like crazy.

She wasn't the only one taking things to the next level. Even though I had my cosmetology license, I wanted to perfect my craft. After my conviction was overturned and Charlene came back to work, I took an apprenticeship at a local hair salon. Without so many troubles hitting me at once, I was able to finally focus on something that brought me happiness.

I'd learned so much from Ms. Joy who, ironically, had earned her license in prison, too. Most of the girls at the shop had done time. I didn't want to say I felt right at home, but I felt inspired. Ms. Joy had one of the most successful shops in the city. She offered me so much encouragement when I told her I wanted to open my own natural hair–care spot. Killian had helped me successfully obtain a business loan, and six months ago, I'd officially closed on my building. It felt so good to have something of my own after not owning anything for most of my life.

When Adrienne climbed out of the car, I ran down the front steps to her. Scooping her up in a hug, I swung her around like I did when she was a kid.

"You're here," I exclaimed.

I couldn't help but smother her cheeks with kisses when I placed her on her feet. All she could do was laugh and try to push me away.

"Oh my God, sissy. Calm down, I haven't been gone that long."

"You were gone long enough. Let me get a look at you."

She stepped back into a little twirl. I felt like a proud mama noticing how much she had changed and grown up. While she could still be sassy, she had matured a lot. A little while after I started therapy, I convinced her and Amiyah to join me. It was something that the three of us could benefit from growing up in that house.

Therapy had helped Adrienne work through a lot of her anger issues, and I was proud of her. The last thing I ever wanted was for her to end up like our mother. Kennedy didn't make it past her first year in prison. Not long after being moved into general population, she was found hanging in her cell. From the story I'd been told, things had been hell for her from the moment she stepped foot on the block.

Child abusers never got it easy on the inside. That was something I'd seen with my own two eyes. While they ruled her death a suicide, I couldn't help but wonder if that was what really happened. Either way, my heart didn't hurt for her death. I felt nothing when I got the call, and I felt nothing now.

Amiyah came running out of the house and down the steps, straight into Adrienne's arms. She'd been damn near living with us for the last seven months.

"I've missed you so much," she declared.

"I've miss you, too, little sister."

The sound of footsteps approaching caused us to turn to the front porch. There stood my man and our biggest blessing, our four-month-old daughter, Kaliyah Marie Lake. She sat in her daddy's arms looking around curiously.

Adrienne squealed as she ran up to them. "Give her to me."

"Damn, I can't get a greeting?" Killian jested.

She giggled. "Hi, brother in-law. I missed you."

Killian and I had gotten married in a small ceremony the summer before Adrienne went off to college. His proposal was just as sweet as he'd always been. He'd kept me out of the house the entire day. I didn't think anything of it because it wasn't uncommon. As we pulled into the neighborhood, he handed me a sleep mask with a grin.

"What's this?" I asked, eyeing him skeptically.

"Just put it on, woman."

"What are you up to, Killian Lake?"

"Layah."

I sighed as I pulled the mask over my face. A few minutes later, the car came to a stop. I heard his door close, and moments later, mine opened. He helped me out and lead me to what I knew was the backyard because we hadn't gone inside.

When we came to a stop, I tried listening for some indication of what he had planned. Alas, I heard nothing but silence. Then I felt the mask being taken off my face. My eyes widened at the sight before me.

Our family stood around with smiles on their faces. The backyard hand been transformed into a romantic oasis. Roses were everywhere. There was a beautiful backdrop with candles leading up to it. In the middle of it stood Killian, motioning me to come to him.

Tears streamed down my face as I slowly made my way to my man. He reached for my hand and pulled me into him.

"Alayah Chambers, you are the love of my life, my best friend, and my soulmate. I've carried you in my heart since I was seventeen years old. If I'd known then what I knew now, I would have made you mine sooner just so I could love you longer. I know the journey you've had has been less than stellar. You've suffered, but more than that you've overcome. I'm so proud of you. Watching you take back your power has been the most beautiful experience.

"You are so worthy of everything you've gained back and even more worthy of what is to come. I love you with every beat of my heart, every part of my soul. If you'll have me, I want to spend the rest of our lives making you happy."

He reached into his pocket and pulled out a black velvet box. Dropping to one knee, he presented it to me. Inside was a beautiful teardrop diamond ring. One hand flew to my mouth as he reached for the other.

"Will you marry me, Alayah? Will you do me the honor of becoming my wife?"

I had no words...none. All I could do was nod repeatedly. He slipped the ring on my finger and stood. I couldn't control my sobs as I fell into his arms.

Killian had always given me the best form of love. It was pure and unconditional and made me feel seen and heard. Nothing compared to him. Watching him be a father to our unexpected bundle of joy brought me the most happiness next to being his wife.

The relationship with him and my sisters was one of mutual love and respect. He understood that while they were young adults, they still needed parenting. In turn, they respected his stance on many aspects of their lives. If Killian and I said no, there was no pushback, which surprised me.

"Hi, TiTi's baby," Adrienne cooed in Kaliyah's face, causing her to grin.

"Don't hog her, Adrienne," Miyah fussed.

"You're here with her all the time. Let me love on her. Kiki, tell that girl I'm your favorite auntie."

My baby grinned. I think she loved them fussing over her. She loved attention and smiled anytime someone talked to her.

"Y'all take my baby on in the house," Killian said. "I'll grab your bags, Adrienne."

"Thank you."

She headed inside with Amiyah fussing the whole way. I shook my head.

"I can't with them."

Killian chuckled as he wrapped his arms around my waist.

"Isn't this what you wanted—all of you under the same roof?"

"It is." I wrapped my arms around his neck. "My girls. My baby. My man. What else could I possibly need?"

"You know what I need?" he asked, peering down at me lovingly.

"What's that, Mr. Lake?"

"My favorite set of lips."

I giggled. "Which set?"

"While I'm partial to both, I will take the ones on your face until I can get to the others tonight."

I squealed as he lifted me in the air and swung me around. I wrapped my legs around his waist and my arms around his neck. Our lips collided in a sensual kiss. My heart was so full.

The sound of the horn blowing broke us apart as both my aunt and uncle and Killian's parents pulled into our driveway. Kareem and his family parked on the street, and Londyn parked behind them. I could see Bridget, Ellie, and Collin making their way down the sidewalk from their home. Looking down at my watch, I saw that everyone was right on time. We were celebrating Adrienne being home the best way we knew how…by throwing something on the grill.

I smiled. Years ago, I never imagined this life for myself. A life outside of prison walls didn't seem to be in the cards for me. Now here I was. I had the healthiest relationship with my siblings. I was surrounded by family and friends. I was a wife and mother. My future was bright, and my freedom was my own.

Through the secret I carried and the secrets revealed, I'd found solace.

I was home.

THE END

BONUS SCENE

Carissa Joe: Inmate #253981

I WATCHED THIS bitch walking around like she was safe for far too long. It had been months since she was placed in our unit, and I'd been itching to touch her. Every time I looked in her face, I saw my baby girl.

I remembered the countless sleepless nights she had because of her nightmares. I remembered her telling me her story. The number of tears I wiped from her face was a shame. Children were a blessing. How any mother could subject their child to what Kennedy did was baffling.

Alayah was more than just a prisoner to me. She was the child I never got to have—a sweet innocent soul that never deserved to be behind bars. I didn't raise her, but I nurtured her...protected her...loved her.

Prison was too good for a bitch like Kennedy Chambers. Every woman on the block knew who she was. The ones closest to Alayah had been giving her hell. She'd been spat on, slapped, had piss thrown on her, and she'd been jumped.

She deserved to suffer. She deserved to pay for everything she'd done. While I hadn't touched her—yet—I was going to make sure she got what was coming to her. Her sentence was justice in the eyes of the law, but street justice was about to be served.

I casually left my bunk and took the short walk down to Kennedy's. When I peeked inside, she was laying there with her eyes closed. The door was slightly ajar, so I slipped inside. Pulling the makeshift noose from beneath my sweatshirt, I approached her bed.

Like a thief in the night, I quickly tied it to the top bunk and slipped it around her neck. Her eyes flew open, but before she could scream, she was hoisted upright. Her eyes widened, and she clawed at the noose.

"*Aht aht*, bitch," I said, pulling tighter. "You thought you were safe, huh? You thought you were gonna live out the rest of your days after what you did to my baby? I got to love the child you abused like she was my own. I told myself if I ever got my hands on you, you were a dead woman."

I watched the life slowly draining from her face, and it gave me so much satisfaction.

"How does it feel, Kennedy," I taunted, "knowing you're about to die and no one can save you?"

Her eyes bulged, and her face was blood red at this point. Slowly, she began to go limp.

"It's almost over, pretty girl. Isn't that what your man used to call Alayah while he raped her?"

The sweet sound of her last breath brought a smile to my face. Her body was fully limp at this point. I tied off the makeshift rope and positioned her to make her death look like she was responsible before slipping out as easily as I'd slipped in.

"I got her for you, baby girl."

COURAGE to *Love* AGAIN

KIMBERLY BROWN

JAHQUEL J.

RICH *and* ROTTEN

A NOVEL

SUMMER'S ECHO

ROBBI RENEE

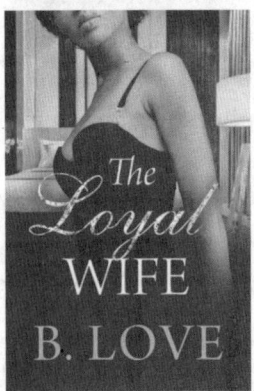

The *Loyal* WIFE

B. LOVE

DANIELLE MARCUS

THICK OF LOVE

A NOVEL

SHADOWS OF JUSTICE

A TOPHER DAVIS THRILLER

BRIAN COPELAND

TARRIS MARIE

BLAQUE PEARLE

#ANOVEL

SOLDIERS OF LOVE

BEAUTIFUL SCARS

N'TYSE & UNTAMED

USA TODAY BESTSELLING AUTHOR

CASSIE VERANO

90 DAYS *to Love*